What readers have said about previous Collins & Clark books

'This was a very good enjoyable read. The banter between colleagues is very funny and fits well into this book between the serious parts.'
Neil Mullins
★ ★ ★ ★ ★

'What a joy this novel is to read. There is non-stop action and intrigue to keep you turning the pages and two very likeable protagonists with some good repartee to keep you warm and amused.'
Elaine Tomasso

'Clive, Michael, and Agnes make a great team in this British procedural. It's sometimes easy to forget what it was like for police in the days before CSI, DNA, and surveillance cameras everywhere but McGrath has written a cracking good mystery story that reminds you of the basics.'
Kathleen Grey

A Death in Summer: 1965
A Collins & Clark Story

Jim McGrath

ISBN-10: 1-912605-02-3
ISBN-13: 978-1-912605-02-6 (j-views Publishing)

Published by j-views Publishing, 2018

© 2018 Jim McGrath

All rights reserved. Without limiting the rights under copyright reserved above, no part of this publication may be reproduced, stored in or introduced into a retrieval system, or transmitted, in any form, or by any means (electronic, mechanical, photocopying, recording, or otherwise) without the prior written permission of both the copyright owner and the above publisher of this book.

This is a work of fiction. Names, characters, places, brands, media, and incidents are either the product of the author's imagination or are fictional representations of the same.

Body set in 11pt Brioso Pro, chapter titles and headings in Motorway

www.j-views.biz

publish@j-views.biz

j-views Publishing, 26 Lombard Street, Lichfield, UK, WS13 6DR

A DEATH IN SUMMER: 1965

1965 Police Attitudes, Terminology and Equipment

Attitudes to black and ethnic minorities joining the British Army or police

The views described by Clark are typical of what existed in all three armed services and police forces throughout the United Kingdom in the mid-1960s.

Terminology

The murderer in this book would today be called a serial killer. However, that term was not in use in 1965. Robert Rissler from the FBI Behavioral Science Unit first used the term in about 1972 and it took more than 10 years to become widely used in the United Kingdom.

Separate forensic teams did not exist in the 1960s. Usually a single officer in each station was designated as a Scenes of Crime Officer and he (it was nearly always a he) could enlist the help of other officers as and when required. The same officer was also responsible for photographing the crime scene.

Police equipment in 1965

There is disagreement as to when police personal radios came into common use. They were certainly not in common use in 1965 and therefore there is no reference to them in this story.

Geography, dialect and poetic licence

Birmingham lies to the south of the Black Country and Handsworth marks the border. Although they are neighbours, the differences in attitude, accents and customs remain significantly different. Simply put, if you want to insult someone from the Black Country you called them a Brummie.

The Black Country has no clearly defined borders, but it is usually defined as "the area where the South Staffordshire coal seam comes to the surface". This includes Brierley Hill,

West Bromwich, Oldbury, Blackheath, Cradley Heath, Old Hill, Bilston, Dudley, Tipton and Walsall but not Wolverhampton. However, using other criteria, it is accepted by many people in the region that Wolverhampton is part of the Black Country.

Each town has its own version of the Black Country dialect and none of them share any resemblance to the typical "Brummie" accent. The following few words are used by Clark and other characters throughout the book to give a poor impression of how a person from West Bromwich might sound.

Ain't = will not	Wi = we
Bostin = good/great	Wiek = week
Dain't = did not	Wem = we are
Kidda = friend	Yow = you
Summut = something	Yowm = you are
Tarrar or tarrar a bit = goodbye	Yam Yam = person from the Black Country

Many readers have been remarked on the accuracy of the Birmingham locations used. So as not to mislead anyone, I need to say that while most of the streets, locations and buildings referred to in my books do/did exist, I have also invented a few of my own when the story required it.

Acknowledgements

Once more I must acknowledge a huge debt of gratitude to David Brown. David served in the West Bromwich and Lichfield Police Forces for ten years during the 1960s and early 70s before becoming a social worker. He has acted as technical advisor, grammarian and critical friend. As a painter of considerable talent David understands the creative process and is a constant source of encouragement and support. He has also painted the cover for this book.

I would also like to say thank my nephew Stephen McGrath, who served in the Staffordshire Police for over twenty-five years. Stephen has given me a rare insight into the attitudes of police officers which has helped me to create the characters found in this book.

Thanks again are due to my fellow Lichfield writer Hugh Ashton, who is a constant source of encouragement. He is also responsible for the design and layout of this book. How he does all this and still manages to turn out his own thrillers and Sherlock Homes stories is beyond me.

Contents

Part 4

A DEATH IN SUMMER: 1965

JIM McGRATH

A COLLINS & CLARK STORY

J-VIEWS PUBLISHING, LICHFIELD, ENGLAND

Prologue

Hockley, Sunday 20 June 1965, 22.00hrs.

The small man in the corner of the storeroom was immersed in his work. What he was doing was not complicated, but he found enormous satisfaction in completing the work perfectly. He knew how lucky he was. Most men had a job which they endured. He had a career, a calling, a vocation. How fortunate it was that he'd discovered his life's work when he was just twelve years old.

As he wound the lint around the cardboard his mind went back to his twelfth birthday. The August night had been hot, moist and sticky. Thunder was in the air but the storm had yet to break. The birthday boy lay on top of the bed sheet. The bedclothes lay crumpled at his feet. He was naked accept for his underpants which he'd pulled down to his knees. He was gently massaging his limp penis. He'd been doing this for the last twenty minutes but nothing had happened.

Just that afternoon his only friend, George, had bundled him into the boys' toilets after school and said that he wanted to show him something which would change his life forever. Locking the cubicle door, George unzipped his flies and pulled out his semi-erect penis. 'You're twelve. It's time you learned how to wank,' he said with all the confidence of someone who had discovered how to do it just three weeks earlier. It only took a couple of pulls on the lamb's tail for George's cock to grow long and hard. The man remembered how the crown of his friend's cock had been blue and shiny. A couple more tugs, and George doubled over and gave a low moan as if in agony. A thick, white fluid splashed against the cubicle wall and dripped onto the floor.

Grabbing a fistful of toilet paper, George wiped himself dry. Now embarrassed, he said, 'That's how you wank off. Try it tonight and you'll thank me tomorrow.'

Well he'd tried, but nothing had happened. He was about to turn over and go to sleep when he heard screaming from outside. Pulling his pants up, he rushed to the window and peeked out from behind the curtains. Mrs Sims, the pretty young blonde housewife from across the road, was standing in front of her house screaming. Thick black smoke billowed out of the open front door and flames were visible in the front room and the bedrooms.

The young boy's gaze shifted from Mrs Sims to the licks of flame he could see and back again. Both fascinated him. Mrs Sims was nearly naked. She was wearing a pair of white nylon knickers, a white bra and a white suspender belt with a red rose in the middle of the waist. One stocking had become detached and lay crumpled around her left ankle. She was the most beautiful sight he'd ever seen. The tears on her face glinted in the light from the flames. Her glistening face contorted in pain as she screamed for someone, anyone, to help her children trapped inside the burning house.

The road was starting to fill with people, and the boy saw his father rush out. Pushing the window up, he stuck his head out and smelt for the first time the heady mix of burning leather, carpet, cloth, wood and paint. As people gathered around Mrs Sims, a man carrying his jacket and tie and with his shirt tail outside his trousers, slipped out of the side entry of the Sims' house and hurried away towards the main road. The boy knew it wasn't Mr Sims. He worked nights at the hospital.

People were now shouting and running about as if noise and movement would do some good. Over the din he heard his father shout, 'Someone get up to Mrs Smith's at 23 and call 999. We need an ambulance and the fire brigade.' A young man in his twenties sprinted away from the group and headed for the only phone in the road. As he left, two men wearing busmen's uniforms ran around the corner, the back of their cream and blue bus blocking the bottom of the street.

The boy immediately recognised the conductor. He was a regular on his school route, a small but well-muscled Pole who was happy to give any boy who misbehaved or annoyed other passengers 'a clip round the ear.' Both men ignored the crowd and looked about for something they could use as a ladder. The driver grabbed the three-foot high iron railings that separated Mrs Sims' house from her neighbour's and with the conductor's help yanked it free from its moorings and placed it against the wall. The makeshift ladder reached almost to the bedroom window.

The conductor went up first. As the driver started to follow, the boy's father grabbed the bottom of the "ladder" and held it steady. Reaching the window, the conductor smashed a pane of glass with his elbow. A yellow, blue and red sheet of flame engulfed his head momentarily. He screamed out and patted at the flames dancing in his hair and trying to set fire to his heavy serge uniform. Satisfied that he wasn't alight, he reached through the broken glass, released the catch and pushed the window up. Then he slithered through the opening into the darkness beyond.

Silence enveloped the crowd as he disappeared into the smoke-filled room. Twenty, forty, sixty seconds had elapsed since the Pole had disappeared into the blackness. People were becoming fearful. The driver moved to follow his friend when a figure appeared at the window grasping a baby in one arm and a screaming, bawling toddler in the other. A cheer went up from the crowd, which now numbered nearly thirty people. Passing both children to his driver, he struggled out of the window. Wracked with coughing, he was unable to move. He sat on the window ledge, his face black and eyes blinded by smoke. His chest heaved as he tried to drag in the oxygen he so badly needed. A crash sounded behind him and the remaining panes of glass shattered into a myriad of needle-sharp projectiles. He arched his back and cursed in Polish as they lacerated his neck and head. Still blind, he eased himself forward and was about to jump when the boy's father rushed up the ladder, grabbed him by the arm and led him down.

The fire burned freely for a further five minutes before the sound of bells announced the arrival of the fire brigade, who quickly doused the flames.

Disappointed that the flames had gone, the boy returned to his bed and relived what he had seen. He thought of Mrs Sims and what she'd looked like in the firelight. Her white underwear, the dark patch between her legs, her face beautiful in its fear and agony. The surprise on the conductor's face when he broke the window and was momentarily engulfed in flames. The smell of smoke and the taste of burning carried by the gentle shifting breeze. Each fragment of memory was etched on his mind in Technicolor. For the first time he realised that he had an erection, rock hard, hot to the touch. He brushed his cock with the palm of his hand. Suddenly his body convulsed in a spasm of exquisite agony that spewed sperm over his stomach and hand. It took all his self-control not to cry out in painful ecstasy. When it was over he smiled, the tip of his tongue, flicking lizard-like between his lips. *George was right,* he thought, *this will change my life.*

Three more times that night he played with his very own lamb's tail. Each time he embroidered the events he'd seen. The image that released his fourth and final orgasm of the night was of Mrs Sims trapped in the bedroom, her body pressed against the window, flames licking at her face and hair, screaming as her underwear caught fire, revealing her breasts and the dark V between her legs.

Stepping back from his work, the man took a penknife from his inside pocket and walked to the end of the storeroom, where he scratched the initials TK inside a heart on the doorframe. He knew that his signature would not survive the fire but he was an artist and *every artist should sign his work,* he reasoned. Feeling in his breast pocket, he took out a packet of Senior Service cigarettes and lit up. After taking four drags, he checked the tip of his cigarette to ensure it was burning brightly. Carefully he slipped the unlit end into the book of matches, and then placed the lint-covered matchbook on the bed of tissue paper and cotton wool soaked in lighter fluid and packing material that he had prepared earlier. Most of the cigarette lay outside the nest but when it had burnt to within an inch and a quarter of the end it would ignite the matches and set the lint and tissue paper alight. Surrounding the nest was the company's own packing material and hidden in it were four small plastic capsules of lighter fluid. They were his insurance policy. Not enough accelerant to show up in tests, but more than enough to ensure that when the thin plastic skins melted, the fluid would spill out and the entire shelf of packing material would burn.

He checked his watch. 10.18pm. It would take three minutes for the cigarette to ignite the book of matches. Within seconds the nest would be aflame. The fire would spread rapidly, aided by the lighter fluid and packing material. By 10.30 the storeroom would be a blaze, and by 10.40 the first flagons and plastic barrels of chemicals would start to explode. The result would be total devastation and the end of another medium-sized engineering company in Birmingham which had fallen on hard times.

It was time to go to call his principal and take up his position across the road and watch his handiwork play out. It was a shame that there were no workers, other than the night watchman, left in the building. He would have liked to see the young typists and sales clerks running from the building in their bright summer skirts and dresses. The image of women screaming as they ran from the building in panic took hold of his mind. Trapped women. Burning clothes. Fear and panic. For thirty seconds he luxuriated in the images that played across his mind. He hadn't been hunting for a long time. He'd been working so hard. He deserved a reward. He'd start looking tomorrow. But for now, he had to concentrate on the job in hand.

Outside, he crossed the deserted street and headed for the two red telephone boxes outside the newsagent's. Lifting the receiver, he pushed four pennies into the black coin box and dialled a local number. When his call was answered he pressed Button A, waited for the line to clear, and then said, 'Just calling to say that your package has been delivered.'

'Excellent. The balance of your fee will be paid into your account tomorrow morning.'

Part 1

Thursday, 24 June 1965

Handsworth, 16.00hrs

Michael Collins was enjoying his three-month secondment to CID. But today had been a washout. Detective Inspector Hicks had been in with Superintendent Wallace most of the day. Meanwhile, Sergeant York was on sick leave with shingles, and the criminals of Handsworth seemed to be on holiday enjoying the summer sunshine. Checking his watch, Collins realised that Clark would probably be in the canteen enjoying a bit of snap. Sure enough, he found his friend sitting alone at a table, staring blankly into a half-empty cup of tea. 'You look like you've lost a pound and found a penny. What's getting you down?'

'Yow know, just the usual stuff. Why am I here? What's the purpose of life? Is there a God? Will Albion ever win the League again? Why does tea make yowr cup go brown but not change the colour of yowr pee?'

'Well, if that's all that troubles you, I can set your mind at rest. You're here because you're not there. Your purpose in life is to catch crooks and piss off senior officers. It's best to believe there is a God, because according to Pascal's Wager, if you don't and you're wrong you'll spend eternity in the soft and smelly stuff. And if there isn't a God, you'll never know you were wrong. Albion will never win the League again because you're a heathen and don't believe in God and your pee isn't affected by tea, because all tea drinkers are fitted at birth with a small strainer that removes the tannin before it reaches our kidneys.'

'Well thanks for clearing that up. Makes me feel a lot better. It must be hard living with all that knowledge crammed into yowr tiny head.'

'Na, it's easy. I just make it up as I go along and some ejit nearly always believes me. Want another cuppa?'

'Why not, now that I know it won't turn me pee brown.'

While standing at the counter waiting to be served Collins heard Clark call his name. Turning, he saw that Inspector Hicks had just sat down and Clark was holding up three fingers.

Seconds later Collins laid three scalding hot mugs of tea on the Formica-topped table. Stepping back he shook his hands vigorously and blew on his fingers. 'Sod it, that's hot.'

'Yow see what I have to work with, Boss. Dumb as ditch water. Don't even know that tea straight out of an urn is hot.'

Collins gave Clark a two-fingered salute and sat down opposite the Inspector. 'What's up, Sir?'

'I'm off on the Senior Officers' Course until Monday night. With York sick, I tried to cancel but the Super insisted I go. So I need you and Clarkee to do me a favour.'

'No problem,' said Clark. What is it?'

'The Super has agreed that until I return, O'Driscoll will take charge, and you can keep Collins company in CID until York returns or we find an experienced Detective Constable. There's nothing on the go at the moment that can't wait until Tuesday, except the manager of the Empire Cinema has called in complaining about a couple of bikers. They've been seen during the interval hanging about near the manager's office.'

'And he thinks they might be casing the joint?' said Collins.

'Got it in one. Pop and see him and give him a bit of protection if he needs it. OK?'

'Will do, Boss,' said Clark.

'Until Tuesday you pair and Sergeant O' Driscoll are this station's CID section. Anything big kicks off, you call me and I'll be back within a couple of hours. Now, look me in the eye and tell me I can trust you not to burn the bloody place down while I'm away.'

With the boss gone, Clark asked, 'How much trouble does he think wi can get into in four days?'

'Based on our record, more than we can handle. So let's keep it nice and quiet until he gets back.' Collins looked at his watch. 'Fancy having a chat with the Empire's manager before you go back on beat?'

'Why not? He might give us a few free tickets.'

Twenty minutes later, Collins and Clark were chatting to the larger-than-life manager of the Empire Cinema, Handsworth. Nigel Booth had been in cinema management since he left school in 1935. Starting as a trainee projectionist, working for the J. Arthur Rank Organisation, his rise to manager of the second largest cinema in Birmingham had been steady rather than spectacular. His years spent climbing the greasy pole meant that what he didn't know about cinema management could be written on the back of a postage stamp and still leave space for an address. Leaning back in his padded chair, his well-maintained beer belly overflowing his trousers, he ran a hand thorough his thinning grey hair, which he had tried to dye black without success, and said, 'Thanks for coming, lads. I appreciate it. It might be nothing, but better safe than sorry.'

'OK, so what's up, Nige?' asked Clark.

'Like I say, it might be nothing, but twice this week the girls and me have seen two blokes walking about up here on the third floor during the intermission. But the signs are pretty clear and the stairs are roped off, so there's no reason for any member of the public to be up here by mistake.'

'What did these guys look like?' asked Collins.

'Well that's it. We're showing *The Sound of Music* but these fellers are late teens – early twenties at most – and wearing black leather jackets and jeans. Typical bikers.'

'Not exactly your everyday *Sound of Music* fans then,' said Collins.

'Exactly.'

'Did yow see both of them?' asked Clark.

'Just the one. Janice came up with the night's takings and told me that a bloke was hanging around outside. So I went and had a look. He said he was looking for the lavatory.'

'What did he look like?' asked Collins.

'About five foot eight. Stocky with pimply skin, curly ginger hair and crooked nose.'

'And when were this?' asked Clark.

'Monday night. Janice tells me that the other guy was taller, about six foot. Slicked back black hair this time, leathers and jeans. She says he had Harley written in studs on the back of his jacket. He was here Wednesday.'

'So what do yow think they were up to?'

'We bring the cash up from the box office, kiosk and usherettes' takings just after the main film starts or after the intermission in long films like this 'un. I think they were checking out what we do. You know, planning a robbery.'

'And how much are you holding?' asked Collins.

'*Sound of Music* is a huge hit and we're cheaper than the Gaumont, so we've got full houses every night. That's easily £350 by itself, plus another £200 from sales of sweets and ice cream. So say £500 a night. Our worst day was Monday and we still took over £380.'

'How often do you bank the money?'

'It varies. But there can be anything up to a week's takings in the safe.'

'How much is it now?' asked Collins.

'About £3,000. I missed banking the takings for last week.'

'OK,' said Clark. 'I'll tell yow what we'll do. I'll pop home and slip into civvies and be back before the intermission just in case Billy the Kid and his mate show up.'

'Thanks. I'm really grateful. I don't mind telling you I was worried. Other than the projectionist, who's older than me, all the other staff are women. I'm afraid if anything happened, we'd be useless.'

'Don't worry about it. One of us will be here each night until things settle down,' said Clark. 'What time did yow say Janice will be moving the takings?'

'About 9.15.'

'No problem. I'll be here.'

Collins was welcomed home by an over-enthusiastic Sheba who was waiting for him inside the front door, her tail banging on the parquet floor. She continued to jump up as he walked across the hall. Collins knew she wouldn't stop until he made a fuss of her. Bending down, he started to tickle her chest. Immediately the pitch black Staffordshire Bull Terrier lay on her back, legs in the air, and waited for her tummy to be tickled. Collins obliged.

'You spoil that dog,' said Agnes.

'I know. But she's worth it. Aren't you girl?' Standing up, Collins kissed Agnes on the lips. 'And if you'd let me, I'd like to spoil you as well.'

'We'll see,' said Agnes. 'First wash your hands. I've made a Waldorf salad with new potatoes and ham. It will be a change from all that fried food you eat on duty.'

Although he would never admit it Collins loved a good Waldorf salad. He'd never tasted one before Agnes had served it up the previous summer, and he knew this would be another cracker. 'Did Jamie get off OK?' he asked.

'Him and 39 others. They should be nearing Paris just about now.'

'Well let's hope he enjoys his first trip abroad and that he learns some French.'

'He will. It's amazing how much you can pick up in five weeks when everyone around you only speaks French.'

'If you say so. I'm still trying to understand you English.'

Agnes smiled, hesitated and then said, 'I had a phone call today from Aubrey. He wants to meet me on Wednesday.'

Collins put his knife and fork down. He'd met Aubrey only twice and he didn't like the man. 'What does he want?'

'I don't know. But when the Deputy Director of MI5 says he needs to speak to you on a matter of some importance, you don't refuse his request.'

'You know I don't trust that man? He's not interested in people, just what they can do for him.'

'I realise that he will use me and anyone else if he needs to but we go back to before you, my lovely Irishman, were born. I owe it to him. Besides he probably just wants some advice or information. He'd never place me in any danger.'

'If he does, I'll put him in hospital, darling. And you can take that to the Bank of England.'

'Oh, I do like it when you act all Neanderthal,' said Agnes and laughed.

'I was trying more for dark and dangerous,' said Collins. This only made Agnes laugh even more. With no other option left to him, Collins joined in. Agnes was still giggling when Collins led her to the settee in the lounge.

Friday, 25 June 1965

Handsworth, 09.00hrs

Overnight, O'Driscoll had dropped a couple of files in the Inspector's in-tray. Collins picked them up and started reading. As far as he was concerned, a good police file was a as exciting as any best-selling thriller. Alas, the pickings were sparse this fine summer morning. A household domestic that resulted in the wife being taken to hospital with a broken jaw, several broken teeth and numerous cuts and bruises. Most of the damage had been caused by the hubby's use of a knuckle-duster, but she was refusing to press charges.

The second case contained very little paperwork. Station Officer Stan Wold had submitted a possible suspicious fire notification at Hadley's Engineering in Hockley. The mid-sized company had been burnt to the ground the previous Sunday. There was no evidence of arson, but the Fire Officer had been unable to rule it out. 'Covering his arse,' muttered Collins as Clark kneed the door open and entered carrying two cups of tea and holding a Kit-Kat between his teeth. Placing both cups on Collins desk he grabbed a chair and pulled it over. 'Whatcha doing, kidda?'

'I was just going through the Inspector's files. Anything happen last night?'

'Na, quiet as the grave. There was no sign of any rockers. But I did get a free ice cream and a packet of Butterkist.'

'So my turn tonight.'

'Yeah. Play yowr cards right and that Janice might just slip you a free Kia-Ora during the interval.'

'As long as that's all she slips me.'

'Yow know, yow used to be an innocent clean-minded young lad. Now look at yow. I mention a simple drink and yow have to attach a sexual connotation to it. Yowr mind has been corrupted by the job.'

'And who's to blame for that?' said Collins.

The phone rang and Clark picked it up. It was the Charge Room. He listened for thirty seconds then said, 'We'll be there in five. Tell Thompson to keep an eye on them until we arrive.'

'What's up?' asked Collins.'

'Thompson has just spotted two rockers in Ron's café. He says they fit the description given us by Booth.'

Collins was on his feet and heading for the door before Clark stood up. 'We'll take my car,' he said.

'No we won't. Last time I were in that bloody bone shaker I could hardly get out of it. Whatever possessed yow to buy a red MG Midget? Poor old Victor must be turning in his grave at the waste of his hard-earned money.'

'You're just jealous that I saw the MG first. Besides, Victor would be on my side. He lived life to the full, God rest his soul. Besides what did you buy? A dark green Morris 1100 that can only get up Hamstead Hill in second gear. That's what I call a waste of money.'

Clark parked his Morris 1100 opposite the café. Thompson was standing in the doorway of the Soho Second Hand Shop and had a clear view of the two rockers. Collins and Clark walked over to the shop window and pretended to be fascinated with the Box Brownie and Polaroid cameras, 8mm projector, cheap watches, old train sets, snooker cues, fishing tackle and other tat that filled the window.

'How long they been in there, Tommy?' asked Clark.

'Maybe twenty minutes.'

'And you're sure it's them?' asked Collins.

'Well, they match the description read out by Ridley at Roll Call.'

'OK then. Let's go and have a chat.'

The café was empty except for the two young men sitting

in a U-shaped booth near the counter. The rockers clocked Thompson's uniform and tried hard to look disinterested. Clark locked the front door and turned the door sign from Open to Closed. Gerry, behind the counter, nodded at Clark and disappeared into the kitchen. He knew what was about to happen.

Collins slipped into the seat next to the bigger man and Clark sat down beside his ginger friend. 'How yow lads doing?' he asked. 'Making last minute alterations to yowr master plan are yow?'

'What the fuck you on about?' asked the smaller man.

'Does yowr mother know yow swear like a trooper?' asked Clark.

'Fuck you,' said the man and tried to stand up. Clark grabbed the youth's balls and pulled him down. 'Be a good lad and sit down and I might give yow yowr balls back before lunchtime.'

The youth's face had turned puce and he was finding it hard to breathe. 'Now wem going to ask yow and yowr mate here a few questions and if I like yowr answers I'll relax me hold on yowr family jewels. But if yow mess us about then yow'll be walking funny for a month of Sundays. Nod if you understand.'

The young man nodded vigorously and Clark relaxed his hold a little.

'Do yow want to do this, Mickey?'

'No, you seem to have it all in hand.'

'OK. I don't care which of yow answers but remember, lie and laughing boy here gets it. Understand?' Both men nodded. 'Good. What's your names?'

The taller one answered first, his lower lip trembling he looked like he was about to cry. 'I'm Harry Moore, he's Robert Swan.'

'How old are you?'

'We're both 19.'

'And where are yow from?'

'Hockley.'

This was not what Clark had expected. Harry looked set to wet himself and could hardly answer the questions quickly enough.

'So what were yow doing casing the Empire Cinema last Monday and Wednesday nights?'

'We weren't casing it,' said Swan. 'We just went to see *The Sound of Music*.'

'Twice in a bloody weik?' asked Clark.

'It's our favourite film,' said Swan.

Clark squeezed hard. 'Don't mess me about, sonny. The only reason you'd go to see it twice in a weik is if yow had something for nuns. Which would be bloody disgusting and force me to squeeze harder. So why were yow at the film?'

It took Harry all of five seconds to break. 'Last week we were at the Palladium in Hockley. They had *The Wild One* on. Great film. Then this big bloke got talking to us at the interval. Said he was an insurance salesman and wanted to put a scare into the manager of the Empire, so he'd stop stalling on buying an insurance policy. Said all we had to do was go to the pictures on Monday and Wednesday and during the interval take a walk round the third floor and let the staff see us. You know, act a bit suspicious like.'

'And what were in it for yow?'

'He gave us a tenner apiece.'

'And what did this guy look like?' asked Collins.

'About 50, six foot, big belly, going bald,' said Swan. 'We dain't break any laws, did we?'

'What colour hair did he have?'

'Grey, but you could see he'd tried to dye it.'

'And you've never seen him before?' asked Collins.

'No never. I swear,' said Moore.

Clark stood up. 'Yow pair are going to sit nice and quietly here while I have a chat with me mate. If yow move an inch, Constable Thompson here is going to hit you with his truncheon. Ain't that right, Tommy?'

'Dead right, Clarkee.'

Moving to the front of the café, Collins leaned against the front door and asked, 'What do you think?'

'I hate to say it Mickey, but that pair don't have the bottle or the brains to organise a robbery from a blind man selling matches.'

'I agree. Are you thinking what I am?'

'If yow mean six foot and a big belly, then yeah, I am.'

'In that case I've got an idea.'

'Now remember what the Inspector said. Yam dangerous when yow get ideas. What is it?'

'Let's get this pair on ice and I'll tell you.'

It didn't take Swan and Moore long to accept 24 hours' free board and lodging at the station when Clark pointed out that the alternative was to be charged with assaulting a police officer in the course of his duties, especially when Clark had two witnesses to call upon if required.

Nigel Booth hadn't arrived for work when Janice let Collins and Clark into his office. She explained that the first showing wasn't until 2 o' clock and Booth usually arrived half an hour before lights down and always left half an hour after the end of the main feature. Both men were still drinking their tea when Booth bustled into his office. 'Hiya, gents. Sorry to keep you. Janice just told me you were here. Got any news?'

'Indeed we do. I think we've scared off your would-be robbers,' said Collins, smiling.

'That's great,' said Booth. 'How did you manage that?'

'A bit of luck really. One our constables saw them on Soho Road. When he started asking questions about what they had been doing here on Monday and Wednesday they legged it. They'd have to be bloody stupid to try anything now when they know we have a description of them,' said Collins. 'So yow see, yam in the clear.'

'That's great news. But you're sure they won't be back?'

'Well criminals are seldom blessed with an excess of brains, but even the dumbest would think twice about doing a job when they'd just been chased by a copper,' said Collins.

'Never underestimate the stupidity of people, is what I say,' said Clark. 'So just keep an eye out for them and call us if yow see anything.'

Handsworth, 22.30hrs

'What time do you make it?' asked Collins.

'Yow got a watch.'

'Yeah, but it's not luminous, is it?

'Well why did you buy it then, yow pillock?'

'Because I liked it.'

'Well next time, like a practical watch. That way yow won't have to keep asking me. It's just gone 11.'

'Film ended at 10.25. He hasn't come out has he?'

'Na. Wi can see both entrances from here.'

'So, Ollie, do you think we should wander over?' asked Collins.

'Why not, Stanley?'

As they crossed the car park Clark said, 'How come I'm Ollie? Yam much bigger than me.'

'Yeah, but I'm tall and slim like Stanley.'

'But I ain't like Ollie. I'm wiry and small.'

'That's OK. I've told Ruth to fatten you up. You'll grow into the role.'

'Bollocks.'

Clark had done a quick recce of the locks at lunch time and had assured Collins that the quickest and easiest way into the Cinema was via the side entrance. He wasn't wrong. Two minutes and they were in. Taking the back stairs, they moved silently up the darkened stairway. As they neared the third floor they could hear desk drawers being pulled out and thrown against the wall. A loud crash signalled a filing cabinet being upturned. The sound of a bottle breaking was quickly followed by a head hitting the office door and a cry of pain.

Collins and Clark exchanged glances. Clark moved in front of Collins and flattening himself against the wall and moved quickly down the corridor. The plush red carpet cushioned the sound of his steps. At the open door he stopped and listened. There were no voices. All he could hear was the sound of one man breathing hard.

Holding up one finger, he stepped into the doorway. 'What yow doing, Mr Booth? A bit of late spring cleaning?'

Booth froze and turned around slowly. Blood flowed from a cut in his hand where a piece of glass was embedded in his palm. His face was covered in blood and snot, his nose broken where he'd smashed it against the office door. There was a demented look of rage in his face which didn't disappear at the sight of Clark and Collins. Screaming, head down, he charged. Clark side-stepped the charge and landed a right jab on the side of Booth's cheek, who stumbled and fell into Collins, who caught him and laid him gently on the floor face-down. He lay there motionless, and then began to sob. Great heaving, pitiful sobs that shook his entire body.

Clark bent down grasped Booth's right arm and slipped the cuffs on him before snapping it onto the left wrist. Booth winced as the cuffs clicked shut and his life changed forever.

Saturday, 26 June 1965

Handsworth, 04.30hrs

It was raining when Collins and Clark stumbled into the station's car park with the first faint signs of dawn appearing in the sky. Both men were dog-tired. Booth had been interviewed and charged with attempted theft from his employer. No one else had been involved in his master plan. His reason for trying to rip off his employers was simple. He was 50 years old. He'd spent 35 years in the business and two weeks ago a soft-faced 24-year-old git, who'd never shaved in his life, had told him that the company were making him redundant. There would be redundancy pay. However, he'd have to wait until he was 65 for his pension. Worse, he knew there was no chance of another job in the business. Even if he was willing to take an assistant manager's job, no one wanted an experienced cinema manager under them. He'd pose too much of a potential threat.

When he told his wife that he was being let go, she informed him that she was leaving him for another man and would be seeking a divorce. When he asked why, she had said 'I need a man who can get it up,' and walked out.

'Yow have to feel sorry for the poor bastard.'

'I do. But he's a prat to think he'd get away with it. What did he expect? That we'd catch the pair of rockers and think they were lying about an insurance man and ten quid apiece and he'd disappear with the money? Hasn't he ever seen a robbery film? Doesn't he know that everyone who pulls an inside job is always caught? Especially when they're bloody amateurs.'

His key in the door of his new 1100, Clark stopped. 'What were yow on about earlier? Who was covering their arse?'

'What?' asked Collins, his tired mind befuddled and

incapable of linking Clark's question to anything he'd said about Booth.

'This morning. Yow were reading the Boss' pending files. Just as I came in yow said something about someone covering their arse.'

'Oh, that. It was a report from some Station Officer. He has a fire which might be arson. But there was no evidence that it had been started deliberately. My guess is he didn't do much of a job investigating it and decided to cover his arse by sending us the notification.'

'Was the guy's name Stan Wold?'

'Could have been.'

'Tell yow what mate. Yow get off. I'm just going to pick up the file from O'Driscoll.'

'Well don't wake him for God's sake. The poor bloke's only just got to sleep.'

Handsworth, 11.00hrs

Collins walked into the kitchen and was greeted by Sheba. Wagging her tail furiously, she brushed against his legs and demanded that he pat her head and stroke her back. Collins was happy to comply. Opening the fridge, he looked for a slice of corned beef he could give her, but finding none, he threw her a piece of curled–up mature Cheddar cheese that was hiding at the back of the top shelf. Sheba caught it in mid-air and swallowed it down in a single gulp.

Collins was finishing breakfast and looking for Sheba's lead when the phone rang. Before he could get the full number out, Clark said, 'Mickey, what yow doing?'

'I was just about to take Sheba for a walk. Why?'

'Tell yow what. Take her for a walk down to the station and I'll meet yow there.'

'What for?'

'For a mate.' Before he could reply, Clark hung up.

'Well Sheba, old girl, it seems you won't be chasing any rabbits today.'

Twenty-five minutes later Collins arrived at the station with Sheba in tow. Clark was sitting by himself in the canteen, a self-made brew in front of him. 'Kettle's just boiled. Make yourself a cuppa. Stan will be here any minute.'

Collins released Sheba, and tail wagging, she bounded over to Clark, looking for food and a good tummy rub. She got no food but Clark was happy to rub her tum.

With tea in hand, Collins sat down opposite his friend. 'So what's this all about?'

'Yow've never met Stan, have yow? He worked just around the corner at Stafford Road Station. But he'd left for the Central Fire Station before yow arrived. Best ladder monkey I ever met. But don't tell him I said that. He's not the kind to do a poor fire investigation. If there were no evidence of arson and he's still worried enough to send in a report, then I'd bet me pension that sommut is up. The least we can do is listen to what he's got to say.'

'Fair enough,' said 'Collins, 'but we could have heard it on Monday.'

Clark refused to be drawn by Collins' comment and both men sat in friendly silence, sipping their tea and playing with Sheba, while they waited for Wold. When Stan arrived, he was nothing like Collins had expected. At 5 foot 9 and only a little over eleven stone it was hard to imagine Wold carrying a man down a ladder from the third floor of a burning building. But looks were deceptive, and although he would be 49 next birthday he could still bench press 220 pounds and run the mile in under 5 minutes. He also had two awards for bravery on his file.

'Mickey, I want you to meet an old mate of mine, Stan Wold. He's one of the better ladder monkeys that you'll come across. Unlike most of them he's got half a brain.'

'Pleased to meet you, Mickey. You and this stunted cretin here made quite a splash with the shoot-out at the scrap yard last year with that bastard Bishop.'

'Wi don't know nothing about that, do wi Mickey?'

'Not a clue.'

'Have it your own way.'

'Wi usually do. But like I said on the phone, we want to talk to yow about the Hadley fire yow chucked our way last week. Why did yow send it in if yow have no proof of arson?'

Stan placed his hands on the table and interlaced his fingers. He was thinking how best to explain a feeling. 'For a long time now, I've been convinced there's a bloody good arsonist for hire in Birmingham. In the last five years, I've had a string of shop, warehouse and factory fires that I know damn well were started deliberately but I couldn't prove a bloody thing. Whoever the sod is, he doesn't make mistakes and never leaves any clues.'

'So why do yow think it's the same man? Same MO, is that it?' asked Clark.

'This might sound daft, but it's the complete lack of clues which I think is the pattern. He's like a bloody ghost.'

'And you're sure that there is only one of them at work?' asked Collins.

'No. But logic and experience tell me there is only one. You see, most arsonists are pathetic wankers. No style. No brains. They just like to play with matches and watch the flames. The chances of having two or more skilled arsonists operating in any city, at the same time, outside of London are pretty slim.'

'Do you know how he sets the fires?' asked Collins

'I can't be sure, but I reckon on some he uses a lit cigarette as a fuse, tucked into a book of matches. The cigarette burns down, ignites the matches, and sets fire to surrounding materials and all traces of how the fire started are destroyed.'

'Sounds a bit risky to me. Timing is almost guesswork and what if the cigarette goes out, or the matches don't ignite the other materials? He's stuffed,' said Clark.'

'That's why I'm here. I think he waits outside, watching. Only leaving when the fire takes hold.'

'Hang on,' said Clark, 'Yow think he goes back in if the first attempt fails?'

'Correct.'

'So, you're here to check if we have any burglars on file who like to play with fire. Is that it?' asked Collins.

'Got it in one.'

'I'll talk to the Boss when he gets back on Tuesday and ask him to send a message to all the stations in Brum,' said Clark.

'And I'll speak to Alf in records and see if he's got anything,' said Collins.

'Thanks, lads, that'll be a big help.'

'Were Hadley's Engineering the last fire?' asked Clark.

'As far as I know. Why?'

'Well it ain't far from here. I were thinking maybe Mickey, Sheba and me might wander down and have a shuftie before heading home.'

'Be my guest. The tatters will have been all over it in the last week but you can still see where the fire started, near where the chemicals were stored. I can give you a lift if you like.'

'That's good of you, but Sheba gets very snappy in cars and the last place you need to be is in a confined space with a Staffie that's scared,' said Collins.

'Fair enough. Once again, thanks for taking a look. I appreciate it, lads.'

The walk to Hadley Engineering on Icknield Street, Hockley took twenty-five minutes. The once prosperous factory had occupied a five-acre site. Now, with the exception of some outbuildings at the rear of the property, the fire had destroyed everything. The factory, stores, loading bays and offices had all disappeared in the course of a single night. All that was left for Collins and Clark to see were a few retaining walls, blackened with smoke and soot, charred rafters, doors and their frames, and plenty of broken glass and sheets of asbestos that had done nothing to stop the conflagration.

As Wold had predicted, all of the metal, from filing cabinets to office machinery and factory equipment had been pinched by the tatters within 48 hours of the fire. The only metal remaining was the blackened heavy machinery. Even the roof lead, which would have melted into unrecognisable blobs, had been hoovered up by the city's metal vultures. It was the tatters who bought scrap for a few pennies, or pinched it, sorted it, and sold it to the scrap metal merchants who in turn sold it on to the foundries who melted it down for reuse. Without the thieving and scrounging abilities of the despised tatters many Birmingham firms would be out of business. Avoiding the black sludge that the Fire Brigade hoses and the previous night's rain had created, Collins and Clark stepped gingerly onto the rubble. Sheba had no such inhibitions and delighted in running around a site that contained thousands of new smells for her to enjoy. 'If this were started deliberately, then the bastard knew what he were doing,' said Clark.

'That's what I was thinking. So where were the chemicals stored?'

'Over there. The crater in the ground shows where the explosion were. That was where the flammable chemicals were stored. I'll bet yow a quid to a bent penny he started the fire near there.'

'OK. Let's have a look at it. Any idea what we're looking for?'

'Na. I think Stan is right. This guy's a pro. He makes sure that any clues are destroyed in the fire.'

Collins and Cark spent the next ten minutes picking over the burnt debris but found nothing. The destruction was almost complete. Very little had survived the blaze. Turning to go, Collins tripped over a door frame and landed hard on the floor, his hands disappearing into the black mud beneath him. 'Bollocks,' he exclaimed and started to stand up. His supporting foot slipped on the black, oozing mud and he fell again but this time banging his head on a partially burnt door frame. Looking up, he saw Clark laughing. 'If yow could just land on your face next time yow could audition for the Mitchell Minstrels,' said Clark.

Collins glared at his friend. Pushing himself up onto his hands and knees he saw the carved initials TK inside a heart on the doorframe. *Even a dirty old storeroom could be used for love when required,* he thought, and smiled. 'Make yourself useful and give me a hand up,' he said.

'Piss off. Yam covered in muck. Get yourself up,' said Clark and headed off, followed by Sheba.

Even me fecking dog doesn't want to know me, thought Collins as he followed, wiping his hands in his handkerchief. With each step he took he could feel his filthy wet trousers slap against his legs and hear the squelch of muck in his shoes. *Marvellous. Just marvellous,* he thought.

Monday, 28 June 1965

Handsworth, 09.40hrs

Collins was just finishing his report of their meeting with Stan Wold, and Clark was making paper aeroplanes and trying to see if he could throw them into a wastepaper bin he'd placed by the filing cabinet when Sergeant Ridley poked his head around the door. His expression was serious. 'Sorry, lads, we've got a sexual assault. It's a nasty one. The poor woman is pretty shook up. I've put her in Interview Room 1.'

'We'll be there in a sec,' said Collins. Knowing full well that it had to be serious for Ridley to leave the Charge Room.

'Nice way to start the week,' said Clark.

As soon as they saw who was in the interview room both men knew they'd been had. Turning to Collins, Clark whispered, 'I'm going to rip Ridley's balls off.'

'Yoo hoo,' cried Mrs Angela Williams. 'Just the man I need to speak to, Sergeant Clark.'

This time it was Collins who whispered in Clark's ear, 'She likes you, Clarkee. I'll leave you two to get better acquainted.'

'If yow do I'm going to kick yowr balls into your gob.'

'Well if you put it like that, how could I refuse your request to stay?'

Angela Williams was one of the Thornhill Road regulars. She was over 80 and had a figure like a 20 stone tin of Heinz baked beans. Collins and Clark sat down and waited for the usual list of crimes against the poor woman.

'I'm sorry to bother you, but they're at it again.'

'Who are at it again?' asked Clark already knowing the answer.

'Why, men of course. I mean, I only have to walk down the street and I can see the licentious looks they give me. Undressing me in their mind. Putting their hands in their pockets so they can feel themselves. You can't imagine how terrible it is to be wanted by so many. To be seen as nothing more than a body to be used for men's pleasure.'

Collins started to smile and bit his lip hard to stop himself from laughing. Only a month on the beat, Sergeant Ridley had dispatched him to take a statement from Mrs Williams concerning an alleged sexual assault by a neighbour. When he'd arrived she explained that in the last year she had been sexually violated by a range of men on a near nightly basis and that daily she had to endure men sexually assaulting her and exposing themselves to her on the street. It had been at that point he'd put away his notebook. Mrs Williams was someone every new probationer was sent to. Part of their initiation into the force. Twenty minutes later, as he was leaving, Collins noticed two framed wedding photos standing in pride of place on the sideboard.

Mrs Williams followed his eyes and for the first time since he'd arrived her face broke into a broad, generous smile. Picking the photos up she pointed at the bride and said, 'That's me. I was 19 and that handsome man was my husband. The picture was taken in 1902. We made a lovely couple.'

'That you did,' said Collins and meant it. The photo showed a tall slender girl with a gleaming smile, white satin skin, long dark hair and a figure that would turn a cardinal's head. 'What happened to your husband?'

'He went away to France in 1914. He never came home. I don't know why,' she said sadly and replaced the photo on the sideboard.

Collins reverie was interrupted by Clark saying, 'What I meant was which particular man is bothering yow this time?'

'A black man! He lives next door to me. He came up to me in the street yesterday and as bold as brass, asked if he could carry my shopping for me. But I knew what he was after. I told him what he could do with his "bag carrying". It's the white skin you know. They can't resist it.'

'And he lives next door to you?'

'Yes.'

'What does he look like?'

'How would I know? They all look the same to me.'

'Do yow know his name by any chance?'

'I heard some coloured woman call him Winston.'

'OK, Mrs Williams, someone will pop round and speak to him.'

'Sooner rather than later, I hope.' With that Mrs Williams stood up and waddled out the room.

'We're not really going to send someone round are we?' asked Collins.

'Not in the way she thinks. We need to warn the poor bugger. When she gets sommut in her head she can make a man's life hell on earth. It were a bit before yowr time, but she shoved burning newspaper through some poor bloke's letter box. Luckily it burnt out before it could set fire to anything.'

'Why wasn't she committed back then?'

'The man felt sorry for her and refused to press charges. Do us a favour and drop in on the bloke on yowr way home and warn him.'

'OK, I'll look in on her latest boyfriend. But you owe me a cuppa and a doughnut.'

As they left the interview room they found the corridor congested with six coppers including Sergeant Ridley, all bent double laughing. 'Yow can laugh now, Ridley, but I promise I'm going to do yow when yow least expect it,' said Clark.

Hurst Street, Birmingham, 15.00hrs

A small man with blond hair and pale skin walked past the Birmingham Hippodrome and the Old Fox pub where Charlie Chaplin used to drink when he was starting out in the music halls. Cautious as always, he slowed down as he approached the newsagents and looked both ways, and satisfied no one was watching, he stepped into the shop.

'Hello, Mr Tubbs. How are you today?' asked the middle-aged man behind the counter.

'Not bad, thank you. Could do with it being a bit cooler. I don't like the heat. Got anything for me?'

'I believe I do.' The newsagent pushed through a red, white and blue plastic string curtain and disappeared into the rear office-cum-storeroom. Seconds later he reappeared holding an envelope addressed to Mr Tubbs. 'Just the one, Mr Tubbs. It's postmarked Luton. More work away from home, I suppose?'

'It might be. It might be. Never know in my game. Anyway, here's next month's rental for the box. You can keep the change.'

'Very kind of you, Mr Tubbs.'

Tubbs slipped the envelope into his inside jacket pocket and left the shop. Despite the threatening clouds, it was still hot, but not once did the man consider taking his jacket off. As he walked past the Hippodrome, a young woman, a little over five foot tall, with blonde hair and wearing a white mini-dress with yellow flowers decorating the neckline, skipped down the theatre steps. Tubbs saw her and immediately felt a jolt of excitement. His decision was instantaneous. He dropped back a few feet and began to follow her. The hunt was on.

She seemed to be in a hurry, walking purposefully towards Bull Street where she would catch her bus. As she joined the queue for the number 16, Tubbs hung back casually inspecting the window displays in Greys Department Store. He stopped by the display which showed two mannequins dressed in tennis whites and carrying rackets. The girl's reflection was particularly clear at this angle.

The girl ran a hand through her shoulder-length hair, found a knot and spent a few seconds smoothing it out. When the number 16 bus arrived, Tubbs joined the end of the queue and followed her on. He found an aisle seat two rows behind her and sat down. The girl had sat beside an old dear in a hat which had last been fashionable in 1952. The old woman said something and the girl smiled. The pair didn't stop talking until the bus approached the junction of Holly Road and Hamstead Road. She stood up and moved towards the open platform at the rear of the bus. Tubbs waited for one other person to pass him before he too stood up and followed. As she skipped off he heard her say, 'Thank you,' to the conductor and flash him a bright smile.

Condescending bitch, he thought. *Pretending to care for the little people when all she's doing is lording it over everyone she meets because of her looks and what rests between her legs.*

He watched the girl cross the road and head towards number 51A Hamstead Road, a large, three-storey corner house built at the end of the 1890s and now converted into flats. *Perfect,* Tubbs thought. She stopped by a row of mailboxes, unlocked the second box and took out a single letter. Holding it in her teeth, she opened the front door and stepped into the hall.

Tubbs crossed the road and walked casually past the house. He tried to read the name on box 2 but couldn't. No matter. At the corner he turned down Gibson Road. The back garden of 51A was nearly 30 yards long and the fence was badly in need of repair. He could clearly see the back of the house and garden through the many broken planks. He was barely 20 yards down the road when he saw the young woman open the French windows to her flat and step into the garden. *Perfect,* he thought. *Absolutely perfect.* Then he saw the pool in the middle of the lawn. *Not a problem.*

Handsworth, 17.30hrs

Collins had spent most of the afternoon waiting for Booth's case to be heard in the Magistrates' Court. The cinema manager pleaded guilty to the attempted theft of £3,277 12s 8d of his employer's money. As he had no previous convictions and given that he had recently been made redundant, his wife had left him and he had virtually no chance of obtaining a similar job at his age, the judge decided that a fine was the most appropriate sentence. Nigel Booth left the court a broken man, with a criminal conviction, a broken nose, facial bruising, and a cut hand.

As he drove down Holly Road, Collins remembered his promise to Clark and pulled up outside Mrs Williams' house. As usual, she was sitting in her front window watching the world pass by and keeping watch for the Peeping Toms that travelled from far and near to spy on her. As Collins stepped from the car, she recognised him and pointed to the house on her left.

Collins trotted up the garden path and rang the bell. Almost immediately a large black woman holding a mop opened the door and said, 'Whatever you're selling I'm not interested.' Collins showed his warrant card and the woman's tone changed. 'What do you want, officer?' her voice a mixture of concern and defiance.

'I'm looking for a man called Winston. I just need to have a quick word with him. He's not in any trouble.'

'My Winston is a good boy. He'd never do nothing wrong.'

'As I say, he's not in any trouble.'

'All right then, come in and wipe your feet on the mat. I've just washed the hall.'

Collins followed the woman along a still wet tiled hall, past the stairs and into a small sitting-room, then out through the kitchen to the garden. Whatever image he might have had of Winston, it was not this.

Winston was no more than 17 but built like a full grown man. As tall as Collins, he must have weighed a stone and a half more, and all of it was muscle. He had his eyes closed and was doing chin-ups on the upturned frame of an old metal swing and was counting '51, 52...' His biceps and chest were bulging, the veins clearly visible through his smooth black skin. His entire torso was covered in sweat and gleamed in the sunlight. Despite his size and power, his face was that of a very young Sidney Poitier.

'Winston, will you stop that. There's a policeman here to see you.'

Opening his eyes he released his grip and dropped to the ground. 'What do you want, Mr Policeman? I've not done nothing.'

'I know you haven't, Winston. It's just that a good deed you performed yesterday was misunderstood.'

'You mean the old woman next door?'

'Yes.'

'God, man, she's awful.'

His mother clipped him round the ear, 'Don't take the Lord's name in vain. You were taught better than that.'

'Sorry, Momma. All I did was ask if I could help carry her shopping. Man, she was awful. Started calling me names and all sorts. It was so embarrassing.'

'Well, with Mrs Williams no approach from a man ever goes unpunished. We know that you were just trying to help. But please don't talk to her again. Avoid contact if you can. Otherwise she will make your life, and ours, a nightmare. OK?'

'Sure, man. No problem. I don't want no trouble. You see, I'm hoping to join the Army.'

'Well with your physique, I don't think you'll have any problems getting in.'

Winston bowed his head, an embarrassed smile playing around his lips. 'Well, we'll see. I need some references and all I've got is one from my old school in Jamaica and one from our Pastor.'

'I've told him they won't carry much weight in this country,' said the boy's mother.

'Sounds like you've only recently arrived?'

His mother answered for him, 'I came over first, five years

ago. My sister has been looking after Winston back home until I could afford to bring him here. He's only been with me for three weeks.'

Collins looked at the man-boy and remembered how alone he'd felt in this strange country when he'd first arrived three years ago. And he'd only crossed the Irish Sea. On impulse he said, 'I've got a friend who might be able to give you a few pointers about the Army. I'll see if he'll have a word with you. Give you a few tips.'

'That would be great, man,' said a smiling Winston.

Tuesday, 29 June 1965

Handsworth, 9.00hrs

Detective Inspector Hicks arrived at work at 7.45 and spent the first half-hour speaking to the Super about the Senior Officers' Course and his plans for the future. When he finally made it into the office he read Sergeant O' Driscoll's reports and those submitted by Clark and Collins on the Empire Cinema case. He'd just finished when Collins and Clark walked in.

'Well, you pair didn't take long to sort out Mr Booth. Well done. Anything not in the report?'

'No, Boss,' said Clark. 'Other than me cadging a few free tickets and some Butterkist it's all there.'

'OK. Anything else happen while I was away?'

Collins looked at Clark who said, 'Yow explain. I'll only start laughing.'

It only took a few minutes for Collins to outline their meeting with Station Officer Wold, and their visit to Hadley Engineering. He ended his report before the part where he fell face first in the muck. But Clark finished the story, embellishing both the results of the fall and their walk home afterwards. To his credit, Hicks managed to keep a straight face.

'Do you think there is anything in Wold's suspicions?'

'I do, Boss. I've known Stan for years and I'd always trust his instincts.'

'What about you, Mickey?'

'The report didn't ring any bells with me, Sir, but after visiting the site I think Wold may be on to something.'

'Why?'

'I'm not an expert on fires but the damage seemed too complete, too perfect. The fire was started at the exact spot where it was guaranteed to do the most damage and it was started when only the night watchman was in the building.'

'Did the watchman see anything?'

'Not according to Wold. We'll check it again,' said Collins.

'Do that, but it doesn't look as if we have the evidence to say that the fire was started deliberately. Until we do, it stays the Fire Brigade's problem, but just in case I'll send out a warning to all stations. Anything else going on?'

No Sir,' said Collins. 'There's just the raid on Denzel Hamilton's place tonight. Ridley asked if we'd be in on it as they're a bit short-handed.'

'Well I think I'll give that a miss. But you should get off early and get some kip. It could be a very long night.'

'Thanks, Sir,' said Collins.

Handsworth, 21.00hrs

The final briefing for the raid was at 21.45hrs. Clark was early and he found Collins, wearing his uniform and nursing a brew in the canteen. Sitting next to him was Sergeant Ridley who was leading tonight's little outing. 'Now what you've got to realise is that fishing a river is entirely different from fishing down the local cut. Canals ain't natural and the water flows at a more even pace than most rivers...'

'Am yow lying about your latest fishing exploits again, Sarge?' asked Clark.

'I don't need to lie. I've got the pictures to prove what I caught.'

'Well I grant yow, yow do have a lot of pictures of yow holding a bloody big fish but that ain't proof that yow caught 'em.'

'For that I'm going to save all the worst jobs just for you over the next week, Constable Clark. Now, if you'll excuse me I've got a raid to plan.'

Clark slid into the vacated seat. 'I thought I'd save yow from Ridley. He can put yow in a coma when he gets going about fish.'

'And you can't when you start talking about the Albion.'

'That's totally different, that's educational. Anyhow, did yow see Mrs Williams' black admirer?'

'I did and her admirer is 17 and a really nice lad. I explained the situation to him. He'll steer clear of Williams in future. He wants to join the army so I said I'd ask you to speak to him.'

'Why did yow do that?'

'You'll understand when you see him.'

'Bloody hell. I ask yow to do a simple job and yow get me giving advice to some black kid about joining the Army.'

'It will only take 20 minutes.'

'No it won't. It'll take about 20 seconds.'

'How come?'

'The lad's coloured. Even if he was accepted, which is unlikely, the other squaddies would crucify him.'

'Why?'

'Yow know why. I ain't saying we're as bad as the American Army was during the war. But the squaddies just won't stand for it and the officers know that.'

'So the lad is wasting his time?'

'Yeah. If he wants to join up he should try the Foreign Legion. They'll take anyone, provided they're fit.'

At 21.45 hrs, the men crowded around two Black Marias in the station yard. 'Right, lads,' said Ridley. 'You all know the drill. I'm not expecting any trouble from Denzel and his mates. As he told me the last time we did him, he earns more in an hour on these gambling parties than it costs him in a court fine. So tonight I want you to pick up some of his punters. If we charge them with illegal gambling, it might discourage others in the future. So no bells and lights. We pull up nice and quiet and catch the lot of them. OK?' A chorus of 'Yes, Sarge' rang out and the twelve men started to climb into the paddy-wagons.

Clark slid in beside Ridley, who was driving the first van and Collins jumped in the back with three other officers. The Austin engine coughed once, then caught and the van trundled out of the station and headed for Oxhill Road.

As they passed St Augustine's School annex, they began to hear the music. They still had 300 yards to go. At 200 yards, the road became a dual carriageway and they could see that the party had spilt over onto the footpath and central reservation with people drinking, singing and hand jiving away to *The Clapping Song* by Shirley Ellis. At 100 yards, they couldn't hear what the man sitting next to them said even if he was shouting. At 75 yards, Ridley pulled into the side of the road and got out. All eleven officers gathered around. 'Well lads, this ain't what I expected. I was told he was having his usual gambling night. This looks like an open door Hogmanay party in bloody Glasgow. There must be 50, 60, or more of them.'

'Easily,' said a voice from the back, 'An' some of 'em look bloody enormous.'

'You ain't scared of a few nignogs, are you?'

'No, but I am scared of an entire bloody tribe.' A round of nervous laughter ran around the group.

'So what are going to do?' asked Ridley. 'If we stay here much longer, they'll notice us and it will take a bit of time to get help from other stations.'

'Well I ain't going home,' said Clark. 'It looks like a bloody good party to me.'

'Why don't I go and call the station, and the rest of you can follow Clark in from a safe distance?' said Collins. This time the laughter was louder but still tinged with a touch of fear. Only an idiot took on a group of more than 30 Caribbean men when you were outnumbered 3 to 1.

After a silent pause in the conversation which no one wanted to break, Clark said, 'OK, that's settled then. Me and Mickey go in first and try and find Denzel and get him to shut the party down. If that don't work, we arrest him and all hell breaks loose.'

'With us in the fecking middle of it, again,' said Collins. 'And where did the "Mickey and I" come from?'

Collins tried to look casual as he walked towards the party. If this went wrong, he and Clarkee could get seriously hurt. As usual, Clark seemed entirely unconcerned about what might happen and strolled along as if he was walking his beat on a summer night with not a soul in sight.

When Clark reached the gate, a black man of about 40 stood up and blocked his way. He towered over the small policeman. His short-sleeved shirt was barely able to contain his arms and chest which could only have been built by spending hours in a gym, or working eight hours a day doing heavy manual labour.

'What do you want, bloodclot?'

'I want to see me mate Denzel,' said Clark showing his warrant card.

'What if he don't want to see you, man?'

'He will. Tell him Clark needs to speak to him.'

'I'm not your messenger boy.'

'Na. Yowr too old for the job. Tell one of yowr mates to deliver the message. We'll wait.'

Clark leaned against the neighbour's wall and began to whistle. Collins joined him in trying to look nonchalant. As he waited, he remembered his favourite cowboy film, *Rio Bravo*. He tried to look like the sober version of Dean Martin in the film, calm, cool, afraid of no man; while inside he felt like the down and out drunk version.

A crowd was gathering on the pavement as people started to come out of their houses to see the two coppers who wanted to speak to Denzel. As they waited, a tension built among the crowd and transmitted itself to Collins. He knew that the wrong word or action could lead to a major punch-up, maybe even a riot.

After what seemed like an eternity to Collins but was probably less than five minutes, Denzel appeared at the top of the steps. 'Clarkee my man, what you standing there for? Come on in and have a drink on the house. This is my birthday party.'

'I know for a fact yowr birthday is in December.'

'So what, man? If the Queen can has two birthdays why can't I?'

'Fair point. But just come down and let me have a quiet chat with yow.'

'OK, but only 'cause you asked so nicely.'

Clark moved about six feet further away from the crowd as Denzel walked down the steps to join him. Turning his back on the spectators, Clark leaned on the next door's wall and started to talk to Denzel, quietly. Collins couldn't hear a word of what he said. After about two minutes both men stood up and shook hands.

As Denzel walked back to the house the big man asked, 'What's happening, man?'

'The party's over for tonight,' said Denzel.

'Bloodclot man, it's not over. It's just starting. Are you going to let a pigmy boss man shove you around? I'll show you how we deal with white imps in Bermuda.'

Storming over, the big man bent down and shoved his face in Clark's. 'Now, whitey, you tell Denzel that the party ain't over until I say so.'

Without flinching, Clark said, 'The party's over,' then turned his back on the man.

Instantly, the man grabbed Clark's shoulder and spun him around. His massive clenched fist was already on its way to Clark's face. At the last moment Clark spun 90 degrees to his left and ducked as the punch flew over his head. Simultaneously, he grabbed the man's wrist with both hands and dug his hips into his groin. Pulling downward on the arm, he dropped low and the man sailed over his shoulder and landed flat on his back. A great whoosh of air escaped his lungs as he hit the edge of the pavement. Before he could recover, Collins placed his knee on the man's neck.

'Don't struggle, mate, or I'll shift me weight and accidently crush your hyoid bone and yow'll be dead. Now pat the floor twice if yowm going to behave.' Clark pushed down with his knee and immediately the man beat the pavement twice with his hand. Clark stood up. No one was talking, and the music had been turned off, meaning that Clark's best sergeant-major's voice was heard by everyone at the party. 'Yow've all had a good night, and now it's time for yow to say goodnight to Denzel and go on home.' No one argued.

Within ten minutes the road was cleared. As they walked back to the Black Marias, Collins finally asked, 'What the feck did you say to Denzel?'

'I told him that if he dain't stop the party there would be trouble. And if any copper got hurt in the punch-up I'd wait for him one night and put him in hospital for six months.'

Collins smiled. He knew that Clark would have carried out his threat if anything had cracked off. Even more importantly, so did Denzel. 'Well all I can say is, good man yourself. That was well handled.'

'Ta. But we'll need to have a word with Denzel next week. His parties are getting out of hand.'

Wednesday, 30 June 1965

Handsworth, 09.30hrs

Agnes was already up when Collins rolled into the kitchen at 9.30. 'Good morning, sleepyhead. What time did you get in?'

'It was nearly one. I didn't want to wake you so I slept in my old room.'

'What happened?'

Collins described the events of the night before. Everyone agreed that in terms of undertaking a raid it had been a complete disaster. However, given the circumstances, Clarkee had been brilliant in avoiding a potential riot. 'You know, darling, I've known that man for 18 months now and he still surprises me. When you first met him you said, "He's a lot more intelligent than he lets on". In terms of policing he's a genius.'

'It's nice to be right some of the time.'

'Don't hide your light under a bushel. You're right most of the time. That's why this ejit loves you. Will you marry me?'

'No.' said Agnes with a smile and sat on Collins' lap. 'But you could take me to bed and ravish me tonight.'

'How can I refuse an offer like that? I'll be home early. Anyway, what are you doing today?'

'I told you I'm meeting Aubrey.'

'Indeed you did. Well, all I'll say is, be careful. He's after something.'

'Of course he's after something. But I'll have to go to find out what.' Looking at her watch she jumped up. 'It's a twenty to ten. I'm supposed to be there at ten.'

'You'll make it.'

Birmingham, 10.00hrs

Collins had been right. Agnes parked on Colmore Row, opposite St Paul's Cathedral and marched into the foyer of the Midland Hotel just as the grandfather clock near the reception desk chimed 10. Sir Aubrey was sitting in a Queen Anne armchair in the foyer and rose to greet her with a kiss on the cheek. 'My God, Agnes, I don't know how you do it, but you look younger every time I see you.'

'Now I'm worried, Aubrey. Compliments on meeting mean you want me to do something for you.'

'Well yes. But nothing much. Let me tell you about it over a coffee.' Taking Agnes by the elbow, he gently steered her towards the lounge. Sir Aubrey waited until the waitress brought the coffee and a selection of Viennese pastries.

'Now I'm really worried. Viennese pastries at ten in the morning. Unheard of. So out with it. What do you want?'

'Do you remember Anatoli Petrov?'

'Of course I do,' said Agnes as her heart missed a beat. 'We worked together in Berlin after the war.'

'I'm sorry, but I have to ask you. Were you two ever lovers?'

'No,' lied Agnes. 'I think Anatoli would have liked that, however, it would have been a very stupid thing to do on my part, even if our love-making was not being filmed by the KGB.'

'Quite. So why would he give me this poetry book and include in it a message addressed to you?' Sir Aubrey withdrew a small book from his inside pocket and passed it across the table.

The cover was black, plastic imitation leather with the title embossed in silver; *An Anthology of War Poems from the Great Patriotic War* by The Moscow Writers' Group. Agnes opened the book. There was no inscription on the title page and the work of about 30 writers was listed in the table of contents. Agnes scanned the page and found Anatoli's entries. He had submitted two, *Leningrad under Fire* and *A Cold Night in Berlin*. The first poem meant nothing to her but the second, she recognised immediately. 'Where's the message?'

Sir Aubrey passed it to her, 'He hid it between the plastic cover and the card it was pasted onto.'

Agnes read the message, which was in Russian,

"Dear Agnes, the time for me to leave dear Mother Russia has come. Meet me at Kings Cross Station on Friday 9/7/65 at 21.00hrs, in the buffet. I will speak with only you and you are not to bring back-up. Under no circumstances is MI6 to be told of my pending defection and the news should be strictly controlled within MI5. Anatoli."

'What do you think? Is it genuine?'

'The message is genuine. He always referred to Mother Russia as dear Mother Russia when he wanted to be sarcastic. It was his only criticism of the system.'

'A system he's done everything to support and protect for the last 24 years. Why does he want to defect now?'

'That I don't know. But I'll ask him on Friday.'

'So you'll do it?'

'What choice do I have? He's an old friend, and you don't run out on your friends.'

'No you don't,' said Aubrey and smiled.

'You say he gave you the book about two weeks ago? How did he manage the exchange?' Agnes asked.

'There was a cultural event at the Russian Embassy about two weeks ago. He was keen to give a copy of the book to everyone he could as part of his Cultural Attaché cover. It was quite embarrassing really. The grandly-titled Moscow Writers' Group is a bunch of amateurs who have never been professionally published. This anthology was self-published and translated by one of the members, probably Anatoli.'

'Which implies he's been planning this for some time.'

'Possibly,' said Aubrey. 'Any ideas why he chose Kings Cross?'

'When we were working together Anatoli said that even in Russia it was well known that prostitutes frequented the back of Kings Cross Station. He said that made it a perfect place for a Russian spy to meet someone. No member of the

KGB would ever query the need for a Russian male to visit the ladies there.'

Sir Aubrey smiled. 'I'll send a car to pick you up on Friday the 9th, say at 2pm?'

'Fine.'

Handsworth, 11.30

As Agnes drove away from the Midland, she remembered the dark freezing night in Berlin. The only time she and Anatoli had made love. *When was it? December 1945. A lifetime ago.* She shivered involuntarily as, unbidden, the memories of the sudden blizzard that had forced them to take shelter and how the ice-laced snow had felt on her face came back to her. Worst of all had been the driving wind that seemed to slice through her clothes and skin and encase every bone and muscle in her body with a layer of frost.

For two weeks she and Anatoli had been searching for the renegade spy who was helping Nazi war criminals escape to England. They had spent the day on another wild goose chase and now the snow made it impossible to get back to the comparative comfort of the bomb-damaged hotel where they were staying.

Huddled together in an abandoned basement for warmth, Anatoli had told her that he loved her, and for a single night she let him believe that she loved him. Agnes smiled as she remembered their lovemaking. Hands fumbling between layers of clothes. Mouths crushed hard together. It had been swift, strangely erotic and very satisfying for two people that had seen only death and despair in the previous 12 months. Afterwards, Anatoli had held her in his arms and said, "I will write a poem for you. For, I know we can never be together. That is all right. We are after all on different sides now. But like that film you took me to see, "I will always remember Berlin." A few days later he had presented her with the poem.

Agnes slipped her Rover past Collins' MG Midget parked

in front of the garage and stopped. She slipped the key in the lock and stepped into the empty house. *Michael must have taken Sheba for a walk,* she thought.

Running up the stairs, Agnes paused by a floor-to-ceiling tapestry showing a medieval jousting scene. Pushing the duelling knight's kneecap, she unlocked a narrow door and entered a room that was barely six feet wide but 12 long. The room contained a bookcase filled with box files, a green filing cabinet, one old swivel chair a scuffed desk and a squat black safe.

Dropping to her knees, Agnes opened the safe. It contained no money or gems, only papers, a few files and a flat wooden box. She quickly found the file she was looking for, took it to the desk and sat down. Inside were various documents in English, German and Russian from her time in Berlin. Anatoli's poem was near the back. Holding the two-page poem in one hand she compered it with the copy in the book. She saw the alteration immediately. A single word on line 21 had been altered from *looking* to *watching*. She continued to compare the poems for any other alterations and found none.

The change confirmed two things. Firstly, that Anatoli's message was genuine. Line 21 related to the time of their meeting. Secondly, the change confirmed that he was being watched by the KGB. His insistence that MI5 deal with his defection had to mean that there was a traitor in MI6 who would report any approach he made to their masters in Moscow. He might even know the name of the agent. *I need to call Aubrey. Warn him,* she thought. Replacing the file in the safe, she took out the flat wooden box and opened it. Inside lay a pre-war Mauser 7.65 self-cocking pistol with a wooden handle, 20 rounds of ammunition and a made-to-measure pigskin thigh holster.

Agnes had not fired a gun since 1957 and had renounced violence when she became a Quaker in 1958 but this was different. By attending the meeting on Friday she would not only be risking her own life, but Anatoli's also. She had no intention of going unarmed. Hearing the front door open, she replaced the gun in the safe and went down to meet Michael. She resolved to clean the gun after he went to work.

'How did your meeting go?' asked Collins.

'Fine. I have to go to London Friday week.'

'Fair enough,' said Collins. In the seventeen months they had been together, Agnes had never said anything about what she had done in the war or the years afterwards. For his part, Collins never asked. However, he did wonder if it was the Official Secrets Act or Agnes' natural discretion that stopped her talking. Either way, it didn't matter what she had done all those years ago. All that mattered was that she was with him now. And if, after meeting Aubrey, she had to go to London it must be important. 'Why don't I make lunch before I go on duty? How about pancakes for a change?' he said.

'That would be lovely.'

By mid-afternoon the sun was melting the tar at the side of the road and Collins and Clark were sitting on the yard steps, jackets off, a mug of tea each at their elbow. Clark had his eyes closed, face turned to the sun. Meanwhile Collins was keeping well in the shade.

'Am yow some kind of bloody vampire or what? Why don't yow get yourself in the sun and catch a bit of a tan, yow pasty-faced numpy?'

'I come from a long line of Irishmen who are pale of skin, strong of arm, battle hardened and fearless. We obey no man, and live by one simple rule; never fight in the fecking sun. Ten minutes of that and we look like a cooked lobster.'

'So yow only fight at night, do yow?'

'Why not? Sure, that way we get time and a half.'

'Yow know, it would be real easy to get yow committed. Yam mad.'

'Ah! This is where you pair of wastrels are hiding,' said Sergeant Ridley and plonked himself down beside Clark, wiping his head with a blue striped handkerchief.

'What can I do yow for, Sarge?' asked Clark.

'I thought you'd like to know Zatopek is at it again.'

'I thought he were still inside,' said Clark.

'Got out last week. Good behaviour. Thought you'd like to know, as you've put him away at least four times to my knowledge.'

'Whose Zatopek?' asked Collins.

'Archie Mellon from Aston. We call him Zatopek 'cos he's done 10,000 gas meters in his thieving life,' said Ridley.

'Mind yow, he's easy to catch. Yow can't run very fast with twenty quids' worth of shillings in yowr pockets. If I see him I'll give him a pull,' said Clark.

'Cheers,' said Ridley.

Back in the office, Clark took a call from Stan Wold. Yes, they had issued a notice to all forces in the Midlands and no, they'd received no responses yet. Yes, the station records officer was checking the files for suspicious fires and burglaries that involved fire. And no, he wasn't finished yet. Hanging up Clark said, 'Stan's really got a bee in his bonnet about this guy.'

'Well, let's hope we turn up something for him,' said Hicks. Looking at his watch, he stretched, stood up and slipped his jacket on. 'I don't know about you lads but I'm heading home. Things are as dead as a dodo.'

'Seems like a good idea Boss. Yow coming, Mickey?'

'You get off. I've got a bit of reading to do.' With the office empty, Collins took out a copy of Stone's *Justice Manual,* the standard work on procedures and law in the Magistrates' Court, and Moriarty's *Police Law,* which provided an invaluable guide to the law and regulations for police officers. Barely six months had passed since his probation had ended, and Collins didn't want anyone to know that he was already studying for the sergeant's exam – especially Clark. Ninety minutes later Collins stood up, slipped the books into the bottom drawer and covered them with a writing pad.

Just as Collins started his studies, and less than half a mile away Mr Tubbs was sitting in his car on Hamstead Road, waiting. It was twenty to four, and if Anne Johnson followed the same routine as Monday and Tuesday she would be home within the next 20 minutes.

Tubbs checked in his mirror and saw the number 16 bus appear at the top of the hill. Less than a minute later Anne Johnson stepped off the bus and waited for it to pull away. Before stepping into the road she looked to her right. Tubbs felt a jolt of excitement as she looked directly at him. He imagined that she had seen him but she hadn't, she was looking beyond the little man in his TV repair van. She was looking for cars and other dangers on the road.

Tubbs watched her cross the street and noticed how her yellow pleated miniskirt moved with each step. Just a few inches more sway and he would be able to see her knickers. He could already clearly see the outline of her white bra beneath her yellow blouse. If he had been nearer, he was sure he would have been able to see the top of her bra, as she'd undone the top three buttons of her blouse. He felt himself grow hard and pushed the images that were crowding into his brain away. *Not now,* he thought. *But soon. Very soon.*

Collins was about to head for home when he remembered the night watchman at Hadley's. He'd meant to pay him a visit earlier but forgot. Crossing to the Inspector's desk he picked-up the report from Stan and found the address for Mr Arthur Blenkinsop. He lived just off Icknield

Street, within easy walking distance of Hadley's.

Collins pulled up outside a back-to-back two-up two-down house with a toilet in the yard shared by four families. Finding no bell or knocker on the cheap front door, he rapped on the wood with his knuckles. After a short wait he heard movement and stepped back.

Blenkinsop was pretty much what Collins had expected, old beyond his 69 years, thin and small with arthritic hands and a cough that would only stop when he died. 'Yes? What do you want?' The voice was hoarse and rasping. A heavy smoker's voice.

'Mr Blenkinsop? I'm DC Collins from Thornhill Road Police. I've come to ask you a few questions about the fire. Can I come in? It won't take long.'

'You took your time coming around. But I suppose you'd best come in.' Stepping aside, Blenkinsop opened the door and Collins found himself standing in a tiny front room. A single door, in line with the front door, led to a dining room from which Collins could hear a TV. The smell of freshly fried fish was over powering.

'Sit yourself down. Do you want a cuppa?'

Collins choose the two-seater settee covered in worn brocade that had probably seen 60 years' service. 'No thanks,' he said and sat down. He immediately felt a loose spring dig into his left buttock and shifted position.

'OK, what do you want to know? But I warn you, I told that fireman all I saw.'

'I've read your statement. But me boss just wants me to double check.' Collins paused then said, 'On the night of the fire you say you saw no one outside the factory before the fire started. Is that right?'

'Yes.'

'How about earlier in the week. Did you see anyone hanging about or acting suspiciously?

'Na, no one.'

'When the fire started where were you?'

'Well I do me rounds every hour. The alarm went off at about 10.25. I was at the back of the building. I went to the nearest red phone and called the brigade and then got out of there fast. I ain't paid enough to be a hero or to get blown up by them bloody chemicals.'

'Where did you go after you came out.'

'I walked down to Ickeild Street and stood about 50 yards away from the building waiting for the fire brigade.'

'Did you see anyone?'

For the first time Blenkinsop seemed uncertain. Collins waited. 'I can't say I seen anything important. Just some small guy came out of the phone box on the corner, got in his van and drove away.'

Collins felt the familiar tingle of excitement. There had been nothing in Stan's report about a man in a van. 'Did you mention this to the Fire Officer?' he asked.

'Na. he dain't ask about what I saw after the fire had started.'

Collins shifted position again and with an apologetic smile asked, 'Do you think I could have that cuppa now, sir?'

Thursday, 1 July 1965

Handsworth, 09.15hrs

The station was busy when Collins arrived. A punch-up between rival gangs had kicked off the previous night at the newly refurbished and renamed Oasis Dance Hall, previously The Palms, on Rookery Road. There were 14 youths in custody and all were due to appear in Magistrates' Court that morning. Pushing through the throng waiting for transport to court, Collins headed straight for the CID Office.

'Morning, Sir,' he said and hung his jacket on the coat rack. 'I went to see Arthur Blenkinsop on the way home last night.'

'Who?'

'The night watchman at Hadley's.'

At the mention of the company's name, Hicks put down the report he was reading. 'Well, did you get anything?'

Collins grinned, 'Yeah. Stan asked him if he'd seen anyone hanging about the building before the fire. He didn't ask if he'd seen anyone outside at the time of the blaze.'

'And?'

'He did. Some bloke was making a call from the phone box opposite Hadley's.'

'Did he get a look at him?'

'No, he was too far away. All he could say was he looked small against the phone box. But he did see him drive away in a Morris Minor van.' Collins paused for effect. 'He says it was light grey and had a sign on its side for carpet fitting.'

'How could he see the sign and not see the bloke?'

'The car drove past him on the other side of the road.'

'What car drove past who?' asked Clark from the door.

'The car that you and Collins are going to be looking for.'

'What?'

'Collins will explain. I have a meeting at Central CID.'

As soon as Hicks had left, Collins and Clark headed for the canteen where over a cuppa Collins briefed him on what he had found.

'He dain't get a registration number?'

'No. Too much to expect from an old man.'

'OK, I'll try and track down the car. It will be hard without at least a partial number plate.'

'Fine, I'll get the phone books out and ring around the carpet fitters.'

Handsworth, 15.00hrs

Tubbs parked on Holly Road and walked 150 yards back to Hamstead Road. He was dressed in brown overalls with a small badge above the breast pocket that read Greenhough Electrical Ltd. and carried a metal tool box. He could feel the sweat start to break out all over his soft pale body and his mouth go dry.

Crossing the road, he strode confidently up to the front door of 51A and slipped a skeleton key into the Yale lock. It didn't fit. Calmly, he removed it and tried another. He wasn't worried or flustered. He was just another workman trying to get into a property using the keys the landlord had given him, and was having trouble finding the right one. He even took the time to confirm the name on mailbox 2, Anne Johnson. His heart fluttered as he recalled how she had looked yesterday. The yellow blouse through which he could see the outline of her white bra and a yellow pleated miniskirt. *God, she likes to tease,* he thought. On the fourth attempt, the lock clicked open and he stepped into the surprisingly cool hallway.

For two minutes, he stood there listening. He was an expert

at listening and waiting. There were no voices or footsteps to be heard in the house. No doors were opened or closed and there was no sound of a radio. If anyone was in, then they were sleeping.

Flat 2 was directly in front of him, at the end of the hallway. The lock was another Yale, and this time he chose the right key on the second attempt. His heart was now beating hard. He never felt this way when he was working on a professional job. It only happened when he was working for pleasure – and what a sensuous pleasure it was to be standing in Anne's lounge. In her private lair. Walking on her carpet. Touching her things.

The room was sparsely furnished but everything in it from the drop-leaf table to the two-seater settee was bright, modern and tasteful. He ran a hand across the back of a rocking chair in the corner and felt the smoothness of the wood beneath his gloved fingers. *You'll burn nicely,* he thought and smiled his little smile which exposed the tip of his tongue.

Crossing to the French windows, he withdrew the key and pushed a small piece of swarf into the keyhole before replacing the key. He checked to see if he could open the windows. He couldn't.

Stepping into the bedroom, his heart rate increased further and he could feel the sweat on his palms inside his gloves. Moving to the bed, he picked up a pillow and buried his face in it. The smell of Anne Johnson's hair and scent swept over him and for the first time he realised that he had an erection.

Replacing the pillow, he went to the chest of drawers. He pulled out each drawer in turn, starting at the bottom. The first three contained clothes, gloves, belts and nightwear. Not what he was looking for. As he opened the top drawer, he saw a jumbled pile of panties, bras, suspender belts and in the corner a collection of stockings and tights. He plunged his hands into the soft fabrics and had to resist the urge to take off his gloves and feel the precious, secret garments. Quickly now he started to rummage through the drawer. He found a pair of plain white nylon knickers, but there was no matching bra. He'd have to use one of his own. However, he did find a white suspender belt with a red rose in the middle of the waistband. Lastly, he selected a pair of sheer nylon stockings before closing the drawer.

Turning, he noticed for the first time a wicker laundry basket. His nostrils flared and his heart beat a little faster. Lifting the lid he saw a pair of plain white cotton knickers and lace bra. *It's the one she was wearing yesterday,* he thought as he picked it up and buried his face in its softness. The bra smelled just like her pillow. Fresh and flowery. A cheerful summer smell.

Returning to the bed he noticed that his hands were trembling as he carefully laid out each item of underwear on the powder blue candlewick bedspread. Each item was positioned just as they would appear if Anne were lying on the bed wearing them. As he folded the left stocking down to ankle length he could no longer control himself. Through his clothing he rubbed his penis as he thought of how Anne's clothes would burn in the fire he was about to set. He conjured up the smell of smoke in his imagination and he came with a low moan and a great shudder.

Picking up the underwear, he opened his tool box and placed them in the bag he'd brought along. *I don't want you getting dirty do I?* he thought. He then removed the only other item in the box, a brown paper package that he had prepared the night before. He was pleased with how ordinary it looked. There was nothing to distinguish it from the thousands of other small parcels delivered daily in Birmingham. Even the cancelled stamps he'd stuck on amounted to the correct postage. Taking his pen he added Anne Johnson's name to the address.

He had one more job to do before he left. Looking around the room, his eyes were drawn once more to the old style Shaker rocking chair. Turning it over, he carved a very small heart, about the size of a halfpenny into the underside of the right rocker before scratching TK in its centre. Even if the chair didn't burn, no one would see it there.

Standing in the hall, he checked that Anne's door was locked, and then placed the package at the foot of the door, just as anyone would if they had taken in a parcel for their neighbour.

He checked his watch. It was 15.30. If Anne followed the same routine as the previous three days, she'd be home within the next 20 minutes. He'd wait and watch from a safe distance.

Tubbs did a U-turn on Holly Road and parked about twenty five yards from the junction with Hamstead Road. He had a clear view of the house. His pulse rate had increased and his mouth was parched. He fumbled for the half-full bottle of Corona lemonade in the passenger well, found it, and took a long swig. It was flat and warm, but it slaked his thirst.

Five minutes later, he saw the number 16 bus slow down, stop and Anne Johnson cross the road. She was wearing a red miniskirt and white blouse today with black kitten heel shoes. *She looks so sure of herself,* he thought. *She thinks that she can have her choice of men. Well you little bitch, you're about to find out you can't.*

He watched her check the mail box before opening the front door. His penis pushed against his zipper but he stayed in control. He didn't want anyone to see him playing with himself. He started to count. He'd reached 132 when he heard a muffed bang from inside the house. Twenty seconds later the front door opened, and a woman, her hair and clothes on fire stumbled from the building. He rolled down the window so that he could hear her screams. That wonderful, familiar feeling of power, lust, and fulfilment rose up as he watched the burning clothes stick to Anne's skin. He was particularly excited by the bright red and yellow flames that had engulfed her skirt. Most of her hair had been burnt away, but some, he was pleased to see, was still burning. Her face was blackened. She had almost reached the pavement when she collapsed face down. Turning on her side, she raised an arm skyward as if in supplication to the heavens, then crumpled to the ground and lay still.

A middle-aged black man raced across the road, ripping off his jacket as he dodged traffic. Reaching the girl, he began to slap out the remaining flames that were still licking at her head and body. Others were now gathering quickly. There were maybe twelve in the crowd when a small explosion shook the windows and a huge flame erupted from the open front door. Two young girls in the crowd screamed, and most present hunched their shoulders and moved further away from the house and the body on the path.

Time to go, Tubbs thought. As he pulled away and turned right onto Hamstead Road, he wound the window fully down and breathed deeply. The smell of smoke and burning was in the air. He couldn't resist smiling, his tongue tasting the smoke. He was happy. He had his trophies and his memories.

Tubbs' workshop, 16.30hrs

Twenty minutes later, Tubbs stood in a long room measuring 20 foot by 8 which had been divided into two rooms, each measuring 10 foot by 8. The door in the centre of the partition was open, and he could see a radiogram, TV, armchair and a cabinet on which a two-ring electric hob rested. Beside it was an electric kettle. A small, cosy bolthole.

The room he stood in was very different. It contained a queen-size bed and a bedside cabinet, both of which he had taken from his parents' house. The two shorter walls and ceiling were covered in mirrors and arranged in a semi-circle were six mannequins. One was naked, but covered with a long piece of muslin through which its shape was easily discernible. The other five were identically dressed. Each wore a white bra and panties, a white garter belt with a red rose in the centre of the waistband, and clear coloured stockings. In each case the left stocking lay crumpled around the dummy's left ankle. On the stomach of each mannequin was a three-inch strip of red Dymo tape which bore the embossed name of a woman.

Bending down, he withdrew the bra, panties, garter belt and stockings that he had taken from Anne Johnson's flat. Removing the muslin from the naked mannequin, he ran his hands over its body, then laid the dummy on the bed. First, he rolled the stockings up the doll's legs, then slipped the panties onto its body. His hand shook as he ran his fingers over the stretched panties. Pulling it away, he fitted the garter belt around the figure's waist and attached the suspenders to the stockings. Starting to feel aroused, he lifted the mannequin and placed the open bra around the dummy's stomach, hooked it closed and then slid it up her torso and arms. Lastly, he adjusted the straps. He picked up the dressed mannequin and returned it to its place before standing back to admire his work. Just two adjustments to make. He centred the red rose in the middle of the doll's waist and then rolled down the left stocking, leaving it in a crumpled pile around the mannequin's ankle.

He felt the tension of the day drain from him, to be replaced by the glorious peace of expectation. Stripping, he pulled on a pair of white nylon knickers, a red garter belt and sheer stockings. He then took a pair of black, patent leather kitten heeled shoes, size 6, from the bedside cabinet and stepped into them. He was finally ready.

Approaching the mirrors he walked up and down, all the time watching his reflection. He was particularly pleased by the sight of his penis peeping above the waistband of the knickers. After five minutes, he could wait no longer and moved to the mannequins. Taking each in turn, he rubbed himself against the hard plastic and soft fabric. On the fifth mannequin, he realised that he could no longer control himself and rushed to his latest girlfriend and climaxed over "Anne's" ankles.

Part 2

Friday, 2 July 1965

Handsworth, 08.40hrs

The morning sun was in Collins' face as he drove along Hamstead Road. Nearing the corner of Holly Road he stopped and got out of the car. This was his first sight of the destruction caused to 51A Hamstead Road that last night's local TV news had reported. The entire three-storey house had been gutted and blackened. Tendrils of smoke were still curling into the air from the furniture, carpets and appliances that the firemen had raked out of the house and the stench of burning wood, plastic and metal filled the air. *God, that looks bad,* he thought. Seeing the burnt image of a human figure on the pavement he crossed himself and said a Hail Mary and a Glory Be for the repose of the young woman's soul. He was about to return to his car when Stan Wold stepped out of the house.

'Stan, what happened?'

'I was just on me way to see your gaffer. This is a bad one, Mickey. The worst I've ever seen. Some bastard sent an incendiary device to a young woman. It ignited when she opened it. Burnt her to death. She managed to get out of the house but died where you're standing.'

Collins looked again at the black stain that was half on the pavement, half on the drive and said, 'You don't think it's your "mate", do you?'

'No, this was very professionally done, but it was personal. The bastard wanted to kill this one girl and he made sure he did just that. Probably a jilted lover or boyfriend. She was a pretty girl. She wouldn't have lacked for company.'

'So where did it actually happen?'

'Come on. I'll show you.'

Stan led Collins down the blackened and water-damaged hall into what was left of Anne's flat. The flames had destroyed carpets, furniture, curtains, doors and every personal item that she had possessed. The French windows were broken and lay open. A pile of debris, raked from the flat, sat on the patio. A black, charred mess.

'Let me show you something,' said Stan.

Collins followed him over to what was left of the French windows. 'Have a look at the lock.'

Collins bent down. The lock was soot-stained but largely undamaged. It still had the key in it. Out of habit, he tried to turn the key. It didn't move. *Must have been damaged in the fire,* he thought. 'What am I looking for?'

'You've already found it.'

Collins hunkered down and looked at the lock again. Removing the key he saw something bright and silvery stuck in the lock. 'What's that?' he asked.

'My guess is it's a piece of metal. Swarf, probably. Now that didn't just jump into the lock by itself. Someone put it there. My guess is that the bastard who torched the place put it there to stop the girl escaping into the garden.'

'But why do that? The bomb would kill her anyway.'

'When you're on fire you try to run away from the blaze. The quickest way out would be into the garden and there's a pool in it. So he cut that route off, forcing her to run out the front.'

'But why would he do that?'

Stan said nothing, letting Collins think it through as he himself had done earlier. Slowly, realisation dawned. 'The bastard. The fecking bastard. He wanted her to go out the front because he was watching. My God, that's evil.'

'I told you, it was the worst I've ever seen.'

Collins moved into the garden, looking for some fresh air and feeling sick to his stomach. The mound of debris on the patio was still radiating heat. What remained of an old Shaker rocking chair had tumbled down the heap and now lay upside down on the lawn. The back had been badly burned but the seat and rockers remained largely untouched. He picked it up by a leg and was about to throw it back onto the heap when he saw the heart and the familiar initials it encased – TK. His hand shook and his voice was unsteady when he said, 'Stan, I've got something.'

Handsworth, 14.30hrs

Events moved quickly once Inspector Hicks designated the house and garden a crime scene and took charge. The Scenes of Crime officer and four PCs, who had been drafted in to assist him, started a fingertip search of the flat, garden, and the charred and mangled furniture. It was slow going.

Collins and Wold visited Hadley's Engineering.
Although anything of value had long since been pinched, no one had been interested in a piece of charred wood, and Collins quickly found the burnt and broken door frame he was looking for. Stan took a picture of it *in situ*, and selecting a one pound lump hammer from his toolkit, he removed the door frame from the few bricks it was still attached to. Carefully, both men lifted the frame into the back of Wold's fire van. They knew that the engraved initials might provide valuable information about the arsonist such as whether he was right- or left-handed, an estimate of his height, while identification of the tool he'd used might identify his trade or training.

Back at the station, Collins and Wold headed for the canteen where they were joined by Clark and Inspector Hicks. None of the men had eaten for several hours and all were only too happy to tuck into some reheated Irish stew. 'So where do we go from here?' asked Wold.

'I've been thinking about that,' said Hicks. 'This guy's been living in the shadows for years. He thinks he's invisible. Untouchable. That no one knows about him. I think it's time we gave him a nasty surprise. Shine a big bright light on him. Call him a few names. Belittle him. Maybe he'll make a mistake. What do you think?'

'One thing I know about arsonists is that they all have giant egos. Push him, insult him, needle him and you'll get a reaction, all right. My only worry is we might get the wrong reaction,' said Wold.

'I think wi should take the risk, Boss. At the moment wi have nowt. Yow should give a press conference. Appeal for witnesses,' said Clark.

'I agree,' said Hicks. Lighting up a Gauloise, he pushed his plate away and sat back thinking. When he spoke he was smiling. 'If this guy has an ego he's going to be pissed off that finally he's been found out. Think how much more pissed off he would be if a wet behind the ears young bobby was in the papers explaining how he broke the case.'

'Hang on a minute Sir, I've never done a press conference in me life. I'd make a pig's ear of it.'

'No you won't, because I'll be there at your side. You'll just have to nod in the right places. And if you're asked a question just speak clearly and be yourself.'

'Bloody hell, Sir, if I do that no one will understand me accent.'

Turning to Wold, Hicks asked 'What do you make of the letters? Are they his initials?'

'I doubt it. I don't think our man would be so careless as to leave his initials behind. More likely a nickname. Or perhaps the initials are somehow related to his first fire. Truth be told, Inspector, they could mean anything.'

'So we keep an open mind on what TK stands for. What are you going to do next?' asked Hicks.

'I'll circulate what we know to all brigades in the country. See if any of them have ever come across a TK and I'll double-check our records,' said Wold.

'OK. Let me have a copy of your memo and I'll send it to all police forces in England, Scotland and Wales. If that's it, I'll see you all at the press conference.'

Handsworth, 17.50hrs

The press conference was held in the canteen, the largest room in the station. The papers had been on the story since yesterday and the room contained reporters from the *Mirror, Sketch, Daily Mail* and *Express* as well as their upmarket cousins, the *Guardian, Telegraph* and *Times*. Local reporters were also well represented but their elbows weren't as sharp as those of the Fleet Street hacks and had been pushed to the back. A single ITN camera had been hastily installed in one corner of the room

Collins walked into the room behind Inspector Hicks and tried hard to control his breathing. Working on a local paper in Ireland for a couple of years covering church and social events had not prepared him for this. Fortunately, Hicks was a natural. Sitting down he said, 'Gentlemen, I'm going to read a prepared statement, after which I will take a small number of questions.' The room settled down and Hicks launched into his statement.

'Yesterday, a young woman, Anne Johnson, was sent an incendiary device which on opening exploded and covered her in inflammable material. She managed to stagger into the road before she collapsed and died from her injuries.

'This was a heinous and vile crime perpetrated on a young woman who had her whole life in front of her. I wish to extend the heartfelt sympathy of all the officers serving in the Birmingham Police Force and Fire Brigade to her family and friends.

'However, thanks to Detective Constable Michael Collins, who is sitting next to me, we now know that the perpetrator is

linked to the recent fire at Hadley Engineering in Hockley. In conjunction with our colleagues in the Fire Brigade and other police forces throughout the country, we are now looking for other cases of arson that fit this man's M.O.

'We believe that Detective Constable Collins has provided us with the essential clue which will lead us to finding the perpetrator of these sickening and cowardly crimes. However, we would ask that any members of the public who saw anything suspicious in the vicinity of 51A Hamstead Road between 3 and 4pm yesterday to contact us immediately. Similarly, anyone who saw anything suspicious at or around 10pm on Sunday, 20th June, near Hadley Engineering in Hockley should contact Thornhill Road Station or their local police station.'

Looking up, Hicks said, 'I will now take questions.'

The reporter from *The Times* asked, 'What is the nature of the evidence that links the crimes you spoke of?'

'At this stage I'm not at liberty to say.'

The *Mirror* man jumped in next, 'Are you expecting to make an arrest any time soon?'

'I think with the evidence we now have, I'm confident of making an arrest in the near future,' lied Hicks.

The reporter from *The Birmingham Mail*, directed his question at Collins, 'Detective Constable Collins, what do you think of the man responsible for this awful crimes?'

Collins hesitated. Then remembered what Hicks had said and responded honestly. 'I think he's a cowardly louse who preys on innocent woman. He should hang for his crimes, but with abolition now nearly certain I hope he rots to death in a prison cell.'

Hicks immediately jumped in and said, 'Thank you, gentlemen,' and walked out of the room with Collins close behind.

Back in the CID room he turned to Collins but before he could say anything Collins said, 'I'm sorry, Sir. It just came out.'

'Don't be sorry. I left because you gave them the headline for every paper in the country tomorrow, "Cowardly louse, should hang". If that doesn't piss the bastard off nothing will.'

Birmingham, 18.35hrs

Mr Tubbs rose from his chair and switched off the ITN News. *The fools,* he thought, *do they really think I can't see through their pathetic attempts to provoke me? Morons, all of them.* But no matter how hard he tried to dismiss what he had just heard, he couldn't understand how they had linked the house fire with Hadley's. The targets had been entirely different. *What the fuck do they have?* His mind screamed. For the first time in his career he felt concern. A panic-inducing worm of doubt and uncertainty had started to wriggle its way into his brain.

He crossed to the cupboard and took down a bottle of gin and poured two inches of the colourless liquid into a tumbler. Returning to the overstuffed armchair by the bookcase, he sat down and went through every facet of the two fires. There was no similarity between them. The ignition methods used had been different. There was no connection between the two targets. He'd certainly not left any fingerprints or even footprints behind. Was it possible that they had been on his trail for some time and could link the Hadley fire to other commercial fires? But if that was the case, why had they not questioned him? How much did they really have on him?

Did they have witnesses from two or more fires who had described him? Was that really likely? He'd never worn the same overalls twice and he always changed the number plates and signage on his van. At best they'd know he used a Morris Minor van. No, they were bluffing. They had nothing on him. But still he worried.

That young Irish bastard on the TV had ruined the entire day for him. He'd been looking forward to celebrating with his special friends again and that bastard had spoilt it for him. *How dare he suggest that I should hang? Well he won't stop me,* he thought. Picking up his toolbox, he went upstairs to work. A *bit of work will calm me down, then later I can have some fun.*

Exhausted, but unable to sleep, Tubbs lay awake, fretting, turning and cursing. For the first time in his life the thought, *They're coming for me* entered his mind and it made him angry. Finally, holding his limp penis for comfort, he fell into a fitful sleep at 2am. It was 5.13 exactly by the alarm clock when he awoke and sat upright, *Fuck,* he thought, *they've seen my sign. That has to be it. It's the only thing that could link me to both fires.* But then sweet rationalisation quickly followed. *They won't know what it stands for. If they think it's my initials they'll never find me. I'm safe,* he thought and smiled his little smile with the tip of his tongue protruding between his teeth, rolled over and went back to sleep.

Saturday, 3 July 1965

Handsworth, 09.25hrs

Collins had never seen the station in such turmoil. Ever since Hicks' TV appearance the night before, the phones had been ringing non-stop. Two morning papers had led with the headline, *Cowardly louse should hang,* and all had quoted what he'd said. The effect had been astonishing. People were queuing out the door in reception to talk to an officer. Collins had barely seen Clark, and although he was responsible for co-ordinating the operation, he'd spent most of the morning answering phones.

In a lull in the calls, Collins slipped into the canteen and grabbed the phone behind the counter. Dialling Newtown Station, he asked to be put through to Inspector Race. After a short delay, the Inspector demanded, 'Yes? Who is it?'

'It's DC Collins at Handsworth Sir. I was wondering if ...'

'I've already beaten you to it, lad. I've sent two PCs and two WPCs to give you a hand. That was what you were calling about, wasn't it?'

'Yes, Sir. I'm really grateful.'

'Don't be. I want this bastard caught. He killed that poor girl, maybe others. We have to put the bastard down.'

'Yes, Sir. You said "Maybe others". Do you have something on him?'

'I'm not sure. I'm just going through all the fires we've had on the patch in the last three years. There are a couple that we thought suspicious at the time but we had nowt to go on. When things settle down maybe you and that Black Country shite of yours, Clark, can pop down and take a look.'

'Will do, Sir. And thank you.'

There was no response from Race, just the sound of him hanging up. Collins replaced the phone and smiled to himself.

Race liked to pretend that he was a cynical misanthrope but the truth was that he'd do anything to help a fellow copper or a member of the public. But if you broke the law, he could be as persistent and bloody-minded as Jean Valjean.

As he hung up, Clark walked into the canteen. 'So this is where yow've been hiding, yow skiving toerag.'

'I'll have you know, Constable Clark, that I've just arranged for four coppers from Newtown to give us a hand. Race asked me to give his love to that West Bromwich shite Clark.'

'I bet he did, but as he's sending four to help I'll forgive him.'

'Have you got anything yet?'

'Yeah, the guy who tried to smother the fire with his coat reckons he saw the guy. Oh, and Mrs Williams wants to speak to yow. Says it's important.'

'It always is.'

'Speak to her now, will yow? She's annoying the punters.'

'OK, where is she?'

'In Reception.'

Collins headed for Reception. Of all the days for her to call, this had to be the worst. But he knew that she would not leave until she had seen him or whichever copper she had selected. 'Mrs Williams, how are you?'

'I'm fine. I want to report ...'

'As you can see, we're a bit busy now. Could I see you tomorrow? I promise I'll call around and you can tell me who's been acting in a lascivious manner towards you.' Taking the old lady by the arm, he tried to lead her towards the door but she shook free.

'It's not about me. It's about the man who burnt that poor girl. That's what happens when a man becomes obsessed with a woman, and I should know.'

'I know it's terrible, but you're perfectly safe, I assure you.'

'Will you listen to me? I saw the man!' she almost shouted.

Collins released her arm and looked her in the face. 'You saw the man?'

'Yes. I was in the window watching for Peeping Toms and

I saw him. He walked up Holly Road, past my house and got in his van. Then he turned around and drove down the road and stopped by Mrs Reynolds' house. He stayed there until the girl came out. The one on fire.'

'Could you describe what he looked like?'

'Of course I can. When there are so many men after you, you need to make sure you can describe them to the police.'

Collins wasn't sure if he should take Mrs Williams seriously. It could just be another of her fantasies, but there was something different in the way she spoke and acted today. 'OK, Mrs Williams, why don't we go to my office and you can tell me all about it?'

The CID Room was empty. Inspector Hicks was speaking to Anne Johnson's parents in the Super's Office. Mrs Williams plonked herself down in York's chair and Collins said, 'I'm just going to get Constable Clark to sit in and hear what you have to say.

Collins found Clark in reception still separating visitors and callers into fantasists, timewasters, possibles, and probables. As usual, his charm was working well. 'Let me get this right, you have evidence that the Duke of Edinburgh is the arsonist, and that it's all part of his initiation into the 39th Level of the Supreme Masonic Lodge and his ascension to the Lizard Throne.'

'That's right.'

'Well do me a favour, Mr Eisen, and piss off.' Turning, Clark saw Collins, 'I thought you were in with Mr Wilson?'

'No, I'm still talking with Mrs Williams. I think she may have seen something, but you know her better than me. I need to know if what she's saying is fantasy or reality.'

Collins sat down opposite Mrs Williams, and Clark took up his favourite position in any interview, leaning against the door. 'OK, Mrs Williams. Please tell me and Constable Clark everything you saw yesterday afternoon.'

'I was in my front room when I saw this workman walk up to his van. He'd parked it outside Mr Jennings' house two doors down on the opposite side of the road. Well, he got in and turned it around and drove towards Hamstead Road. He only went about 100 yards, then he pulled up. I thought he had another job to do but he didn't get out of the car. He just sat there. I was surprised.'

'Why did you think he was doing another job?'

'Well I can't be certain, but I think he came out of the house that caught fire. I didn't see him leave the house, but he crossed Hamstead Road right in front of it.'

'I see. But why did you think he was working?'

'Well he had one of those metal toolboxes and he was wearing a brown boiler suit.'

'And you saw all this from your front windows?'

'I'm not nosey, if that's what you mean. It's just that with all the flashers and Peeping Toms trying to get me I have to keep track of them.'

'I'm not suggesting you're nosey, Mrs Williams, I'm just very pleased that you were so observant. But you said you were surprised…?'

'That's right, he sat in his car until that poor woman came running out. He must have been really hot.'

'Did you get a good look at the man? Could you describe him?'

'I saw him right as rain as he walked up the street. A small man, only about five foot four. He wasn't fat but he looked a bit podgy. '

'Anything else?'

'He had blond hair and pale skin."

'And you say he was wearing a brown boiler suit?'

'Yes, it had a badge on it.'

'Could you see the badge? '

'Not really, but I think it had a lightning bolt on it.'

'Why do you say that?'

Because his van had a lightning bolt on the side and under it was the name Greenhough Electrics.'

'What type of van was it, Mrs Williams?' asked Collins, praying that she'd say a grey Morris van.

'Oh I couldn't say. I don't know anything about cars. All I can say is it was dark blue.'

Collins felt his heart sink but managed to keep the disappointment from showing on his face.

'Yow must have a great memory to remember so much, Mrs Williams,' said Clark.

'Oh, my memory is terrible these days. That's why I write everything down in my record books.'

'Record books?' asked Collins.

'Yes. I keep a description of every flasher, Peeping Tom and rapist I see,' she said proudly. 'How else can I report them to you?'

'Do yow have the book with yow?' asked Clark.

'Oh, yes,' said Mrs Williams as she rooted around in her shopping bag before pulling out a school exercise book and handing it to Clark.

Clark opened the book and his face broke into a smile. He handed the book to Collins. Each page was divided into three columns. The first was the date and time. The second was a full description of the sexual perverts who were constantly assaulting Mrs Williams and the third was details of their cars – if any. It was immediately obvious to Collins that Mrs Williams wasn't familiar with most car makes as she'd resorted to describing the many cars rather than just give their make and registration number.

Turning to the entries for Thursday, Clark read, "Small blond man, with pale skin and soft features, about 5 foot 4, walked to his car in a licentious manner and turned it around and drove down the street. He stopped outside Mrs Reynolds.' He may have been thinking about coming back to take me. But when the woman ran out of the house on fire he drove away in a dark blue van with a lightning bolt on it."'

Clark nodded at Collins who said, 'Mrs Williams you've been a big help. Constable Clark here is going to take your statement and I'm going to get someone in with the Identikit – and he'll try to construct a likeness of the man from your description. Is that all right?'

'Perfectly. But I'd like a cup of tea, please.'

'I think we can arrange that.'

On the way to Interview Room 1, Collins collared the admin assistant and asked her to take two teas and iced buns to the CID room. If Mrs Williams didn't want her cake, Clark would scoff both. Collins recognised the second witness as the man who had used his coat to beat out the flames that had engulfed Anne Johnson. Eighteen hours on, he still looked shocked. A grey tinge lay beneath his ebony skin, his eyes distant, still seeing the burning body of a young girl. 'Hello again, Mr Wilson. How are you feeling today?'

'Sick, man, sick to my stomach. I keep seeing that poor girl. But you know what's worse? I can still smell her burning flesh.'

'It must have been terrible, but you did everything you could. You even gave us a statement, which must have been difficult for you. So what's brought you back? Did you forget something?'

'It's like I said to Mr Clark. Yesterday, I told you about what I did but it was only when I saw you on the news last night that I remembered the man in the van.'

'What man?'

'A workman. He had brown overalls and was driving a dark green van with the name of some electrical shop on it.'

'What made you notice him?'

'He turned right out of Holly Road. He was driving very slowly. Looking at what was going on.'

'That's pretty normal when there's a fire.'

'I know. People everywhere like to watch other people's misery, just like in Barbados. But he slowed down and wound his window down. And I think he was smiling. I can't be sure.'

'OK. Can you describe the car?'

'It was a Morris van, I think, dark green. With a lightning bolt on the side.'

'Would you be able to describe the man to our identikit officer?'

'Yes, but I only saw his face.'

'That's not a problem. I'm going to take your statement and I'll get the officer in after that. But before we start can I get you a tea, coffee or a sandwich?'

'I could do with a rum. Settle my nerves.'

'I don't think we can run to a rum, but I think I know where I might find a drop of whisky for your tea.'

'That's better than nothing, man.'

As Collins headed for the canteen, he saw Mr and Mrs Johnson being ushered out of the Superintendent's office by Inspector Hicks. Anne's parents were both in their late forties, but with their red-rimmed eyes, deathly white skin, and the unutterable pain and despair etched on their faces they looked twenty years older.

Steeling himself, he walked over to the Inspector who introduced him to the bereaved couple. 'I just wanted to say how sorry I am for your loss. It's a terrible thing that's been done.'

'Thank you,' said Mr Johnson, his voice cracking. 'Just do one thing for me. Catch the bastard.'

'We will, sir. I promise.'

It was lunchtime before things started to calm down and Collins and Clark were able to bring Hicks up to date on what they had found out. 'Well, Boss, we may have our second and third pieces of evidence linking TK to both fires.

'Mr Blenkinsop, Mrs Williams and Mr Wilson all saw a small van. Blenkinsop and Wilson think it was a Morris Minor. But they can't agree on the colour, it might have been grey, blue or dark green. They also disagree over what signage was on it. Blenkinsop says it was for a carpet fitter, but the other two say it was for an electrics company.'

Clark was interrupted by PC Hartford, the Identikit officer. He apologised for the interruption, laid two pictures on the Inspector's desk and said with a hint of triumph, 'That, boss, is our killer.'

Inspector Hicks picked up the pictures and held one in each hand. He was joined by Collins as he studied them. 'My God, they do look alike,' he said.

'It's the same man, Sir,' said Hartford. 'I'd bet me next wage packet on it. The two witnesses saw the man from different angles and each of them will have noticed slightly different features. That's the only reason the pictures aren't identical.'

'OK, so what do we do with them? Go public or just circulate them to police and fire brigade?' asked Hicks.

'It's difficult, Boss. I'm sure wi would get a reaction if wi went public, but it means tipping our hand. The bastard could easily do a runner,' said Clark.

'I agree. Up to yesterday he was invisible to us and the fire brigade. My bet is that he could disappear and stay lost if he wanted to.'

'So wi keep it to ourselves, Boss? asked Clark.

'For now. But get these pictures out to every police and fire station in the country.'

'Right, Sir,' said Collins.

'What wi going to do about the van, Sir?' asked Clark.

Hicks took a long drag on his cigarette, let the smoke out slowly, and continued to sit there thinking. Finally, he said, 'The only thing we can be fairly sure of is that a Morris van was seen at both fires. The colour and signage on the van is in dispute. But my gut tells me that it's the same van. Which means that TK is a clever bastard who is happy to change the colour and signage after every job. If he's willing to re-spray the car regularly, then it's near certain he switches the number plates as well. So all we really have to go on is his picture and the make of his van. Sorry lads, but it looks like you wasted a day's work chasing down the car.'

'Can't be helped, Boss,' said Clark. 'I saw the kid's parents this morning they looked desperate. I don't mind wasting a few days if wi catch the bastard.'

'They seemed decent people. Do you think they'll be all right, Sir?' asked Collins.

'My guess is they're ruined for life.'

'Did they give us anything we could use?' asked Collins.

'No. She'd been working at the Hippodrome as an assistant stage manager since breaking up from Bristol Old Vic Theatre School for the summer. Her parents don't think she was seeing anyone in Birmingham.'

'Do yow want us to go down and have a chat with the people at the Hipp?' asked Clark.

'Wouldn't do any harm. Show them the picture. Maybe one of them saw him. It's a long shot...'

'But it's worth a try,' said Collins. 'We'll check the surrounding shops and pubs as well.'

'Here, mind who yow're volunteering. I want to get home for six tonight.'

'Hot date?'

'Very funny. It's Mam and Dad's anniversary. Ruth's cooking dinner.'

'OK, Cinderella, I'll get you home for six. But first, I need something to eat.'

Hurst Street, Birmingham 14.10hrs

A quick lunch of fish and chips meant that Collins and Clark were at the Hippodrome by 2pm. Everyone who had worked with Anne had liked the cheerful, intelligent, and creative young woman. Two men admitted to asking her out without success. As one said, "She was a bit out of my league but I thought it was worth a try."

Copies of the two pictures were handed around but no one recognised the man or could remember seeing him hanging about the theatre or in the vicinity.

'What now?' asked Clark, as they stood on the steps of the theatre.

'Let's try a few of the shops. If he works around here he probably uses the tobacconists, newsagents, pubs and cafés. You take the pubs and cafés, and I'll check out the newsagents and tobacconists. I'll meet you in the café on the corner.'

'Fair enough.'

Collins could see three newsagents and one specialist tobacconist from where he was standing and started walking. Clark headed for the Old Fox Pub opposite the theatre.

The first newsagent and the tobacconist had looked hard at the pictures. Screwed up their brows in concentration and then said, 'Sorry. Never seen him around here.'

The second newsagent's shop was tiny. Not much bigger than a kiosk with a front door and a bell that rang as Collins pushed his way into the shop. A middle-aged man, dirty grey-haired, with rheumy eyes and a ruddy complexion, stepped through the plastic strip curtain and said, 'Good afternoon, sir. What can I get you?'

Collins showed him his warrant card and said, 'I'm trying to find this gentleman. Do you recognise him?' Collins handed the man the pictures.

The man looked at the Identikits and immediately said, 'No. Never seen him.'

Collins felt a slight shiver. *The bastard's lying,* he thought. 'Would you mind taking another look at the pictures please? This is important.'

'Why what's he done?'

'We just need to speak to him.'

'I see,' said the man and looked at the pictures again. This time he studied them carefully. 'I'm good with faces, Constable. Like, I saw you on the news last night. But I've never seen this man before in my life.'

'Well thank you Mr...?

'Hastings, Alan Hastings.'

'If you do remember anything, please call me at Thornhill Road Station.'

'Will do. But like I say, I don't know him.'

Hastings waited for Collins to walk away from the shop before he locked the front door and went into the cubbyhole of an office that lay beyond the plastic strip curtain. Along one wall was a row of six pigeon-holes, all of which contained at least one letter. Directly beneath the letter rack was a single pedestal desk. Hastings knew that all his postal address customers were dodgy. Some were using his shop as a drop for dirty photos that had been developed in London. They were always the easiest ones to recognise from the thickness and feel of the envelopes. He'd often enjoyed a pleasant 20 minutes looking at the contents of envelopes he'd steamed open. Some pictures he didn't like, the ones with queers in. But the women and young girls were a real treat. Others were letters from married men to their fancy women or vice versa. Some were just business deals, probably shady. But he didn't care. He had 34 customers and charged £6 rental a month for his very discreet service. That amounted to £204, plus tips, per month for doing nothing.

He'd steamed open all of Mr Tubbs' envelopes but they only ever contained a telephone number plus a time and date. No names, no addresses. Nothing. And now the coppers were looking for him in connection with those fires. Pulling the desk out, he wriggled between the desk and wall, a task made more difficult by the row of pigeon-holes and his beer belly. Hidden behind a wooden box that looked like the cover for a gas or electric meter was a cheap galvanised safe that a lad of 15 could get into with a tin-opener. He lifted it onto the desk, spun the dial and pulled out the expanding index file.

As he opened the file he smiled. This was his pension. Another year and he'd sell up, and then those customers who had left an address or phone number would be contacted by a friend of his. Nearly every customer he had ever had was represented in the folder, along with details of the correspondence they had received and where appropriate, Xerox copies of their correspondence and/or photographs which he'd held back for his private collection.

Tubbs' record was just a single sheet of paper listing the full contents of every message he'd ever received. At the top of the page, circled in red, was a phone number. Mr Tubbs had emphasised that it should only be used in an emergency. *Well this was an emergency*. One that Hastings expected to benefit from.

Clark was sitting in a window seat drinking his tea when Collins sat down. One look at his young friend's face was enough to tell him that he'd found something. 'OK, yow grinning baboon, what'cha got?'

'Mr Alan Hastings, the newsagent, is a lying little toerag of the first order. He recognised the pictures but claimed he didn't.'

'Yow sure?'

'Certain. And it's a pound to a penny that if we run a check we'll find that he has a record. He smells of prison.'

'OK. So what do yow want to do?'

'Have me cuppa and then the pair of us can go and see him again.'

Hastings dialled Tubbs. The phone rang out for nearly 30 seconds before it was picked up and Tubb's familiar high-pitched voice said, 'Yes, who is this?' It sounded as if he was in a church or an echo chamber.

'It's Mr Hastings from the newsagents. I'm sorry to call you but I thought you should know that a young policeman, the one who was on TV last night, has been around asking questions?'

'What about?'

Hastings found the echo disconcerting and tried to ignore it. 'He had two pictures of someone who looked just like you. He asked me if I recognised the person in the pictures.'

'What did you say?'

'Nothing, Mr Tubbs. Nothing at all. You've always been one of my very best customers. Over the years you've been appreciative of the service I've provided and this has been reflected in your very generous tips.'

There was silence on the line. Hastings wondered if he had been too subtle with his threat. He didn't want to be blatant. Better if Mr Tubbs decided how much his silence was worth. Early in his blackmail career Hastings had discovered that he often underestimated what people were willing to pay to keep their actions secret. Now he always let them suggest a price.

Finally, Tubbs said, 'I'm very glad to hear that. This is obviously a misunderstanding on the part of the police. However, I can do without any aggravation just now. I think the best thing I can do is send you a little something for your trouble and continued silence.'

'That's very kind of you, sir. I hadn't expected anything. I was just looking out for my favourite customer.'

'Of course. But good service demands a reward. You should get it Monday morning.'

'Thank you, Mr Tubbs.'

Tubbs hung up, his normally pale complexion crimson with anger. 'Fuck, fuck and fuck again,' he screamed at the empty workshop. Standing still he forced his anger down into his belly and started to think: *How the hell did they get a picture of me? If they have a picture then it's only a matter of time before someone recognises me and they track me here. I have to get away. Cut all links with this place.* As a plan of action started to form in his mind, he began to relax. He took a piece of paper and pencil from one of the work benches and sat down. For the next fifteen minutes he listed what he had to do. Finished, he sat back and read what he'd written. It was a good plan. It was simple. It would work. But something was missing. Leaning forward he added "Kill the Irish cunt and that Inspector." Only then did his secret little smile appear on his lips, his tongue moving between his teeth.

Hastings was pleased with how his telephone conversation had gone. He was sure that Tubbs would be co-operative. *He had no backbone.* All soft, flabby skin with *nothing but fear and self-doubt inside. No, he'll be easy to handle and good for a fair few quid,* thought Hastings.

For Hastings, it had been a surprisingly good day. He decided that he deserved a reward. For the first time in a week he thought of Nicki. She was a bit older than his usual girls, nearly 18, but she was small, firm and a snug fit. He decided to give her pimp a ring and see if she was available. Ten minutes later he'd closed up for the day and was on his way to Johnny's. As he drove, he decided to make a night of it. First Nicki, then a few hands of cards and a drink, and maybe he would finish the night off with the new tart, Debbie. Johnny said she was 11 but Hastings reckoned she was nearer 13.

By the time Collins and Clark had returned to Hastings' shop it was locked up and he'd gone. Like all the shops making their money from those working in the wholesale markets, he would be closed on Sunday. Collins cursed himself for not asking Hastings for a home address. A quick call to the station and he asked WPC Milne to find the address and to check if Hastings had done time.

Arriving back at the station, Collins and Clark went looking for Milne. Five years out of the army, she had retained her military bearing and can-do attitude. Word was that she wanted to make Sergeant within five years, a tall order for a man, nearly impossible for a woman, many thought.

They found her in the records room. 'He lives in Quinton,' she said, 'and he did four years in Winson Green for blackmail in the mid-50s. I've written his address down.'

'Many thanks,' said Collins. Then looking at his watch, he asked Clark, 'We've just got time to get to Quinton and get you home in time for the ball, Cinderella. Want to come or go home?'

'Let's go and see the sod. I ain't been intimidating for days. I don't want to lose me touch.'

'No chance.'

Hastings' house was off the main Wolverhampton Road, tucked away in the corner of a cul-de-sac. A privet hedge that looked as if it hadn't been cut in 10 years surrounded the front garden and hid much of the house from the path. The lawn was brown, half dead and weed-strewn. The house matched its surroundings, a detached dormer bungalow with the paint peeling and the slates under both the bedroom and lounge windows cracked and chipped.

'It don't look much like an entry for *Home and Garden,* does it?' said Clark.

'True but it does reflect the owners' unique style,' said Collins in a flawless upper-class accent with just a touch of campness. 'Notice how the grass reflects his hair style. A few strands spread unevenly across a browning dome. The paint a mirror image of his lined face, and the general forlorn look, which is in total sympathy with his overall appearance.'

'Bloody hell, yowm getting worse. I'm starting to think yow need to see someone.'

'Why? I thought it was pretty good.'

'Yow would. Yow'm tone deaf.'

There was no car in the drive. Just a large oil stain. Vigorous knocking on the door confirmed that no one was home.

'Shame to waste a trip,' said Clark. 'Fancy a butcher's?'

'Why not?'

Clark was through the Yale lock in 20 seconds. The Chubb took slightly longer.

'You're not getting slower in your old age, are you?' asked Collins, stepping into the house.

'Piss off.'

'I'm just saying maybe you need glasses.'

'And yow'll need a bleeding doctor if you don't shut up.'

'That's another sign of old age. Becoming crotchety.'

Clark responded with, 'Bollicks,' and headed into the lounge. Collins went up the stairs. The air was stale and smelled of fried food and old chip papers, and the carpet, decorated with beer and tea stains, felt sticky underfoot.

The bedroom was a tip, with dirty clothes and bed linen littering the floor. Collins checked the wardrobe and chest of drawers. Nothing. Then Clark called up. 'Mickey, come and have a look-see at this.'

Clark was standing in the middle of the lounge, a tea chest by his feet. In neat piles beside it were over 100 pornographic mags and about a dozen Standard 8 movies. 'He's got wide tastes, has Mr Hastings. He likes animals as long as them with a naked woman. And there are loads with girls who should be home playing with their dolls. Then there's the rape mags. He seems to like them best. I'm not sure what we can do him if they're for his own use.'

'I don't think we can do anything, possession isn't an offence under the 1959 or 1964 Obscene Publications Acts. Unless we can prove he was planning to distribute.'

'Bloody hell, anyone would think yow been studying for

yowr sergeant's exam already.'

'Na. I'm just a collector of dirty mags who likes to know his rights. Now let's get you home for your Mam and Dad's big night. We can have a chat with Hastings at his shop Monday morning.'

Sunday, 4 July 1965

Handsworth, 11.00hrs

Collins returned from Mass but found it hard to settle. His mind kept returning to the case. He tried to read his copy of the *News of the World* but couldn't concentrate. Finally, Agnes laid her *Sunday Times* down and said, 'For goodness sake, go to the station and do some work.'

Collins smiled and stood up. 'You know me so well. I won't be too long.'

'Take your time. Dinner's not until five.'

Collins kissed the top of Agnes' head. She raised her face to him and he kissed her lips. *I must be mad,* he thought. *I could be spending me afternoon with the woman I love, and what am I doing? Going to bloody work.*

The station was quiet when he arrived, but when he pushed the CID door open he found Clark sitting at his desk reading the statements of all those who had called in the previous day. 'How's it going?' he asked.

'Nowt to write home about. The best stuff we got was from Mrs Williams and Mr Wilson.'

'I'll give you a hand.'

'Cheers, but let's grab a cuppa first.'

Sitting in the deserted canteen, Clark took a sip of his tea, sat back in his chair and asked, 'How's Agnes?'

'Grand, thanks.'

'I'm surprised that a good Catholic boy like yow is still living in sin. Haven't you asked her to marry yow yet?'

'Sure, I've asked her dozens ahh times.'

'And she's said no?'

Collins nodded yes. 'I'm not sure why. I think she might

be worried she's too old for me. But I can't be sure. Agnes doesn't wear her feelings on her sleeve, but I think she loves me.'

'That's bloody obvious to a blind man. Ruth knew it first day she saw yow pair together. It was the snowball fight in the back garden. And Agnes had only known yow for a couple of days then.'

'What should I do then?'

'Don't ask me, mate. I'm a man. Not even Einstein could unravel how a woman's mind works. But my advice is to hang in there. Eventually she'll weaken and say yes.'

'Come on then, let's get back to work.'

Both Clark and Collins were disappointed when they finished empty-handed at 5pm. They'd found nothing new in the more than 60 statements that would help them catch the arsonist.

Returning home, Collins heard Agnes moving around in the kitchen. Putting his hands around her waist, he pulled her to him and said, 'I love you, Agnes Winter,' and gave her a long gentle kiss on the mouth. Laying her head on his shoulder she said, for the first time, 'I love you too.' They kissed again but this time it was hard and demanding. Without breaking the embrace, Agnes reached behind her and turned off the gas. Dinner could wait.

Agnes and Collins had just finished washing up when the phone rang. Collins picked it up. It was the station, but this time Ridley wanted to speak to Agnes. Taking the phone, she said, 'Sergeant Ridley, how can I help you?'

'One of the officers found a young girl badly beaten up while on patrol today. She says she has nowhere to go. I was hoping that you might be able to take her in for a few days until she's feeling a bit better.'

'I'd be happy to. I don't have any guests at the moment. Do you want me to pick her up?'

'If you could that would be great. I'm short-handed just at the moment.'

Twenty-five minutes later Agnes arrived at the station to be greeted by a garrulous Sergeant Ridley and a very taciturn Joanne Munroe from Handsworth whose father had thrown her out of the house.

Fifteen minutes later Joanne was shaking hands with Collins, who noted the strong smell of hospital coming off the girl, who was apparently 19, but looked around 15. She was a bottle blonde, five foot three tall, with what had been a pretty face until someone had broken her nose with his fist before he really gave her a going over. The result was a badly bruised face with a cut lip and abrasions down the left side where someone had rubbed her face on the road. Every step she took was filled with pain, but she was too proud to let it register on her face.

Collins said, 'It's nice to meet you, Joanne. You're in good hands here. Agnes will look after you and if you want to press charges against whoever beat you up you can speak to me.'

'Thanks,' she said. 'But all I really want to do now is go to bed and sleep. If that's OK.'

'Of course. If you'll follow me,' said Agnes and led Joanne up the stairs.

'Hasn't she said anything about what happened?' Collins asked Agnes when she returned.

'No, nor did she speak at the Station. As yet she hasn't said a word about who beat her or why. But she's suffering, that's for sure.'

'Well, if she's not saying, it's probably "the love of her life",' said Collins.

'Maybe. But time will reveal all. It always does,' said Agnes.

Come on, let's see what's on the box tonight.'

Later that night a loud cry woke both Agnes and Collins. Agnes placed her arm across Collins' chest, 'I'll go,' she said. 'You go back to sleep,' and she slipped on her dressing gown and went to see what the problem was with Joanne.

Monday, 5 July 1965

Hurst Street, Birmingham, 09.30hrs

Collins and Clark were still parking when they saw the postman leave Hastings' shop. 'Well at least wi know he's in this time,' said Clark.

A light rain was falling as they crossed the road to the shop, but the day was still warm with a promise of sunshine later. Halfway across the road, they were blown off their feet as the front window of the newsagent's exploded outwards, sending shards of glass flying in a deadly cone-shaped blast. Flames leapt through the open door but quickly receded.

Clark was the first to regain his feet and sprinted towards the burning shop. As Collins tried to stand up he saw that a foot-long sliver of plate glass was embedded in his left forearm. He felt his knees go weak and sat down hard on the road, just as Clark emerged, dragging Hastings behind him.

Clark half-dragged, half-carried Hastings to the other side of the road, then went back to help Collins. By the time he had propped Collins up against the wall of a sewing machine wholesaler's, the postman had sprinted back to see what was going on. Clark looked at him and shouted 'Stop gawping and find a fucking fire extinguisher.'

People started to pour out of shops and stood watching the fire from a safe distance. A young woman said, 'I bet it's the gas main.'

But a middle-aged man, who'd survived the Birmingham Blitz, said, 'Don't be bloody daft, woman. The gas main would level the bloody street for 30 yards in every direction. No, that was a small bomb.'

Hastings was in a bad way with his face and arms badly burned. Much of his clothing had either been burnt or blown off. What little hair he had had was gone, and his breathing was fast and shallow. Clark had seen the effects that a small powerful explosion can have at close quarters on many occasions. He knew that there was no knowing what the concussive effect of the bomb would be on Hastings' chest and brain. He opened the man's mouth and yanked out his false teeth which had become dislodged, and Hastings started to mumble, his eyelids fluttering.

Clark moved closer. 'Who did this, Mr Hastings?'

'The safe box. Get the box.' As he spoke, small bubbles of blood formed at the corners of his mouth.

Clark asked again, 'Who sent the bomb?'

'The box. Get the box,' he mumbled. 'Behind the desk.'

'OK, Mr Hastings, I'll get the box. But who sent the bomb?'

Hastings face contorted in pain and he coughed violently, sending a spray of blood and black bile down Clark's jacket. The coughing continued for nearly a minute. 'Tubbs.' Exhausted, he slumped back. Seconds later he twitched once and was dead, his eyes open and unseeing. Clark shook him but he knew it was no use.

'Will this do?' asked the returning postman, holding a red conical fire extinguisher.

'Fine,' said Clark, and grabbed it. 'Look after me mate. Try and stop the bleeding but don't pull the glass out.'

Standing on the pavement, Clark directed the stream of foam through the shattered window and door. The explosion had been designed to kill, not to start a large fire. The shop was wrecked. The counter and wall behind it had taken the worst of the blast. Only half of the plasterboard wall was still standing, and the rest had been spread across the floor of the shop in a million small pieces. The counter had been pushed four feet from its original moorings and lay broken and upended against the opposite wall.

'Watch the floors, Clarkee. Don't fall through,' shouted Collins who was now sitting beside Hastings' body. He felt light-headed and wondered why the road was undulating like a series of waves. He decided to close his eyes. Given that he'd just been blown up and stabbed with a foot-long piece of glass he felt surprisingly relaxed.

With the remaining flames dampened down, Clark pushed his way into the gutted shop. He immediately saw the small galvanised safe resting on the floor where the counter had once been. The explosion had blown it into the shop along with most of the wall.

The postman started to bandage Collins' arm with strips of material torn from his own shirt. His hands were shaking and twice they touched the glass, causing Collins to open his eyes, stiffen and breathe in sharply.

Grabbing the safe, Clark stood up and grinned. Jogging back to his car, he placed it in the boot. No Central Division copper was getting a look at it before he and Collins had gone through its contents.

The first fire engine arrived within six minutes, and the first police car soon after. Clark flashed his warrant card and said that they would provide full statements after Collins had been taken to hospital. The PC recognised Clark and knew his reputation. Wisely, he decided not to argue with the little man. Eight minutes later Collins, was lying on a trolley in the Accident Hospital being rolled into the operating theatre.

Clark called Agnes with the news, then phoned Inspector Hicks. After that he settled down to wait.

It was nearly 2pm before Agnes and Clark were allowed to see Collins. His arm was heavily bandaged and he was still groggy from the anaesthetic. When he saw Agnes, he smiled and said, 'You can't blame me this time, love. I was just walking across the road when it happened.'

Agnes leaned over and kissed him lightly on the lips. 'You and Clark attract violence like a magnet attracts iron filings.'

'Guilty as charged. Have they said when I can get out of here?'

'They want to keep you in overnight for observation. You

have a concussion and you've lost a lot of blood. An inch to the left and you might have bled to death. They've given you a transfusion but you'll be off work for a few days and then no exertion for a week or so.'

Collins looked over Agnes' shoulder at Clark and grimaced. 'I'm relying on you to keep me up to date.'

'Will do.'

'Have you had a look at what's in the safe yet?'

'No.'

'Well, get back to the station and open it up with the Boss. Call me when you know what we've got.'

'OK.'

With Clark gone, Agnes sat on the bed and held Collins' right hand. She was from a generation who didn't like to show affection publicly, and it was only now that a solitary tear ran down her face. 'When Clive called I was so frightened. He didn't know how serious it was. All he could tell me was that you'd been in an explosion and that a large piece of glass was embedded in your arm.'

'I'm all right, love. You can stop worrying.'

'Yes, I can. But only until you go back on duty.'

Handsworth, 15.00hrs

Clark walked into the CID office carrying the galvanised safe and a bag of tools from his car. He laid the safe on the Inspector's desk. 'I picked this up before the Central boys arrived. Hastings was very keen we find it.'

The Inspector looked at the safe then at Clark and said, 'I have to say, that was a very stupid thing to do. You should have left it where it was.' Then his face broke into a broad smile, 'But I'm bloody glad you didn't. Get it open.'

Clark examined the lock. It was a four-figure combination and he could probably open it in two minutes, but he was in a hurry, and withdrew a hammer and a large chisel from his tool bag. The bottom of the cheap safe had been attached by bending over a quarter inch of metal onto all four sides and spot welding it. Four hefty blows and the first side came loose. Eight more and the floor opened like a door to reveal the expanding file.

'Do we know what we're looking for?' asked Hicks.

'Yeah. Someone named Tubbs.'

The Inspector drew out the papers filed under T. Quickly he found a single sheet of paper headed Mr Tubbs and placed it on the table. 'Looks like we've got a telephone number for your Mr Tubbs. But what do you make of the rest of it?'

Clark scanned the list of eighteen entries. There was a date at the start of each line, followed by a telephone number a time and another date. 'Not sure,' said Clark and handed the sheet back to the Inspector. He then picked up another envelope, this one for a Mr Gibson. Inside were photocopies of letters he'd received from some woman called Jean. A third file had copies of some amateur photos. 'There were a row of pigeonholes over the desk. I think Hastings offered a postal address service for anyone who dain't want certain letters and parcels landing on their doorstep. WPC Milne told us Hastings had done time for blackmail, so my guess is he kept a record of what people got. He was probably blackmailing everyone in the file, but that don't explain why he was blown up today by our Mr Tubbs.'

Hicks continued to examine the single sheet of paper with Tubbs' name on it. After a further 40 seconds he smiled and slapped the desk, 'What if Tubbs was the only one in the file not being blackmailed? What if Hastings didn't know what the dates and times meant, but he knew they were dodgy?'

'Then Collins provided him with the key. And he tried it on with Tubbs.'

'We'll need to check these numbers and dates. See if they correlate in any way to the dates of the fires. But first get onto the Post Office and find the address that goes with Tubbs' number. I'm off to see the Super. We need to call in the afternoon shift.'

While waiting for the post office to get back to him, Clark called Stan Wold at home. It took Stan all of 20 minutes to reach Thornhill Road, and he and Clark headed into the canteen.

'How's Mickey?'

'He'll be all right. He were lucky.'

'I'm glad. He's a good man.'

'That he is.'

'Do you think Tubbs will still be at the address?'

'I don't know. If he thinks he's cut off any link between himself and Hastings and he's feeling cocky he might be. But if he's a suspicious bastard he'll have done a runner,' said Clark.

'My bet is he's done a runner. If Tubbs is TK then he's careful. He'll go on holiday until he's certain he's safe,' said Wold.'

The canteen was filling up with police called back from their patrols, all of them wondering why they were there. A few came over to Clark and asked what was up. He shrugged his shoulders and said the Inspector would explain. He and Wold changed the subject and chatted about the Wimbledon tennis championships that had ended the previous Saturday.

'Did you watch the Final?' asked Stan.

'Yeah. Bloody Aussies won damn near everything. The Men's and Women's Finals plus the Men's Doubles and Mixed Doubles. Why can't wi win a game of tennis?'

'They've got some great players at the moment, Emerson, Stole, Newcombe, Roache and Margaret Smith, not to mention Ron Laver. They've also got the climate and the facilities for the game.'

'So what yow saying is them just better than us?'

'No. I'm saying nearly everyone is better than us. Have you

ever played the game?'

'Na. A bit too poncey for me. Don't get me wrong. I like to watch it and the guys who play are bloody fit, but all the royalty attending and bowing and scraping, that turns me stomach. Besides, wi never had enough money to buy me a racket when I were a kid.'

'I know what you mean. Tennis clubs can be right stuck up places but there are plenty that lets the likes of you and me in. Tell you what, when we catch this bastard I'll give you a free tennis lesson and you won't have to buy a racket. Deal?'

'Deal,' said Clark.

Another hour of increasingly desultory conversation had passed before Inspector Hicks entered and shouted, 'Everyone in the parade room. Now.' As an afterthought he added, 'Bring your drinks.'

Standing at the front of the room, with Clark taking up his usual position by the door with Stan, the Inspector launched into his briefing. 'I know you all want to know what's going on. Well, thanks to Clarkee...'

'And Mickey, Boss.'

'As I was saying, thanks to our very own dynamic duo we have a lead on where the arsonist who killed Anne Johnson lives.' There was a stirring of excitement among the assembled officers. 'Settle down,' said Hicks. 'As I was about to say, the Post Office have just confirmed that a phone number he is believed to use is situated at a warehousing and workshop site that was once part of an old military stores camp. The Ministry of Defence sold it off a few years back and the new owners rent out the buildings. Now this guy is dangerous, so those of you who are authorised to carry firearms can pick up a gun from Sergeant Ridley. Any questions?'

'And those that aren't can get one off Clarkee,' whispered Stan.

'Sorry, did you have a question, Station Officer Wold?'

'No Inspector. Just thanking Clarkee for inviting me along.'

The stores were situated near All Saint's Hospital, Winson Green. The old asylum had been around since 1850 and was still referred to locally as the Loony Bin. Two Black Marias followed Inspector Hicks along Soho Road and turned onto Bolton Road. Seven minutes later they were pulling into the old army depot. It had just gone 6pm and the fierce heat of the day was passing to be replaced by warm, bright sunshine that felt gentle in the soft breeze that had sprung up. The entire barracks looked quiet and peaceful with not a soul in sight.

Shed 14, as it was described on the Post Office's records, lay near the centre of the field. Clark was impressed with Tubbs' choice of location. His workshop was ideally camouflaged among 31 identical buildings. The police convoy stopped and parked up 50 yards away. A quick check revealed that no lights could be seen in the building and nor could any movement be detected. Clark was not surprised. If this was Tubbs' workshop there was no reason to assume he'd be here this late in the evening, but his many years of training had taught Clark caution. He knew that there was always the chance that Tubbs was inside. 'I'll take a quick look-see, Boss, and wave you in if it's clear.'

Hicks nodded in agreement and Clark set off at a quick sprint to the next shed, about 20 yards from Shed 14. Flattening himself against the wall, he took three deep breaths and sprinted to number 14. Keeping low, he circled the building, looking through each window in turn. The shed consisted of a single room measuring about 30 foot by 18. A partition running the width of the building had been built about eight feet from the rear wall. A quick look revealed that it had a couple of chairs, a table and a waist-high cupboard on which sat a two-ring hotplate. *All the comforts of home,* thought Clark. He guessed that an enclosed cubicle in the corner was the lavatory.

The rest of the shed contained three work benches in the centre of the room arranged in an H shape. Various small tools hung on neatly fitted wall racks and there was a metal trolley containing more tools parked against one wall. Pushed against the partition wall was a free-standing metal rack, its four shelves filled with a miscellany of chemicals in bottles, flagons and tins. In front of the shelves was a trap door. *Must be a cellar,* thought Clark. Satisfied that the building was empty, he waved the others forward. By the time they arrived, he'd picked the lock on the shed.

Pushing the door open, Clark and Hicks stepped into the room and turned the light on. 'Well this is bloody disappointing,' said Hicks. 'I thought we were onto something.'

'The evening's young yet, Boss, and there's a trapdoor in the corner.'

'All right men, spread out and see what you can find. Clarkee, you, Wold and me will have a look at what lies below.'

The trap door was chained and padlocked. Clark took one look at it and shouted, 'First one to find me a crowbar or something wi can use as a crowbar gets a free tea and a round of toast.'

A voice from the far end of the room said, 'Tight bastard,' which got a round of laughter.

A short crowbar was quickly found and Clark levered the hasp out of the wood and pulled it away from the opening. The open door revealed ten steps leading down to a steel-reinforced wooden door. Descending first, Clark examined the locks. There were two of them, both German-made, and both looked a damn sight harder to pick than any British lock he knew.

Running his hands around the frame of the door, Clark examined the inset hinges. This was going to take a bit of time. 'We'll have to drill the locks out.'

'Well, before you do that,' said Wold, 'why don't you check

if it's locked?' Clark looked at him as if he was a half-wit but did as he suggested. Turning the handle, he pushed. The door swung inwards. Wold grinned. Clark blushed.

'One nil to the Fire Brigade,' said Hicks

Before stepping into the room, Clark felt for the light switch. As the fluorescent light flickered into life and the familiar hum of the tubes settled into near silence, Wold followed Clark into the basement.

'Fuck me,' said Wold. 'Have you ever seen anything like this before?'

'The mirrors, yes. The mannequins, no.'

Both men stood still searching the room with their eyes. The room was smaller than the workshop but it had also been divided into two. A partition had been built about 10 feet from the back wall. The door in its centre was open and Clark could see the bottom part of an armchair, a stereogram and a TV. They could see no trip wires or other signs of booby traps.

Wold wandered over to the line of 3 naked mannequins covered in muslin while Clark went to the bedside cabinet. The drawers were empty. 'He's done a runner,' said Clark, 'and taken his toys with him.'

'What do you reckon he did with these mannequins?' asked Wold.

'I'm bloody sure you can guess,' said Clark.

Turning, Wold knocked one of the mannequins with his elbow. It rocked on its base and Wold heard a click and the flow of liquid. 'Out. Out,' he screamed and ran for the door. Clark reached the door first and Wold pushed him through it. As he did so a loud whooshing sound escaped from the mannequin, and Wold was hit in the back by an expanding ball of flame. He landed against the door, slamming it shut. In his pain Wold felt Clark push against the door, but he knew it was too late. The two other mannequins had fallen over and Wold had just enough time to think of his wife and children before the concussive force of the explosion scrambled his brains. An all-consuming sheet of flame followed almost immediately and ran along the full length of the ceiling destroying everything beneath it, and incinerating Stan Wold.

When the fire brigade arrived, the fire was out. With no oxygen to sustain it, the initial conflagration had quickly died down. To avoid re-ignition, the door was opened four inches and two hoses directed into the room. Half an hour later, the body of Stan Wold was carried past silent police officers and firemen in a canvas bag. Every man removed his cap or helmet as he passed. It was one thing to be killed fighting a fire. That was the risk that every fireman took. To be ambushed and murdered by fire was an entirely different matter. That was personal, and every man there wanted to find and kill Tubbs.

Back at the station, the afternoon shift signed off in silence and headed home to their families. All of them had the same thought. *That could have been me.* However, the day was not over for Inspector Hicks. He had to accompany the Chief Fire Officer of Birmingham to the home of Stan Wold, and tell his wife and two children that he would never be coming home again.

Clark sat in a corner of the canteen, O'Driscoll beside him. They didn't speak. There was nothing worth saying. Instead they drank several cups of tea each heavily laced with good Irish whiskey.

At 10.30 O'Driscoll went back to the CID Office and Clark headed home. He found Ruth curled up in an armchair asleep with the TV still on. Turning off the TV, he picked Ruth up, and carried her up the stairs. Halfway up, she started to wake and he kissed her on the forehead. 'Go back to sleep, love.' She snuggled into the crook of his neck and was asleep again before he reached the bedroom door. Bending his knees, he pulled the bedclothes down with one hand and gently laid Ruth on the bed. Pulling the covers up, he kissed her lightly on the forehead and went to the bathroom. He was in the middle of brushing his teeth when the tears started to flow. Silent at first, they soon became great heaving sobs. They did not stop until Ruth came and held him.

Tuesday, 6 July 1965

Handsworth, 10.00hrs

Collins was discharged from hospital at 9.30am on condition that he rested for 72 hours. The hospital insisted that Agnes wheel Collins to her car, as any sudden exertion such as standing up quickly could make him feel dizzy.

As they drove home Collins continued to insist that he was perfectly all right and that he would be at work as usual in the morning. Part of his belligerence was down to the news that Stan Wold had been killed by Tubbs. Agnes didn't try to argue with him. She knew that words alone would not deter him. Instead she parked in front of the garage, walked around the car, and opened the passenger door. She made no attempt to help Collins from the car.

Stepping from the car, Collins stood up and took two steps before his legs began to buckle. Agnes caught him and helped him to the front door. Propping him against the wall, she opened the door, before slipping Collins' arm over her shoulder and helping him walk to the lounge. For once, Sheba didn't jump and make a fuss at the sight of her master. She knew something was wrong.

Without speaking, Agnes deposited Collins on the settee and went to the kitchen to make tea. On her return she laid the tea tray with two mugs of tea, four rounds of buttered toast, raspberry jam and marmalade, on the coffee table. Handing Collins his tea, she said, 'I know you want to help find Mr Wold's killer but you will only be in the way at work if you keep falling over and fainting. You need time and rest to replenish the blood you lost, not to mention giving the muscles and tendons a chance to heal. Why don't you check with your records officer and see if he's found any case files that involve arson and burglary and have them delivered to us?'

Collins could see the concern on Agnes' face and relented. 'OK. I'll call Alf and see what he's got. After I've had me tea.'

'Good.'

After finishing off the last piece of toast, Collins sighed contentedly and closed his eyes. Ten seconds later he was asleep. Agnes lifted his legs onto the settee, pulled the heavy drapes closed, and tiptoed out of the room. Forty minutes later, she held his arm as he walked to the phone.

Alf's phone rang for nearly a minute before it was picked up. Alf was a retired police officer who had been re-employed as a civilian to sort out the station's ramshackle records system. It had taken him a year, but he'd finally tamed the chaos. Unfortunately his hearing was deteriorating by the day. This made any telephone conversation with him a long-winded job.

Speaking just one level below shouting, Collins asked, 'Alf, have you managed to sort out the files Hicks wanted?'

'Yes. I've even got a few files from the other stations Hicks contacted.'

'That's great. Can you do me a favour and box them up and send them to my place?'

'No problem. But you do realise that there are nearly over 60 of the buggers?'

'That's all right. Agnes will give me a hand.'

'What am I going to help you with now?' she asked him.

'Well it was your idea that I go through the files at home. The least you can do is have a look at a few of them. '

Forty-five minutes later, two boxes of files arrived in a police van. Sheba sniffed around them for a few moments, found nothing of interest and retreated back to her basket in the kitchen. Agnes refused to let Collins carry either box in case he burst his stitches, and carried them into the lounge herself. Five minutes later, the files were neatly laid out on the dining table. 'Well, what are you waiting for?' she asked.'

'A cup of tea and a biscuit,' said Collins. 'I can't work without a cuppa. And besides I've got a sore arm.'

'Pathetic. I can see I'm going to have trouble with you.'

'True, but you like it when I'm trouble.'

For the next five hours, working through a cold lunch, Agnes and Clark examined each file. By the time they had finished, they had a total of 18 unexplained or suspicious fires which might have involved Tubbs.

Pulling a foolscap pad of paper towards her, Agnes asked, 'What have these fires got in common?'

Collins started to list the common features they had identified. 'All took place within a 30 mile radius of Birmingham. They fall into four categories, shops, warehouses, manufacturing businesses and in two cases private homes where young women lived. All the business fires took place at night when the premises were closed and empty, if you exclude the night watchman, while the house fires started in late evening when the house was occupied. The methods used to start the commercial fires are unknown. There is no evidence to suggest that the commercial fires were started deliberately. However, in each case the seat of the fire was adjacent to flammable materials and the damage caused in all cases was catastrophic to the business. There is no mention of a TK in any of the files.

'In the case of the home fires both were the result of a gas fault and explosion that followed. If Tubbs was responsible for these fires, it means he entered the houses at least once to set up the fire. But no one saw any suspicious characters near the houses in the week before either fire.'

'So he must dress to fit in, which supports your witness' story that Tubbs was dressed as a workman,' said Agnes.

'We know Tubbs was responsible for two fires. Unfortunately that's as far as the hard evidence goes,' said Collins. 'It's so bloody annoying. If only we knew more about Tubbs. What's he like? What does he do with his time? Where does he come from? What's his history? That sort of thing.'

'That's it, Michael.'

'What is?'

'His history. We're looking for Tubbs in the present, a present in which he's very good at covering his tracks. We should be looking for him in the past, when he was developing his skills and wasn't so careful or professional.'

'And other than building a time machine, how do we do that?'

'I don't know a lot about arsonists, but I remember reading that they usually developed their love of fire as children...'

'So if we access records of child arsonists we might find something,' said Collins.

'That might work, but I was thinking about psychiatry. Any child caught starting a fire would have been assessed by a psychiatrist, and I don't think that that there are many who specialise in that field.'

'So how do we find them?'

'I know someone at Birmingham University who might be able to help. I've only met her once or twice, but I think our problem will pique her professional interest.'

Looking at his watch, Collins said, 'Call her.'

After some initial difficulty in getting through to Professor Miriam Barkley, it only took a five minute conversation for her to agree to meet Agnes the following day.

'Well that's good news,' said Collins. 'Now, I don't feel too guilty about going to bed and having a sleep.'

On his way to bed, Collins passed Joanne, who was looking much better then she had just 48 hours earlier. Although several times lighter, the bruising around her face was still there but she seemed to be moving more easily now. 'How are you feeling?' he asked.

'Better. At least I wasn't blown up. How are you?'

'I'm fine. Just a bit tired. If you're looking for Agnes, she's in the kitchen.'

Handsworth, 18.00hrs

Clark had found sleep difficult to come by and was glad to get up at 9am and potter around the empty house. The normality of taking the bin out, checking how the fruit on the two apple trees in the back garden was developing, and making his own breakfast acted as a balm on his troubled mind. He'd seen friends killed in action; shot, or blown to bits by a grenade or shell. One had even been killed by a flame-thrower, but for some reason Stan's death had hit him harder than any of those. He tried to understand the reason why and it kept coming back to the same factor. Stan had died saving him. It didn't matter if he'd slammed the door shut by accident or on purpose – the fact was that closing the door had saved Clark's life, and he felt guilty.

Arriving at work just as the afternoon shift came on duty, Clark found a pall of grief hanging over the entire building. Stan hadn't been one of them, but the general opinion was that he'd died protecting them. The CID office was empty and silent. Clark thought about going to the canteen just to be among the living, but instead found the list of messages that Tubbs had received. With all the excitement of finding Tubbs' workshop, no one had fully examined it.

Clark took the paper and looked for a date that might be connected to the Hadley fire. Examining the last entry first, he saw that the date at the start of the line was eight days after the Hadley fire. The second date was tomorrow. Clark immediately knew what he was looking at. The first date was when Hastings received the letter. The telephone number was that of whoever was hiring Tubbs and the date and time he guessed was when he should call whoever had hired him for instructions.

Picking up the phone, he called the General Post Office and asked them to trace the name and address of the subscriber who owned the last number on the list. With nothing to do now but wait, Clark went for a cuppa and some of the human contact he so badly needed. He wished that Collins was working. He could do with talking to him.

Both Hicks and Clark were in the office when the GPO rang back. The number belonged to Bright and Son, a soft furnishing and bedding warehouse, off Heath Street in Winson Green.

A second call to Companies House and a further wait of half an hour confirmed that the company's last set of accounts had shown a trading loss of £113,000 on a turnover of £540,000. 'It looks like Bright's is going tits up, Boss.'

'So it seems. What does your gut tell you? Is the fire set for tomorrow or is it just a call to arrange the fire?'

'I don't think that Tubbs takes written instructions. If he did, Hastings would have known what he was up to and taken copies. Besides, all the times quoted are during normal business hours and all the commercial fires took place at night. Na, tomorrow is when he gets his instructions and probably finalises the fee.'

'I agree. We need a phone tap on Bright's line. While you're at it, get the Post Office to trace the addresses of all the other numbers on the list.'

'Will do. After that how do yow want to handle it?'

'I think we leave Bright free until we grab Tubbs. If we pick him up someone will blab to a mate or to the press that we have a breakthrough and Tubbs gets tipped off. No, we let Bright think everything is hunky-dory. Than we take him when we have Tubbs.'

The GPO engineer arrived at the junction box 20 yards from Bright and Son Soft Furnishing Warehouse just as Mr Bright left for home in his black Daimler. He saw the man working on the lines but didn't imagine for one moment that it had anything to do with him. The job was completed in less than half an hour. Mr Tubbs' call was scheduled for 10.45am next morning. Now all that Clark and Hicks could do was wait.

Clark heard the scampering of an excited Sheba and the click of Agnes' heels on the wooden floor before the door was opened. He had come bearing a gift, a large mutton bone in a brown paper bag. Without a please or thank you, Sheba jumped up and grabbed the bag from his hand. Turning away, she scurried into the kitchen, out through the dog flap and into the back garden.

'How's the invalid?' he asked as he followed Agnes into the lounge.

'Just getting up. He went for a nap.'

'Not surprising, really. Blood loss does that to yow and the anaesthetic and painkillers are probably still in his system. But he's OK?'

'Yes, he's fine.'

Seeing the files laid out on the table, he said, 'Looks like yow been busy.'

''Not just me. We worked on it together. Here, read the summary,' said Agnes, 'while I call Michael and make some tea.'

Clark took the single page summary and sat at the table. He'd read the summary twice by the time Collins appeared.

'Sleeping on the bleeding job again?'

'Up yours,' said Collins, and flopped into the chair opposite Clark and yawned.

Waving the summary sheet, Clark asked, 'What yow going to do next.'

Collins explained what Agnes had arranged. 'She's due to see the professor tomorrow.'

'That's good. It will be useful background information at

the bastard's trial.'

'You've got something?'

'That we have, Mickey.' Clark quickly brought Collins up to date.

'That's great. I'd love to be there when you snap the cuffs on the bastard.'

'Well there's a good chance you will be. I don't think the fire will be set this week. Unless Tubbs has already done a ...' Clark hesitated. 'Oh sod me. I need to phone the Boss.'

'Why? What's up?'

'I was going to say unless he's done a recce. But of course he's got to do a recce before he can agree the price. He could be there now.'

Agnes arrived with a tea tray containing three teas and several slices of her homemade tea cake liberally covered in butter. She only just managed to sidestep Clark as he rushed for the phone. 'What's going on? Why's Clark acting like a whirling dervish?'

Collins explained and then finished by saying, 'I'll have to go with him. It will take the Boss time to get a watch team out and I can't let him go alone.'

Agnes looked at Collins and knew she would be wasting her time trying to dissuade him. 'Very well. But once the other officers arrive, you come home. You're in no fit state to be on active duty.'

''Yes, Madam,' said Collins and saluted before kissing Agnes on the cheek.

Winson Green, 19.00hrs

Twenty minutes later, Collins and Clark were parked on Halford Lane. Both sides of the road were home to factories and warehouses of various shapes and sizes. During the day the Lane came to life. There was the noise of machines, raised voices, bustle and constant traffic delivering or picking up goods. Now the road was silent and empty. The machines had been turned off and their operators gone home to watch the telly or go down the pub.

The summer sun, still high in the sky, was diffused by the haze of manufacturing smoke and fumes that hung over the street. The haze imbued the scene with a slightly nostalgic look, like a turn of the century sepia-tinted photo of a road with no cars and few people.

'We stick out like a bleeding boil on a bride's nose here,' said Clark. 'Best if we wait inside. Come on.'

'One of us should stay outside.'

'Agreed. But by the look of yow, yow ain't fit to stand, let alone confront this sod.'

'Exactly, which is why I should stay out. I'd only be a handicap to you if I go in. I'll stay by the front door and meet the cavalry when they arrive. If he's in there you'll find him.'

'OK. Have it yowr way. But don't get hurt. Agnes made it very clear that she will arrange for one of her mates in MI5 to kill me if anything happens to yow tonight.'

'Liar. Agnes is a pacifist.'

'Not when it come to yow, she ain't.'

Collins took up position on the steps of the warehouse. Although he wouldn't admit, it he didn't feel at all good. Maybe there was something to this blood loss caper. The headaches had returned and now two miners were drilling away behind his eyes. His head was spinning and he felt sick as he leaned against the pillar that concealed him.

Clark turned down the access road at the side of the warehouse. The wide alley was used for deliveries and shipments and ended in a turning circle and small car park. *Probably for the bigwigs,* thought Clark. Half way down he found an old sash cord window. Slipping the blade of his knife through the gap between the upper and lower window, he pushed against the stiff catch. It had been painted over and was stuck hard.

He was thinking of finding another window or door when he felt it give. Pushing the window up, he crawled through the opening and found himself standing next to a pile of rugs and 12 foot by 9 carpet squares. The room was cavernous, 50 yards by 35 if it was an inch. A balcony ran around the entire perimeter of the storage area. It was there that the offices, canteen and toilets were located. With the exception of clearly marked pathways along which goods were moved, every conceivable inch of floor space was covered in mattresses, bed linen, cushions, curtains, rugs, and rolls of lino, and these were just the stock Clark could see from where he was standing. 'Bloody hell,' he muttered to himself, 'Even a kid could burn this place down.'

Habit compelled Clark to stand still and listen. To check his surroundings. He then started his search by checking the perimeter of the room. All the windows and doors were closed and locked. There was no sign that anyone had broken in. Quickly he trotted up and down each lane. Still no sign of anyone or of any disturbance to the stock.

That just left the balcony, offices and reception area. With one last look at the warehouse he pushed through the swing doors to reception. With a wild scream, Tubbs swung a fire extinguisher at his head. The scream gave Clark a fraction of a second's warning. Automatically he raised his arms and moved backwards, but the extinguisher still hit him a glancing blow on the side of the head and sent him crashing backwards through the swing doors, dazed and unsteady. Tubbs followed quickly. Swinging the fire extinguisher over his head, he tried to cave in Clark's skull. Clark rolled sideways and was caught on the shoulder. Pain shot down his arm. Tubbs followed up with a wild kick at Clark's face which Clark blocked with crossed wrists. Before Tubbs could retract his foot, he grabbed it, twisted it hard to the right and pushed. The twist sent Tubbs crashing to the floor. Landing on his back he kicked out blindly and his heel connected with the top of Clark's head. Clark felt a delicious lightness spread down his body. He was floating and everything felt good. Resisting the temptation to close his eyes, he started to scramble to his feet. It was then he heard the front door splinter and Collins shout, 'Police, the building is surrounded.' Screaming, Tubbs threw the extinguisher at Clark, hitting him on the side of the face, and sprinted towards the back wall. Like a boxer who had taken a nine count, Clark stumbled to his feet. Collins crashed through the swing doors, saw Clark, and grabbed him by the arm. 'You all right, Clarkee?'

'I'm fine. Get after the bastard,' he said before he collapsed unconscious on the floor.

Collins took two steps forward before he too felt the room spin, and had to sit down on a pile of towels before he fell over.

When Hicks and two uniformed coppers arrived at the warehouse minutes later, they found a note pinned to the shattered front door.

"I've taken Clark to Accident Hospital. Tubbs was on the premises but escaped out the back. Check for devices."

It was signed Collins.

The waiting room contained a battered table, four overstuffed armchairs of different colours, a noticeboard that hadn't been updated since the winter and half a dozen ragged *National Geographic* magazines. By the time Ruth had been shown into the room, Clark was in X-ray. 'What happened, Michael?'

'I'm not sure. I think Tubbs suckered him with a fire extinguisher. I wasn't there to back him up. I was outside. When I heard Tubbs screaming and doors banging, I went in shouting "Police" and Tubbs took off. I was about to go after him when Clarkee collapsed and I almost joined him on the floor.'

Ruth looked at Collins' ash-coloured face and the deep black circles under his eyes, and knew that he should never have been anywhere near the warehouse. 'What do the doctors say?'

'They think he's got concussion but they want to make sure it's not something more serious. I'm sure he'll be OK. Before you know it, he'll be back home and you'll be able to wrap him in cotton wool.'

Ruth laid her head on Collins' shoulder and he wrapped his arm around her shoulder. 'I'll do just that, but when he goes back to work the only person I trust to protect him is you. Just as you did tonight, and just as you protected me.'

'I'll always do me best,' said Collins and a sudden chill made him shiver as he remembered the beating he'd taken from Bishop's thugs as part of Clark's plan to rescue Ruth. It had been the worst ten minutes of his life. The damage that fists and a pair of pliers can do in that time to body and mind is unimaginable for anyone who has never been systematically beaten by experts, and it stays with you long after the physical scars have healed.

'I know you will,' said Ruth, 'and so does Clive.'

An hour later the doctor stuck his head around the door. 'Mrs Clark?'

Ruth stood up, took a deep breath, and said, 'Yes.'

'We've had a good look at your husband's X-rays. I'm very pleased to say that there doesn't appear to be any bruising or bleeding on the brain. At this time we think he's suffering from severe concussion and a very minor crack to the top of his skull. Plus some bruising to the face. He was lucky'

'Will he be all right?'

'I'm very confident he will, Mrs Clark. Just to be on the safe side though, we're going to keep him in for 24 hours as a precaution.'

'Good,' said Collins. 'If he tries to discharge himself call me and I'll handcuff him to the bed.'

'Can we see him?'

'Yes, of course.'

Although his face looked as if he'd gone 15 rounds with Muhammed Ali, Clark smiled when he saw Ruth and Collins. Ruth kissed him lightly on the lips and squeezed his hand. 'I was worried about you, Clive.'

'Nothing to worry about, love. He hit me where it were certain to do the least damage.'

'Don't joke about it. You've got a cracked skull. A bit harder and he could have killed you.'

'Not when Mickey's about. Did you catch the sod?'

'How could I? You were passed out on the floor.'

'Yow should have left me and gone after Tubbs. I would have been all right.'

'Maybe, but Michael didn't know that, did he?' said Ruth. 'He did the right thing and you should thank him.'

'But now we've got nothing. He'll disappear and wi might never catch him.'

'We'll soon have the addresses for most of the phone numbers on his list, thanks to you. Over the next few days, Hicks and me will be making a few visits. If nothing else, we'll get Tubbs' bank details. Meanwhile, Agnes will be checking into the medical records of young arsonists.'

'OK. Just catch the bloody sod,' said Clark.

Ruth and Collins sat with Clark long after he'd fallen asleep. It was nearly midnight when she kissed her husband on the forehead and she and Clark slipped quietly away. As she walked back to the car she recited Psalm 23 under her breath in thanks and relief.

Agnes had stayed up for Collins and enveloped him in a silent hug before asking, 'How's Clive?' as they walked to the kitchen.

'He's all right. Has concussion and a few bruises, but

nothing serious.'

'When Inspector Hicks called he said you'd saved Clark.'

'Well don't say that to Clarkee. He was still conscious and fighting when I arrived on the spot. I just helped scare Tubbs away. Anyway, enough about me. How's your day been?'

'Fine. I had my first real conversation with Joanne.'

'Did she tell you who hit her?'

'No, but she did talk a lot about her dead mother and how the death changed her father.'

Collins knew that most violence was dished out in the home and asked the question, 'Did it turn him into a child beater?'

'She didn't say.'

Collins wasn't very hungry, but slipped two slices of bread into the toaster and put the kettle on and played with Sheba while waiting for the toaster to pop and the kettle to whistle.

Fifteen minutes later he locked up, and he and Agnes went to bed.

Wednesday, 7 July 1965

Handsworth, 09.00hrs

Hicks looked up from the report he was reading, saw Collins and asked, 'What are you doing here? You're supposed to be off sick.'

'You're missing York and Clark. As long as you don't expect me to do any running or fighting for a day or two I'm OK.'

'You should be resting. You look bloody awful.'

'I'll survive. I can rest when we've got the sod.'

'OK, if you say so,' said Hicks doubtfully. 'How's Clark?'

'He'll be fine in a day or two. He's more upset about Tubbs escaping than his own noggin. If we don't catch him before Clarkee gets back he'll probably duff us both up.'

'Well in that case, let's get to work. The last of the names and addresses came in this morning. We have 11 in total. The other seven are either unlisted numbers or belong to a telephone kiosk. We've got three, Bright's, Knight's and Hadley's. The others I've farmed out to the local nicks in whose area the fires took place. I've also spoken to the Fraud Squad, and they're checking the bank records of every business we have a name and address for. Once we have the details of any payments they've made to Tubbs, they'll start to talk.'

'Where do you want to start?' asked Collins.

'How about Mr Bright?'

'As good a place as any.'

'We don't have that much on him. So let's go in hard. OK?'

'No problem.'

The front door to Bright's had been boarded up the night before. An old married couple passing saw the damage, tutted loudly and the husband said, *"I don't know what the country's coming to. Sommut should be done about these teddy boys. Me, I'd birch the lot of them."*

The sight of the door and the memory of Clark lying unconscious on the floor reminded Collins of how close Clark had been to death. The man who owned this place had hired Tubbs. He was the one who was responsible for Clark's injuries. Collins was determined to make him pay for that.

Hicks stood back while Collins flashed his warrant card at the receptionist and asked for directions to Mr Bright's office. 'I'll just phone and see if he's in.'

'No you won't. You'll tell me where he is. This isn't a social call,' Collins tone was ice-cold.

The woman looked at Collins and quickly made up her mind. 'Take the stairs on the left and turn right at the top. Mr Bright's office is in the far corner.'

'Thank you. Now, do me one more favour, Don't tell your boss we're on the way up.'

The woman nodded. Bright's didn't pay her enough to upset the police.

The door to Mr Bright's office opened onto the balcony that Collins had briefly seen the night before. The bottom half of the wall was panelled with plywood and the top was glass. A secretary was typing at a desk, and to her left was a door marked "Edward Bright, Chairman and Managing Director".

'Good morning. We're here to see Mr Bright,' said Inspector Hicks.

'I'm sorry, he's in an important meeting. He can't be disturbed,' the secretary said and stood up as if to bar entry to her boss' office.

'Oh I think he can,' said Hicks and nodded at Collins who brushed past her into an office that was three times the size of the secretary's. There was a large desk in the far left-hand corner. Behind it stood an open-fronted Edwardian bookcase containing business directories and catalogues. Nearby was a bank of three new filing cabinets. A tank of tropical fish stood on a table against the right wall and a 12-seat conference table was situated in the middle of the room. The large room looked underfurnished, and not what you'd expect in a successful company.

Five men sat around the table. The small man at the top of the table stood up. He was even smaller than Clark, with slick black hair and a neatly trimmed pencil moustache. He looked like the crook Giulio Napolitani that Norman Wisdom had played in *On the Beat*. When he spoke, his voice was surprisingly deep, 'Who the hell are you to burst into my office? Get out before I call the police.'

'We are the police, and if you don't behave yourself, Mr Bright, I'm going to arrest you for conspiracy to defraud your insurers,' Hicks told him.

'The rest of you gentlemen can push off, but stay in the building. We may need to speak to you later,' said Collins.

The room emptied faster than a brothel in a raid, leaving Bright still standing, a slightly bewildered look of innocence on his face. 'Look, I don't know what's going on. You've clearly got the wrong end of some stick you're holding. My business was broken into last night. I'm the aggrieved party here. That's what I was just discussing with my managers.'

'I don't think you're the aggrieved anything, Mr Bright,' said Hicks. 'We have evidence that you were in the process of arranging for a Mr Tubbs to burn this building, and every item of stock in it, to the ground.'

'And why would I want to do that?'

'Because last year you lost £113,000 and once the fraud boys have a look at your accounts, I suspect they'll find that you're heading in the same direction this year,' said Hicks.

'And how the hell would you know that?'

'While I and my officers were securing the building last night, we noticed that you are carrying a great deal of stock. Much of it is two, even three years old, if the delivery dates on the packing materials is anything to go by. You can't get rid of it, can you?'

'I'm carrying stock because I have orders to fill.'

'No. You're carrying stock because you can't sell it, but you'll price it at full cost when you make your insurance claim.'

'What evidence do you have to substantiate your claims?'

'Your direct telephone number connects you to a known arsonist for hire. He was due to call you today to confirm final arrangements, wasn't he? said Hicks.

'If all you have is a telephone number, than you have nothing. Anyone could have given this man – Tubbs, did you say? – my number.'

'True, but not everyone has transferred money from their account to his, have they?' Hicks asked.

Bright hesitated. His mind racing. *How the hell did they know about the transfer? Are they bluffing? What else do they know?* He looked from Hicks to Collins and back again. They were both impassive. Even if they didn't have a sound case against him, he instinctively knew they would keep going until they did. His decision made, he said, 'All right, I'll tell you everything I know, but I want immunity from prosecution.'

'That only happens in American films, Mr Bright. The British police and courts don't make deals,' said Hicks. 'Tell us what you know and we'll say you co-operated in our enquiries and if appropriate we'll confirm that your information helped us to capture the arsonist. It might be enough to keep you out of prison.'

Bright hesitated. 'How do I know I can trust you?'

'You don't,' said Collins, 'but we're the only hope you've got.'

After what seemed like a long pause, but was barely six seconds, Bright said, 'OK. What do you want to know?'

'How did you make contact with Tubbs?' asked Hicks.

'I asked around and was told that I should go to The Strangeways pub in Walsall and tell the barman I was looking to hire a specialist.'

'We'll require full details of all your contacts, but for the moment, tell us what happened next.'

'The barman made a call and about an hour later a man came in and sat down next to me.'

'What was his name?' asked Hicks.

'Tony. He didn't give me a second name.'

'What did he look like?'

'Over six foot tall, black greasy hair, big nose covered with blackheads. His hands were huge. Filthy fingernails. I'm sure he worked in one of the smelting firms. He smelled of coke and metal.'

'And what did he say?' asked Hicks.

'He wanted to know what type of specialist I needed. I told him I needed someone who knew about fires. He laughed and said that information would cost £100 cash. I said that seemed expensive. He said that he only had three charges. £50 if you wanted a heavy to beat someone up. £100 if you wanted to start a fire or do other serious property damage, and £250 if you wanted someone taken care of permanently. Those were his charges. No exceptions.'

'How did he put you in touch with Tubbs?'

'He took my name and address and said I could be contacted. About two weeks later, I received a note in the post saying if I wanted to continue with my venture I should write to a postal address in Hurst Street and provide a telephone number I could be reached on, plus a date and time for the call. It stipulated that the date should be at least three weeks from the date I received the note and that no other information should be contained in my letter. I was also to transfer £5,000 to a Mr D. Fairbanks account at Lloyds Bank, Holborn, London, before that date. But you know all about that.'

Collins felt the familiar thrill of bluffing and winning but kept any sign of pleasure out of his voice and off his face. 'Did you keep the note?' he asked.

'No. I destroyed it.'

'Was it typed or handwritten?' asked Hicks.

'Typed.'

'And the postmark?'

'Birmingham, I think.'

'But no price was mentioned?'

'No. Nothing at all was said about the job. I assumed that would be discussed when he called me today.'

'Was the note signed?'

'No.'

Hicks asked for the full details of Tubbs' bank transfer which were provided within five minutes by Bright's secretary. 'Right, Mr Bright. You will attend Thornhill Road Police Station tomorrow morning at 9.30, where you will be interviewed under caution and required to provide a full statement of your dealings with Mr Tubbs. We will also require full details of all those who helped you make contact with Mr Tubbs. You may bring your solicitor with you if you wish. Do you understand?'

'Yes.'

'One last thing before we go, were any of your employees aware of your plans?'

'No. I thought it was too risky to involve anyone else.'

Collins waited until they were in the car before saying, 'Well, that was a result, Sir.'

'Yes, it was. We got lucky when he believed me about the transfer.'

'Who do you want to see next, Sir, Knight or Hadley?'

'Neither. Let's get back to the station and arrange for a court order for Tubbs' bank account and see who else has been paying into it. That will flush out the bastards who used unlisted phones and call boxes.'

'Do you think we'll be able to freeze Tubbs' account?'

'More than likely, for all the good it will do. I think you'll find that any money paid into Lloyds was transferred out within 24 hours. It could be hard tracing it.'

University of Birmingham, 16.00hrs

Agnes parked near the University railway station and walked over to the medical school. Professor Miriam Barkley's office was on the second floor and her door was open. Agnes tapped lightly, and looking up, Miriam waved her in. 'Agnes, nice to see you again. Can I get you a coffee? I only have instant.' The small woman was already moving towards the electric kettle perched precariously on the window ledge, her head bobbing up and down as she moved, with her short black hair, streaked with grey, swaying with each movement.

'That's fine,' said Agnes, taking a seat. As Miriam busied herself with cups and kettle, Agnes looked around the small office. It was a typical academic's lair. Bookshelves covered three walls of the room and were stuffed to overflowing with a wide range of psychiatric books and journals. Most were in English, but there were several in German and Dutch. The shelf nearest Miriam's desk contained maybe 20 books with her name on the spine. Other books lay in piles on the floor along with students' assignments and dissertations. The remaining space was barely enough for Miriam's small desk, her chair, and one visitor's seat.

Miriam handed Agnes a black coffee, cleared a space on her desk and placed a small circular tray on it which contained two spoons, milk, sugar, and an open packet of arrowroot biscuits. 'Help yourself,' she said.

Sitting down, a mug of black coffee in her hand, Miriam smiled. The effect was startling. Her smile illuminated her entire face and made her look at least 10 years younger than her 70 years. 'Right. You got me hooked yesterday. So now you're here, tell me all you know about your arsonist.'

Agnes took the summary sheet she and Collins had prepared the previous day and, using it to jog her memory, outlined everything they knew or suspected about Tubbs. When she had finished she sat back and waited. Miriam had her eyes closed, her hands making a steeple, thinking. After several seconds' pause she said, 'The police may catch this man by questioning his customers, but if you want to understand him you need to look at the case of Anne Johnson. There was no financial gain involved in this crime.'

'As far as we know.'

'Yet despite the risk, he stayed behind in anticipation of seeing the poor woman burn to death. That suggests he has an overpowering compulsion to see women, and maybe others, burn. These commercial fires, the ones he performs for gain, have never resulted in anyone's death. He carries them out when the buildings are empty or else when there is just a night watchman, and destruction is assured. If no deaths occur, there is less chance of a police investigation. This suggests to me that he is cold, calculating and professional when dealing with his commercial fires. They are his livelihood, not his passion. He is cautious and does everything he can to reduce risk. No, it was not a commercial fire that first attracted him to flames. You say that the police have been unable to establish a link between Anne Johnson and Tubbs?'

'Correct.'

'Then I would suggest she may have been chosen at random. If not at random, then because she fitted a certain type of woman to whom he is attracted.'

'An Oedipus complex perhaps?' asked Agnes.

'Possibly, but Anne was a young woman. If he was burning women because they reminded him of his mother, I would say that he'd choose more mature victims. No, I suggest it's more than likely that he saw something in his childhood leading him to associate fire with sexual excitement.'

'So you think he has been interested in fire from an early age?'

'Almost certainly. How old do the police think he is?'

'Their best estimate we have is from 27 to 34.'

'Let's assume he was about 12 or 13 when he saw his first fire. 'If he's 34 than he would have been born in 1931. If so, he may well have witnessed incidents in the war when people died in fires. If he's 27 then he might have seen a fire after the war, in a hotel or house in which people were trapped. Either way, such an experience may have triggered his interest in fire.

'That would mean the earliest date we are interested in is 1943 and the latest would be 1950, give or take a year or two,' Miriam concluded.

'You think he saw his "first fire" when he was going through puberty?'

'That's when he would have been most impressionable.'

'So how do we find him? There must be hundreds of children throughout the whole country who started fires during that period.'

'I don't think you need to worry about the whole of England. You've already identified that he doesn't stray far from Birmingham and surrounding towns. This is typical of many criminals who prefer to stay near to home. They find comfort in the known.' Miriam paused and went on. 'Any child caught starting a fire was, and still is, referred for a psychiatric evaluation, and up to quite recently that meant coming here. We have a lot of records from the period in question. Unfortunately, I can't guarantee that they are complete. Mind you, the police will also have their records. Between the two sources, you'll probably have 90 per cent of all incidents.'

'In other words, I have a mountain of files to plough through.'

'Indeed,' said Miriam and then smiled. 'But perhaps there's a quicker way.' Pausing, she moved to the Rolodex on her desk and flicked through it. Stopping at the G's, she extracted a card. 'You know, you should talk to my predecessor, Dr Roger Granger. He was here from 1933 to 1957. A lovely man with a wonderful memory. I'll give you his address and phone number.'

Birmingham, 18.30hrs

Collins found Clark propped up in bed reading *The Grapes of Wrath*. 'Trying to catch up on your reading?' Collins asked.

'Na, I've read it before. It's a great book.'

'I thought you'd be more of a Hemingway fan.'

'I never took to him. He's a bit too lean for my liking. I need a bit of flesh, a bit of description to keep me interested. Speaking of which, what happened with Bright?'

Collins described the conversation that he and the Inspector had held earlier in the day with Mr Bright. Clark smiled when he heard how easy it had been to con the owner into confirming that he'd transferred funds to Tubbs.

'We've passed Tubbs' bank details to the Fraud lads and they're digging into any and all accounts from which Tubbs received funds. They promised us some answers by tomorrow night. Friday at the latest.'

'What about Agnes, has she come up with owt?'

'Don't know. I haven't seen her since this morning. Anyway, what about you? When are they going to let you out?'

'The doc says I can leave in the morning. Seems he wants me to pee before I can leave. I don't understand it me. Since when did a thump on the nut stop you peeing?'

Handsworth, 19.20hrs

When Collins arrived home, he found Agnes sitting in the lounge ready to go out. 'Are you off somewhere?'

'No, we are. We're going to the cinema and then you can wine and dine me on fish and chips afterwards.'

'And what are we going to see?'

'*Goldfinger*. I've not seen any of the Bond films and I think it's time I did. An old friend of mine died last year, and I'd like to see it for him. Besides, we could both do with a break.'

Collins didn't ask who the old friend was. He was too

interested in what had happened that day. 'What did your professor have to say?'

'I'll tell you on the way.'

As they drove home after the film, Agnes said, 'I'm off to see Dr Granger tomorrow. Maybe he'll be able to point us in the right direction. If he can't, then you'll just have to plough through all the hospital files.'

'Let's hope he can help.'

Agnes looked across at Collins. 'What's wrong, Michael? I thought you'd enjoy the film but you seem preoccupied. What's worrying you? Is it the case?'

Michael looked at Agnes and smiled. 'Sure, you can read me like a book. I'm not worried about the case. We'll get Tubbs – eventually. It's just all the talk about spies and missions tonight got me thinking. It's you I'm worried about. I don't trust Aubrey. I never have. He's ruthless in a way that not even Clark is. He's a cold-blooded fish, wrapped in charm and blarney. He'd betray his own mother if it got the job done. What's worse, I think he believes that everyone is expendable.'

'Is that your Irish instinct at work or just your distrust of the British establishment?' said Agnes smiling.

'Both. Tell me I'm wrong.'

Agnes hesitated. How much could she say? How much should she say? 'What you have to understand, Michael, is that in the war everyone was expendable. If we had lost, Britain as we know it would have been wiped off the face of the earth, along with God knows how many people. Aubrey is a child of his time. Just like Clarkee and me, for that matter. I know how Aubrey thinks. I know that he'll use me if it helps him achieve his aims. But knowing that means I am well aware that I have to protect myself and the people I love at all times.'

'Well if you thought that was going to reassure me, you

were wrong. I'm not going to relax until you're home safe and sound on Friday.'

'What I'm doing is not dangerous, my love. I'm just meeting with an old friend. Nothing more,' lied Agnes.

Collins didn't believe her for a minute, but said nothing.

Thursday, 8 July 1965

Handsworth, 09.30hrs

Bright arrived with his solicitor at 9.30. He'd recovered some of his composure and tried to backtrack on some of the more incriminating statements he'd made the previous day, but faced with Hicks' and Collins' records of the meeting, he ended up pleading for a deal of some kind. The interview ended at 1.35 and Bright was charged with conspiring to defraud his insurance company and bailed to appear at the police station on July 31. The only concession he'd managed to wring from Inspector Hicks was that the court would be informed that he had co-operated fully with the police. That, plus the fact that the fire had not actually been set, would probably be enough to keep the businessman out of prison.

Collins left the station and drove to Clark's house. Ruth answered the door. 'I suppose you've come to see the invalid?'

'That I have.'

'He's in the lounge listening to his records. Go on in, and I'll make a pot of tea.'

Looking up, Clark saw Collins and asked, 'What yow doing here? Skiving again?'

'You know me so well. Hicks and I have just finished taking Bright's statement and he's been charged. Now we're hanging about waiting for the Fraud boys to turn up with some information.'

'I've got a feeling that will end in a big fat nothing. This guy is clever. I don't think he will have left a nice clean trail leading from the bank to his front door.'

'Probably not.'

Clark continued as if he hadn't been interrupted. 'No, I reckon the only way we'll get him is if we catch him in the act, or we piss him off so badly that he comes looking for us.'

'And I suppose you have a plan for the latter.'

'Not yet, but when I do I promise that you can have the starring role as the bait.'

'Wonderful. Just what I've always wanted – a lunatic arsonist trying to kill me.'

At 3.25 pm, Detective Inspector Hicks' phone rang and he picked it up, listened for 30 seconds, then said, 'We'll be right there.'

'Come on, Mickey, the boys with the purple pens have arrived.'

'Purple pens?'

'The Fraud Squad. They like to use a different colour ink when checking records than your everyday accountants and auditors. In the Met they used green, here some of them use purple.'

'That's fascinating, Sir.'

Standing in reception were Chief Superintendent Patterson and DC Andrew Morgan. Patterson looked like an old time copper. Solid. Six foot, 13 stone 9 pounds and with a broken nose. He looked like he'd been in his fair share of pub brawls. The clipped grey hair, a neat moustache, broad features, and soft blue eyes gave him the look of everyone's favourite uncle, an image only added to by his green checked suit and rosewood pipe.

What was not so obvious was that Patterson had qualified as a Certified Accountant in 1939. He could add up a column of pounds, shillings and pence with the flick of an eye and analyse a balance sheet faster than most stockbrokers.

'Sir,' said Hicks, 'I didn't expect you to come in person. Would you like to come through to my office?'

'No that's all right. Me and young Morgan here could kill

for a bit of grub. Is the canteen still open?'

'Well, if it isn't it soon will be. Mickey, run ahead would you, and see what's on the menu.'

The afternoon shift was not due to start come in for their snap before 5.30, so all that Mary had to offer was reheated shepherds' pie, and freshly cooked peas with gravy. 'That sounds great,' said the Superintendent, 'as long as it comes with a mug of tea and a slice of bread and butter.'

Five minutes, later Patterson and Morgan were tucking into the mince-filled potato pie with relish. 'Tell the Inspector what you found,' said Patterson.

Morgan put down his fork. Tall, slim, and good-looking in an almost feminine way, he'd only been on the squad a month and was still finding his feet. 'We analysed his Lloyd's account that you gave us. We went back to the day the account was opened on 2 January 1960. There was a total of 49 credits. They followed a distinct pattern. A payment of £5,000 would be paid by an organisation or individual, followed by a much larger sum of variable size within 4 to 6 weeks.'

'We guessed as much,' said Hicks, but didn't elaborate.

Morgan ignored the interruption. 'There were also 19 withdrawals or transfers. Twice a year he transferred money from his Lloyds account to one of four other bank accounts. These accounts are held at different banks in England. He uses four different names, Lloyd, Keaton, Fairbanks and Chaney. There is also at least one annual withdrawal from the Lloyds account. Normally he leaves a balance of £1,000 in the account following these withdrawals. However, last week he withdrew £67,000 in the form of a cashier's cheque, leaving a balance of just £69. The accounts for Lloyd, Keaton, Fairbanks and Chaney were also emptied last week.'

'Well at least we know one thing about him,' said Collins.

'What?' asked Morgan.

'He likes silent film stars.' Morgan looked at Collins as if he was talking gibberish.

'What do you think he does with the cashier's cheques?' asked Hicks.

'The same as you, Inspector,' said Patterson. 'He makes a visit to Switzerland once or twice a year, and deposits the cheques in one or more bank accounts.'

'Untraceable?' asked Collins.

'Absolutely,' said Patterson.'

'We've got the addresses of those customers who were daft enough to use a business or private phone to contact him, but there were six from call boxes. Can you trace their addresses from his bank accounts for us?' asked Hicks.

'Already on it,' said Patterson.

'We questioned one of his customers yesterday and today. He knows nothing about Tubbs. All he got was a few words of instructions through the post and a demand for his retainer of £5,000. If we hadn't intervened, Tubbs would have called him from a phone box with final payment instructions. It's a long shot, but maybe one of his customers can give us a bit more info on Tubbs.'

'For what it's worth, we'll keep ferreting away. You never know what we might find.' said Patterson. 'Get the local nicks who are working on cases to contact me direct.'

'Will do, Sir, and thanks,' said Hicks, 'We appreciate all you've done.'

'Listen Inspector, normally we're dealing with embezzlers and shady businessmen. This bastard is a killer, and if we can do anything to help catch him, we will.'

Birmingham, 15.00hrs

Agnes parked outside an old Victorian house in Erdington that had been built when Prince Albert was still alive. The U-shaped driveway had been designed to take several horse-drawn carriages and the grounds suggested that either a very talented amateur gardener or a well-paid professional attended to the lawns, trees and shrubs on a regular basis with great care and pride.

The man who opened the door was in his eighties, but the gleam in his eye, the firm handshake, and the smile on his lips showed that he had no intention of going into the night quietly any time soon. 'Come in, Mrs Winters. Come in,' he said still holding her hand. Then, looking around to ensure he couldn't be overheard, whispered, 'I called Miriam after you contacted me. She says you can be trusted.' Leaning forward, he almost whispered, 'Can you be trusted?' and grinned maniacally.

Agnes was surprised. Maybe, not all was as well with Dr Granger as she had been led to believe. Seeing the doubt cloud her eyes, the old man burst out laughing and slapped his thigh. 'Miriam didn't tell you? I was well known for my little jokes at the university. I particularly liked it when I caught out one of the bigwigs. Alas, now I rarely get the chance to pull the odd leg or two. Anyway, come in, come in. My wife has left us some sandwiches and cake.'

Five minutes later, Agnes was eating a freshly made ham and cucumber sandwich and relaxing in Dr Granger's personal library. Unlike Miriam's cramped office, Dr Granger had enough space to spread out and arrange his books by subject and then by author. Agnes noticed that one six-foot run of shelving was given over entirely to his own works.

'Miriam told me about your case. Fascinating, absolutely fascinating. I'm a little surprised though, that a civilian and not a police officer has come knocking on my door.'

'I'm a friend of one of the officers investigating the case. As you can imagine, he's busy following up more traditional lines of inquiry.'

'Hmmm! So it was your idea to check the medical records?'

'Yes.'

'I'm not surprised. Typical of someone who worked at Bletchley Park.'

Agnes answered him without hesitating, 'I'm sorry. I've

never heard of Bletchley Park.'

'No, neither have I. It's just a place I visit now and then in my dreams. Oddly enough, I spent a lot of time talking to people there about their dreams and sometimes their demons. One of my most enjoyable dreams concerned a very striking young woman about your height, playing croquet with a chap by the name of Dilly Knox. Her auburn hair was shoulder-length in those days and shone like a golden halo in the bright sunlight. After the grime and filth of London, she really did strike me as the most beautiful thing I'd seen that year. Anyway, you didn't come here to talk about my dreams, so fire away.'

Agnes looked at the old man. She smiled brightly, then winked. Granger laughed and sat back in his chair, a mug of tea nestling in his gnarled hands.

'Have you seen the news coverage concerning the arsonist who burnt Anne Johnston to death?'

'Of course. You'd have to live in Siberia not to have seen it. As soon as Miriam rang off I started to look through my notes from the period in question. The man you're looking for isn't the usual arsonist who sets a fire for the thrill of it. Such people are often poorly educated. This man is someone who, even as a child, would have displayed special attributes.'

'You mean technical skills? An understanding of chemistry and such like?'

'I think such talents may have been present in a latent form, but I was thinking more along the lines of intelligence, arrogance, poor social skills, an outsider who was avoided by other children. Someone who lacked empathy with others, and who had a grossly exaggerated sense of his own importance. A person who wasn't interested in other people for themselves, but only what they could give him. Probably a "mummy's boy" with a poor relationship with his father.'

'A homosexual?'

'I doubt it. His fixation on Anne shows that in his own way he is attracted to women, although I suspect he may be a virgin. If not a virgin then he probably resorts to prostitutes for satisfaction.'

'Anything else?'

Granger paused, unsure if he should share a theory he had been developing overnight. He knew that Bletchley Park had contained numerous geniuses, as well as many people whose only skills were to cook a good dinner and keep their mouth shut. Agnes, he suspected, was in the former group. She would know the value of listening to really stupid ideas. Finally, he decided that she could be trusted with his wild speculation. 'I'm toying with the idea that this man is attracted to certain women. He may resent them, but he probably also wants to worship them. He might actually believe that by burning Anne to death he was giving her a gift.'

'What sort of gift?'

'His one true love is fire. In his mind by burning Anne he was making her into an offering to the Gods. Or maybe he sees himself as Hephaestus, in which case burning a young woman may, for him, be akin to taking a bride. As I say, this is no more than pure speculation on my part.

'Anyhow, I spent several hours thinking about what Miriam had said, checking my journals and trying to recall those patients who had made the greatest impression on me between 1940 and 1952. At about three this morning, I was able to whittle it down to two young men.'

'Did these two youths know one another?'

'Not that I'm aware of. One lived in Coventry, the other in Smethwick.'

'What were their names?'

'The older one was George Tay, the other Martin Grace.'

'Were they ever charged with arson?'

'That I can't be sure of. Certainly in the matters for which they were referred to me, neither stood trial.'

'How can you be so sure of that?'

'That they weren't prosecuted? I was never called as a witness. Of course, it's possible that they were charged with other offences later.'

'So it's back to the police files?'

'Possibly,' said Granger and smiled. 'The officer I dealt with most at that time was Detective Sergeant Osbourne. Before you start ploughing through files, have a word with him.'

'Do you have a contact address for the Sergeant?'

'Indeed I do. My price for divulging it is that you have another cup of tea and a macaroon.'

When Agnes returned home she rang retired Sergeant Osbourne and tried to arrange a time to see him either that evening or early Friday morning. Neither was possible. His wife was in hospital undergoing tests and he would be with her that night and most of Friday. They settled on Saturday morning.

She then briefed Collins on what she'd discovered. 'This is great stuff, darling. I need to report what you've found to the Boss.'

Agnes hesitated, then said, 'He wasn't too pleased the last time I became involved in an inquiry. Why don't you wait until I've spoken to Sergeant Osbourne? There's less chance you'll get in trouble if you can offer the Inspector both a name and address for Tubbs.'

Collins wasn't convinced. Withholding information from your commanding officer was never a wise thing to do. But if he reported what Agnes had found, the police would interview Osbourne and she would be frozen out. Then he remembered that the Inspector was due in court on Friday. Possibly all day. Maybe he did have some wriggle room and could delay reporting the information until Saturday. He decided to sleep on it.

Friday, 9 July 1965

Handsworth, 08.00hrs

Collins awoke feeling almost like his old self. The light-headedness that had been afflicting him since the explosion on Monday seemed to have disappeared, and his arm had stopped aching. He still felt the occasional stab of pain if he stretched his arm at odd angles, but put that down to strain on the 21 stitches in his forearm. However, his good mood disappeared when he remembered that it was Friday and Agnes was meeting Aubrey in London. Try as he might, he couldn't shake off the feeling that something bad was about to happen.

Agnes and Collins ate breakfast together in near silence. He didn't want to let Agnes see how worried he was or presume to tell her what to do, so he remained quiet. When he left, he kissed her and held her tight. All he said was, 'I'll see you later. Take care of yourself.'

Agnes watched Collins drive away, and for the first time allowed herself to think about the risks that attended any meeting with a Soviet spy who was thinking of defecting. She refused to dwell on the risks and shook them off. Anatoli was an old friend and he'd asked for her help. She had to go.

With Hicks in court on a GBH with intent case and Clark still off sick, the office felt dead. Collins had long ago discovered that the little man's personality had a way of filling every space he inhabited, and when he was absent he was missed.

He couldn't face the thought of re-reading the witness statements again, and instead headed to Alf and the records office. Maybe something new had come in from one of the other nicks.

Nine hours later, Collins rang Clark and invited himself around for tea. It was infinitely preferable to returning to an empty house, and besides, it would take his mind off Agnes and whatever it was she was up to in London.

London, 18.00hrs

The Daimler deposited Agnes in front of a nondescript office near Thames House at 5.40. Five minutes later she was sitting outside Sir Aubrey's office under the watchful eye of his secretary, Miss Florin. Clearly Miss Florin had still not forgiven Agnes for calling Sir Aubrey in 1963 and arranging a meeting for the following day without her consent. A capital offence if ever there was one, in her eyes. The same 19th-century portraits of once-important men, now long dead and forgotten, hung on the walls, their eyes judging everyone who dared step into Miss Florin's realm.

Thankfully, Sir Aubrey was not delayed and within a couple of minutes he emerged beaming from his office, 'Agnes, so good of you to come. Miss Florin, might we have tea for four, and break into our reserves and find some cake, would you, please.' Agnes saw Miss Florin stiffen. *First chocolate biscuits and now cake - really!*

Two men rose as Agnes entered the office. She recognised the younger of them immediately as James Richards, who had infiltrated the Eddie Bishop gang and been part of the cover-up that followed the gunfight at H&T Scrap Merchants. The other man was medium height and middle-aged, with a full head of silver grey hair. His three-piece suit said Savile Row, and his tie said Irish Guards. The self-assurance that he exuded spoke of a long history of giving orders and expecting them to be obeyed. 'Agnes, you already know Richards, and this gentleman is a colleague from the Home Office.' Agnes noted that the Home Office representative remained unnamed.

Agnes sat down and immediately asked, 'How many people know about Anatoli?'

'Everyone in this room, plus Miss Florin,' Aubrey told her.

'Have any of you mentioned Anatoli to a colleague or friend?' Agnes asked.

'I think we know enough about security to avoid such basic errors,' said the unnamed man, clearly affronted by being asked such a question by a woman.

'Maybe. But you didn't answer my question. Have you told anyone about Anatoli?'

'No,' said the man his face reddening.

'No,' said Richards.

Aubrey shook his head.

'Good. Keep it that way. It's clear to me that Anatoli believes he is being watched. If that's the case then any KGB friends inside Five – or Six – will have been put on notice to look out for him.'

'Do you think he really does want to defect, or is he part of some disinformation play?' asked Aubrey.

'I don't know,' said Agnes. 'I'll be better able to judge that after I've spoken to him.'

'I'd like to have Richards shadow you tonight,' said Aubrey.

'No,' said Agnes. 'If Anatoli is being watched and Richards is seen, they will deduce that whoever he meets is also with MI5. As it is, they will just see Anatoli talking to a woman about his age. If they question him later, he'll be able to say he was just trying to pick me up.'

'I don't like it. A woman attending a meeting with a leading KGB agent alone is dangerous for both of them. I mean, if something does kick off, what help is a middle-aged woman going to be in a gun fight?' the man from the Home Office said.

'I've seen Agnes in action,' said Aubrey, 'She was as good an operative as any agent, male or female, that I've ever seen.'

'"Was" is the word you used, Aubrey. I apologise if I sound

ungallant, but I suspect you are talking of what Mrs Winter was capable of during the war. She's twenty years older now,' the man said.

'I'm good with a knife,' said Agnes, 'but I'm much better with a gun. I've also kept my eye in with regular target practice,' she lied.

'It doesn't feel right to me. We may only get one chance to land this KGB man.'

'That's true,' said Agnes, 'and I am the only bait that will get Anatoli to take a nibble.'

'Very well, Aubrey, it's your operation. It's on your head.'

'Good,' said Aubrey. 'But all this talk of shooting has reminded me whether you require a suitable firearm, just in case.'

'That won't be necessary,' said Agnes. 'I've my own weapon,' but she made no mention of the Mauser strapped to the inside of her left thigh.

Kings Cross Station, 21.00hrs

At 8.55 Agnes entered Kings Cross Station through the main entrance. The two huge half-oval windows, one each side of the clock tower, always reminded her of a mournful owl's eyes, and she shivered for no good reason. As she walked past posters listing the latest day excursions from London to such exotic places as Oxford (16/6), Portsmouth (19/-), and Ipswich (17/-), she wondered how she would react to Anatoli.

After the war they had worked together for three months, been lovers for one night and good friends for the rest of the time. It had been a different world back then. Simpler in some ways. Your deadliest enemies had worn black uniforms and their cap badge was a silver swastika. Now even friends couldn't be distinguished from enemies, because, unlike the Nazis, they wore no uniforms. Aubrey was right to question if Anatoli really was interested in defecting, or if this was an elaborate charade by the KGB to feed the West lies and disinformation, or to protect one of their own operatives in MI5 or MI6? *Well,* thought Agnes, *I'll soon find out.*

Taking a tray, Agnes approached the refreshment room counter and ordered a tea and a piece of Dundee cake. The room was less than half-full and she had no difficulty finding a table from which she could watch the main entrance and the door leading into the kitchen and from there into the alleyway at the side of the building. She smiled to herself. Old habits die hard. For the first time since the mid-50s she was scouting her escape route.

Sitting down, Agnes observed her fellow diners. It was too early for any of the working girls from behind the station to make an appearance. Some people nervously checked the clock every few seconds to ensure that they would not miss their train. Others were happy to while away a few hours, drinking a single cup of tea, like the old soldier sitting near the counter. Anything was better than constantly walking the lonely streets of London. A few had arranged to meet someone. Like the clock watchers, their eyes constantly scanned the door looking for the man or woman they were waiting for.

At two minutes past nine Anatoli walked in, went to the counter and bought a coffee. Turning, he surveyed the cafeteria. When his eye settled on Agnes he gave the impression that he'd never seen her before, but would like to make her acquaintance.

Crossing to her table, he asked, 'May I sit down?'

Agnes didn't look up, but replied with a muttered, 'Yes.' Anatoli had changed over the years but not much. His six-foot frame was still lean and athletic, even if a few ounces of fat were beginning to show, and his dark brown hair was as thick as ever. Perhaps there was some grey in it now, and his brown eyes may have lost a little of their life but they still contained a hint of kindness, mixed with danger.

Anatoli took out a pack of cigarettes and held it out to Agnes, 'Would you like one?' Agnes shook her head again. Anatoli lit up, then leaned forward, his head bent trying to engage Agnes in conversation. His elbow rested on the table, and his hand holding the cigarette covered the side of his face. This, together with the angle of his head, made it impossible for anyone to read his lips. Keeping his voice low, he said, 'It is good to see you, my friend. Thank you for coming. I wasn't sure if Aubrey would follow my instructions.'

'Why me?' asked Agnes. 'Why Five?'

'Six is, how do you say? Compromised. It's possible that Five has also been infiltrated. The only person I will trust is you.'

'So, why now, Anatoli? Why after a life of service to the Motherland do you wish to defect?'

Anatoli leaned even further in. 'Ever since Brezhnev replaced Khrushchev I have been living on borrowed time. For reasons I won't go into, Brezhnev hates my guts. I have managed to avoid returning to Russia for nearly ten months but now I have been ordered back next Friday. On arrival, it will either be a bullet in the head or a gulag for me. I must defect before next Thursday.'

'Why does Brezhnev hate your guts?'

'It's a long story and goes back to Hungry in 1956. He thinks I got his nephew killed.'

'And did you?'

'Yes,' said Anatoli without hesitation. 'He was a lunatic. All he wanted to do was torture and murder enemies of the state, and if they were young and pretty, so much the better.'

Agnes decided to change the subject. 'What about your wife?'

'She died last year.'

'I'm sorry to hear that. It will be difficult to arrange your extraction at such short notice.'

'It has to be next week.'

'I understand that. I'm just saying that planning will be rushed, and we both know what happens when plans are rushed.'

'I have no choice. But you will look after me, won't you Agnes?' and he smiled.

'I'll try. Where do we pick you up?'

'Here. Outside by the taxi rank at 8.33am. The rush hour traffic will provide cover.'

'Fine. But Aubrey will want to know what information you can provide, in return for your new life.'

'I have been the KGB's leading representative in London, Washington and Paris. I think Aubrey will be interested in my story, starting with the two agents in place within MI6 and more than a dozen Labour MPs, including two ministers, who are members of the Party. Plus a lot of information on Paris and Washington which will prove interesting to the Service and Prime Minister.'

'Can you name the double agents?'

'Yes, but you will still have to gather evidence against them .'

'What do you want in return for this largesse?'

'A new identity, a secure house, £100,000 and a pension for life.'

'You are expensive, Anatoli.'

'Yes, but then I am a poor immigrant coming to England without a single kopek.' He smiled. 'I'm starting again.'

'I think we both know that the former head of the KGB in London, Washington and Paris is anything but a poor man.'

Anatoli inclined his head and said nothing.

'Very well, I'll speak to Aubrey. How do you see the snatch working?

'They must pick me up in a black cab from the taxi rank outside at exactly 8.33 next Thursday morning." He paused. "One last thing. I would like you to be in the queue with me.

If I am being watched, it will look like I've taken a girlfriend.'

'Very well,' said Agnes and stood up, knocking her chair over, and slapped Anatoli's face. 'How dare you suggest such a thing?' she hissed at him, and walked swiftly towards the door.

Halfway across the floor a tall man appeared in the doorway, with broad shoulders, wavy black hair combed straight back, and a loose-fitting suit covering what Agnes knew to be a shoulder holster. Their eyes met, and in that instant the killer realised that Agnes knew exactly why he was here. His hand moved inside his jacket. 'Anatoli, gun,' Agnes shouted, and threw herself to the left, hitting the edge of a table, which fell on her.

The man's gun now was clear of his jacket. Ignoring Agnes, he fired at the quick-moving Anatoli who, keeping low, was heading for the counter before escaping out of the back door. A shot exploded over Anatoli's head, and the tea urn sprouted a leak.

Customers and staff were now screaming and running for cover. A young man grabbed his girlfriend and dragged her to the floor. An elderly man, who moments earlier had been sitting on his own, stirring a cup of tea, had thrown himself across a young mother and her child. Staff were running for the exit door behind the counter.

Fumbling under her skirt, Agnes grabbed the Mauser. The feel of the gun, the adrenalin pumping through her body, and the fear that she had to fight, all combined to trigger her training from 25 years ago. Without thinking, she flipped the safety catch off and from her prone position fired one shot at the man. Her bullet hit him in the chest. A surprised look crossed his face, and he turned to look at Agnes, horror etched on his face. Desperately, he tried to bring his gun to bear on her, but couldn't control his arm. Then his legs gave way and he fell to the floor and lay unmoving.

A second man appeared at the door and aimed at Agnes. She started to raise her gun just as a chair hurled by Anatoli sailed over her prone body and hit the man in the chest and neck. Agnes felt Anatoli grab her hand, pull her to her feet, and push her towards the kitchen. The man raised his gun, took careful aim and fired. A bullet ripped through Anatoli's jacket, and Agnes felt his arm jerk as a bullet left a shallow furrow in his right bicep. Pushing Agnes into the kitchen, Anatoli upended a metal storage cabinet and blocked the door.

Agnes grabbed Anatoli by the hand and ran for the exit. They made it just as the killer pushed his way into the kitchen and fired another shot that slammed into the wall above Anatoli's head. Dropping to one knee, Agnes held her gun with both hands and fired two shots at the killer. The first missed. The second hit the man in the thigh. Screaming like a lost demon, he fell to the floor. Blood gushed from the wound, turning his light grey trousers black and forming a large puddle around him. *Dear God, not the femoral artery,* Agnes prayed.

The alley was deserted. 'Where can we go?'

'Euston. Follow me,' said Agnes. She grabbed Anatoli by the hand and walked quickly away. Within ten yards she realised that her right thigh was had gone dead. *I'm too old to be diving about on concrete floors,* she thought and ignored the pain.

Reaching Euston Road, Agnes turned right. Eyes darting from side to side, she quickly evaluated the level of threat posed by each person she passed. Her right hand rested lightly against her leg. No one noticed that the tall middle-aged woman who walked with such confidence hand in hand with a tall man was holding a small flat gun in her other hand. Shouts and screams were now coming from the buffet but before the first police officer had arrived, Agnes and Anatoli could already see Euston station.

Stopping outside the station, Agnes stepped into the telephone box near the corner and called Collins. Thirty seconds later Collins picked up the phone. Agnes cut his greetings short, and launched into a slightly drunken monologue, hoping and praying that he would understand what she was saying. 'Michael, I'm so glad you're home. I've had a wonderful day in London. I bought some really lovely pieces today. Although the competition was deadly. Deadly. Unfortunately, I have nowhere to put them that's safe. Perhaps you or Mary could think of something.

'Anyway darling, I'm going to catch the next train from Euston. Do come and meet me. You could bring along a couple of Clive's little friends if you like. They could be useful and they are always so amusing.'

There was only the slightest pause as Collins translated what Agnes had said. When he spoke his voice too was light and cheerful. 'That sounds grand. I'll see you soon.'

Agnes smiled grimily and hung up. The pain and stiffness in her leg was growing worse. She resolved to ignore it until later, and linking arms with Anatoli, strolled towards the station entrance. For anyone watching, they were just a middle-aged couple who had enjoyed a good day out in London and were now heading home on the last train to Birmingham.

Automatically, both Agnes and Anatoli waked to the rear of the train. They both knew that if they had to get off in a hurry it would be the safest place to jump from. Thankfully, it was a corridor train and the last carriage was empty. Anatoli stood in the doorway while Agnes limped along to the toilet. Locking the door, she leaned against it. Standing there the full implications of what she had done washed over her. She saw again the bullet hit the first killer and the red stain spread rapidly across his chest. She knew he was dead. Suddenly, bile welled up in her throat and she was bent double over the toilet, vomiting onto the track below. *God forgive me. I killed him. How could I?* Then the trembling started.

Fighting to regain control, Agnes ran the cold tap. A trickle of yellow-tinged water filled the basin slowly. Cupping her hand, she splashed her face twice then wiped it dry with a hankie. A quick application of lipstick and a comb pulled through her auburn hair was enough to tidy her appearance. But her mind remained a chaotic maelstrom. *I killed a man!*

Collins drew up outside Clark's house. The light was on in the lounge and the curtains drawn. Collins rang the bell and the door was opened by Ruth wearing a blue house-coat and matching slippers. The navy blue of the housecoat seemed very similar to the Albion's navy blue stripes, and he wondered if Clark had bought it for her.

Ruth took one look at Collins' face and asked, 'Michael, what is it? What's wrong?'

'I don't have the details but I think Agnes is in trouble.'

'Come in. Clive's in the lounge resting.'

Clark had heard the exchange and was already standing when Collins entered the lounge. 'Trouble?'

'I'm not sure but Agnes just called from London. She was doing a job for that bastard Sir Bloody Aubrey Nicholas. Something's gone wrong. She wants me to meet her at New Street and to bring a gun and Mary.'

'Why does she want Mary?'

'I think she needs some place to stay or hide out, and Mary has several flats for her girls.'

Clark could see how worried Collins was, and said, 'OK. Yow wait here. I'll get a couple of shooters and change. I won't be a tick.'

Part 3

Saturday, 10 July 1965

Birmingham, 00.12hrs

Collins and Mary stood on the platform watching the London train glide slowly into the station and stop. Somewhere in the shadows, Clark was watching them and everyone else on the platform. Not for the first time, Collins missed the smell of burning coal and the hiss of steam that used to accompany the arrival of a train. They watched as the passengers disembarked, some rushing to grab a taxi before they were all gone, others unconcerned, knowing that someone would be there to meet them.

When most of the passengers had disappeared, the door of the last carriage opened and a dark-haired man of about 50 stepped down. Casually, he looked around, saw Collins and Mary and turned to say something to whoever was still in the carriage. Seconds later, Agnes appeared, and Collins realised that he'd been holding his breath. Taking Mary's arm, he walked towards the train.

After Agnes had taken two steps, immediately Collins knew she was hurt. He sped up. Mary embraced Agnes as if they were sisters, and Collins and Anatoli shook hands like old friends. Charade over, they moved quickly towards the exit in silence. Clark followed at a distance.

Collins had parked the Rover 100 in Station Street. He turned the ignition, and waited until Clark had got into the car before saying, 'We're heading to Moseley. Mary's got a flat you can use there.'

'You are certain that no one knows of its existence?' asked Anatoli.

The thick Russian accent registered with Collins and he

thought, *What has that fecker Aubrey got you into, Agnes?*

'In my profession it's necessary to have a number of properties that I or other girls can use which neither the police nor the Revenue know about. Rest assured, it's safe,' said Mary.

'Let's get Anatoli there as quickly as possible,' said Agnes. 'The sooner he's off the streets the better. Michael, has there been any mention on the news about a shooting at Kings Cross tonight?'

'Not that I heard.'

'Good, that means Aubrey was able to contain the situation.'

The flat was off a side road not far from the Edgbaston cricket ground. The house was post-war, and while not as large as many of its neighbours, it was still a substantial four-bedroom house and, unknown to everyone but her solicitor, was owned by Mary, along with four others in the area. Quietly she opened the front door and led the way to the flat on the first floor. Flicking the light on, she crossed to the windows and closed the curtains.

The room in which Anatoli found himself was not what he'd expected. There was a small kitchenette on his right and in front of him was a double bed, small settee and a four-drawer chest of drawers, on top of which were a range of whips, canes and riding crops. Attached to the wall were an array of chains and ropes including a 7 foot high wooden X, with cuffs at each of the four points. The remaining flats in the property were all let to office workers who were seldom at home during the day when Mary's girls were entertaining their clients.

Mary didn't comment on or excuse the unusual furnishings, 'The bathroom is across the hall and I've left some food in the kitchen. It will see you through the next 24 hours. I'll call around tomorrow afternoon. But now I need to go home and get some beauty sleep or else my clients will be complaining that Madame has black rings under her eyes, and is falling asleep on the job.'

'Thank you for everything,' said Agnes, and kissed her friend on the cheek.

'My pleasure,' said Mary and set out to walk the two hundred yards back to her own house.

Agnes kicked off her shoes and said to Anatoli, 'Let me see your arm.'

He slipped his jacket off and rolled up his sleeve. As she had suspected when she examined his wound on the train, the bullet had only grazed the bicep and the pad she had improvised from her slip had stopped the bleeding. Sending Collins to find the first aid kit in the bathroom, Agnes selected a two-inch bandage and wound it tightly around the injury before ripping the bandage and tying it off. 'There, that should hold it,' she said.

Anatoli inspected Agnes's work, pronounced that it was good, and headed into the kitchen to make some tea. Before long Collins could hear him filling the kettle. Clark had taken up a position by the front window and kept a discreet eye on the street below. Unable to contain himself any longer, Collins asked, 'What the bleeding hell did Aubrey get you mixed up in?'

By the time Anatoli reappeared with a tray of tea, coffee and toast, Agnes had provided Collins with the bare outline of what had happened. 'Who were the men that attacked you, KGB?' asked Collins.

'No,' said Anatoli. 'They are Bulgarian. I've known them before. They are part of Colonel Petko Kovachev's, Service 7. It is a new department, only one year old. Its job is very simple. They are trained killers. Their services are available to all governments of the Warsaw Pact. Service 7 specialises in murder, suicides, kidnapping and, how you say, wrong information, against Bulgarian anti-revolutionaries living abroad. Already they have carried out missions in Britain, West Germany, Turkey, France and Switzerland. We were very lucky to escape. I think they did not expect you to have a gun, Agnes. That was the surprise, which saved our lives.'

'Bloody hell. It sounds like something out of a spy book. What are you going to do now?' asked Collins looking at Agnes.

'Tomorrow, I will call Aubrey.'

'Are you sure that he can be trusted?' asked Anatoli.

'Whoever betrayed you, it wasn't Aubrey. I'd stake my life on it.'

'Darling, that's exactly what you're doing,' said Collins.

Agnes gave a weary little smile, 'Things will look better in the morning. Clive, can we drive you home?'

'Ta.'

Standing, Agnes kissed Anatoli lightly on the cheek. 'I'll be here tomorrow afternoon. We can discuss your next move, then and please don't go out.'

'I will stay here. What about your friend Mary, can she be trusted?'

'We have often helped each other out. She can be trusted, I guarantee it.'

'I sleep better if I had a gun and some ammunition.'

Clive hesitated for only a moment before taking out a small .44 Bull Dog revolver from his pocket, a British gun that had been manufactured for nearly a century and which had been used by Charles Guiteau to assassinate James Garfield, the twentieth President of the United States, in July 1881. The little gun only took five shells but at short range it was accurate and deadly, as Garfield had discovered. 'I'll need it back when you're finished. It's one of a pair.'

Anatoli looked at Agnes and smiled, 'I like this man,' and took the offered .44. Clark smiled and pulled out a half-full pack of .44 ammunition from his jacket pocket. 'I like him a lot,' Anatoli said and laughed.

Handsworth, 01.55hrs

Collins sat on the edge of the bed. A bottle of Universal Embrocation rested on the bedside cabinet. He heard Agnes turn off the shower and waited while she dried herself. When she appeared she was wearing a white terry towel dressing gown, her wet hair wrapped in a small blue towel. She looked exhausted. Collins patted the bed beside him, 'Come on, darling, let's see that leg of yours.' Agnes lay on her right side and pushed the dressing gown to one side. The side of her left leg, from hip bone to knee, was a swollen mass of yellow, red, blue, purple and black bruises. 'That looks painful.'

'It is, and it will be worse in the morning when it stiffens up. So slap some embrocation on and let's go to sleep.'

'OK. Mind you, this is going to sting.'

Pouring a liberal amount of the thick creamy white concoction into his hand, Collins transferred it to the injured leg. Instantly, the entire room smelt like any one of ten thousand dressing rooms. Agnes stiffened first at the coldness of the mixture and then at the stinging sensation as the embrocation searched out the scratches, abrasions, grazes, and cuts on her leg.

At 4am Collins awoke. It took him a few seconds for the reason to register. Agnes was lying beside him in a foetal position, gently sobbing. Turning on his side, Collins pulled her to him and held her in his arms. Finally, when there were no more tears to shed for the man who had tried to kill her, she slept. Collins remained awake, listening and thinking about what he'd like to do to Sir Aubrey.

Handsworth, 08.00hrs

When Agnes awoke, she could hear Michael moving about in the kitchen below. She turned over and winced. As she'd feared, her left leg had stiffened up.

Throwing back the covers, she examined the damage. The bruising now extended from her hip bone to below the knee and there was even an isolated bruise on her ankle. *The table must have hit me harder than I thought.*

Slowly, she swung both legs onto the floor and stood. *That wasn't so bad. Hardly any pain at all.* Then she took a step. Pain shot up the left side of her body. *I can't have broken anything,* she thought, and using the bed and dressing table for support, hobbled over to the bathroom. *A warm shower and I'll be as right as rain.*

Agnes wasn't sure which was worse, stinging hot water on her injured leg or the agony of cold water seeking out every scratch and raw bruise. Taking a deep breath, she lathered her hands, told herself to stop being a baby, and started to wash her leg. It wasn't that bad, she decided. No worse than having your skin peeled off by an overly enthusiastic employee of the Spanish Inquisition.

Collins watched her hobble into the kitchen and said, 'You're going to the General Hospital for an X-ray.'

'Oh, don't fuss. It's just bruising.'

'Well, let's leave that diagnosis to the doctors.' Agnes stuck her tongue out, and Collins laughed. 'Very grown-up, I must say.'

'Anything on the news about what happened?'

'No.'

'I didn't think there would be. It probably missed the deadline for the early editions, which would have given Aubrey time to issue a D notice.'

'Do you think the great British public have any idea how often the Government ban the publication of a story on the grounds of public interest?

'I doubt it.'

'So what are you going to do about Anatoli?'

'I'm not sure. I need to speak to Aubrey but I can't rely on MI5. He assured me that the information hadn't been shared with MI6.'

'So it had to come from his end,' said Collins.

'Yes. Probably one of the people I met on Friday.' Agnes took a sip of her tea and played with her scrambled eggs. Knowing that she was thinking, Collins concentrated on eating his breakfast as quietly as he could.

Taking another sip of tea, Agnes said, 'I'm going to ask Clive to interview Sergeant Osbourne about those two lads. No need to let that investigation grow cold. Then I'll call Aubrey. After that you and I are going to the General Hospital.'

'I'm glad you've seen the light…'

Agnes continued as if she had never been interrupted. 'Hospitals are great places to lose anyone who's following you. After that, we visit Anatoli and discuss his options.'

'And what do I do in all of this?'

'You drive, darling. After all, I've got a poorly leg,' she said in a fairly good imitation of Collins' Dublin accent.

Selly Oak, 09.35hrs

Clark had been dreading another day of doing nothing, and had been only too happy to agree to interview the retired Sergeant Osbourne. Following the Bristol Road, he passed the University of Birmingham and the Royal Orthopaedic hospital and continued to follow the A38 for a further half mile before turning left and parking outside Sergeant Osbourne's house. He was now in the heart of Selly Oak, much of which the Quaker Cadbury family had built for its employees and which boasted the distinction of not having a single pub within its boundaries. The houses were a mixture of detached and semi-detached, all with front and rear gardens and built on wide tree-lined roads and streets. It was one of the best examples in the country of large-scale house building for families.

Before stepping from the car, Clark checked his mirrors for any cars that might be following him. None. *OK*, he thought,

Let's go and see the good Sergeant.

Osbourne's front garden looked in need of a weeding, although the grass had been recently trimmed. The paintwork on the semi also looked in need of a touch-up. Clark rang the bell and waited.

When the door was opened, Osbourne held out a hand that was covered in grass stains and freshly dug earth. 'Sorry mate, I weren't expecting you this early. Come on in.'

Clark followed the big man into the dining room at the back of the house. Through the French windows, he saw a woman in her sixties weeding a large rose bed. "That's the missus. She ain't been well, but she got the all clear yesterday. We're trying to get things shipshape again. Fancy a cuppa?'

'Ta, that would be great.'

Before he served Clark, Osbourne took a mug of tea and a digestive biscuit to his wife. She took it, and looking up, raised her cup at Clark, who waved back.

Settled in his favourite chair, Osbourne said, 'Old Granger told me what you were after. Damned if I know how he got my number.'

'Do you remember the lads he talked about?'

'Oh yeah. Right little shits, both of them. George Tay was a big bastard for his age. Only about 14 or 15 but looked like a 20-year-old. He had a few brains and might have become a serious problem for us, but he got in the way of a lorry and the lorry won.'

'He was run over?'

'Sort of. He was being chased across a construction site when he ran in front of one of them earth movers. Squashed flatter than a bug.'

'Why was he being chased?'

'He tried to pinch four sticks of dynamite but was seen by one of the workmen.'

'So he's out of the picture, then?'

'Oh yeah. But even if he were alive and setting fires every week I'd still point you in the direction of Martin Grace.'

'Why?'

'Because he scared me shitless when I interviewed him.'

'How so?'

'Did you ever see *Village of the Damned?*'

'Yeah. Creepy blond-haired kids.'

'That's it. Guy who wrote the book they made the film from, *Midwich Cuckoos,* was from Brum. Martin Grace was just like them kids. I mean, I saw the film years after I interviewed him but as soon as I saw the kids I thought of him.'

'How did you come to interview him?'

'There was a fire across the road from his house.'

'Whereabouts were this?'

'Bearwood, Smethwick. Near the woods. Woburn Road, I think. I can't remember the number. '

'The kids and hubby escaped? asked Clark.

'The husband had taken the kids to Weston-Super-Mare for the week-end. He and the wife were breaking up. Seemed she had a lot of gentlemen friends visit her when he was on nights.'

'Was she on the game?'

'Might have been. Anyhows, she had over £600 in her building society book when she died. Back then that were more than six times the average annual pay for a man.'

'And when was that?'

'End of 1950.'

'How old was the kid?'

'Fifteen. Sixteen at most.'

'OK, but what was suspicious about the fire?'

'That was just it, nothing. The fire brigade put it down to a leaking gas line which blew up.'

At the mention of a leaking gas line Clark knew he had something but kept the excitement out of his voice. 'So why investigate?'

'An old ladder monkey came to me. Told me that about three years earlier they'd had a call to the same house. No one got hurt that time, but he remembered that a kid opposite the house had watched the whole thing from his bedroom. He swore to me that the kid looked like he was wanking off as he watched the fire.'

'Bloody hell.'

'He still lived opposite. So I called on him. He was a real cold fish. He mainly answered yes and no to my questions. When I asked him about the first fire though, I saw something in his eyes. It was only there for a second but I saw it.'

'What were it?'

'Interest, excitement, lust, happiness. It was all of these things. It was like that first fire was the greatest moment of his life.'

'But he didn't have the same reaction to the second fire?'

'No.'

'How come the mother died? Was it the smoke that got her?'

'No she was trapped in her bedroom. She was a bit tipsy. She'd spent the night dolled up to the nines in her local but didn't get a nibble from anyone she fancied. Anyhows, she went home, locked up and headed for bed. About an hour later the fire started. But she couldn't get out of the bedroom. The fire had run up the stairs and along the landing. She was burnt to death as she tried to break the window. From what eyewitnesses say, it took about a couple of minutes. Terrible way to go.'

'What did she look like?'

'Oh, she was a looker in her day, 5 foot 5, trim with a good figure. A natural blonde I were told.'

Clark fixed his gaze on the old copper, 'Between yow and me, mate, I think yow've just told me who killed Anne Johnson. Now all we need to do is find the bastard and prove it.'

Osbourne nodded thoughtfully. 'I told you he was a creepy little shit.'

As he drove back to the station along Soho Hill, Clark spotted Archie Mellon riding a pushbike on the opposite side of the road. Like Pavlov's dogs, Clark's conditioning sprang into operation and he began to salivate at the thought of nicking the little creep for a record fifth time. Turning the car round, he followed him. When Mellon stopped outside a bike shop, Clark parked behind him and got out.

Standing beside the shop door, Clark waited until Mellon emerged. Grabbing him by the shoulder, he spun the rat faced little thief around and pushed his face against the wall. 'What you up to, Archie? I don't see many meters around here.'

Archie recognised the voice and stopped struggling. 'Hello, Mr Clark. I'm just here to get some brake pads for me bike.'

Clark released his hold. 'OK, let's see what you have in your pockets. Turn 'em out.'

Mellon obliged. There wasn't a shilling in sight.

'OK. Let's see what's in your saddle bag.'

Archie walked confidently to his bike and opened the bag hanging behind the seat. It was empty, except for a puncture repair kit. 'See, I've got nowt. I'm clean as a Brillo-scrubbed pan.'

'That I doubt.' Leaning forward, Clark jabbed Archie in the chest with his index finger. 'Don't start doing meters on my patch or I'm going to do you. Understand?'

'Yes, Mr Clark. I won't.'

As he watched the black-eyed greasy git walk away, Clark realised that Archie had only agreed not to do any meters on his patch. That didn't mean he wouldn't be doing meters elsewhere. *Well, that's someone else's problem,* he thought.

Returning to the station, Clark called Inspector Hicks. 'We've got the bastard, Boss. His real name is Martin Grace. He used to live in Bearwood, near the woods.'

'Where did the info come from?'

'A retired copper by the name of Osbourne. He remembered him in connection with a fire that occurred right opposite where Tubbs lived. A pretty blonde housewife got burned to death.'

'Well I'll be damned. When did he come in with the information?'

'That's it, Boss, he didn't. Said he'd left a message with the switchboard but no one rang him back on Friday.'

'Well how did you get onto him?'

'I was following up on a lead that Agnes found.'

'Bloody hell. I should rip a strip off Collins and Mrs Winter for interfering in another police investigation.'

'Yow could, Sir, or wi might just follow up on what she dropped in our lap.'

There was silence on the end of the line. Followed by a sigh. 'You're right. We can't afford to look a gift horse in the mouth.' He paused, thinking. 'It's no use trying to contact the Inland Revenue or Land Registry until Monday, but draft out a request for information and drop it off on Monday before you come to work.'

'Right, Boss.'

'Oh, and well done.'

Clark hung up and called Agnes with the good news and confirmed that he would see her later that afternoon at Mary's flat.

Handsworth, 11.30hrs

Agnes had just finished speaking to Clark when the doorbell chimed. After checking the peephole, she opened the door to the Deputy Director of MI5 and Richards. Shamefaced, Aubrey asked, 'Can I come in?' Stepping away from the door, Agnes limped towards the kitchen followed by both men.

'Coffee?' she asked. Both men nodded. 'So who was the blabbermouth?'

'We don't know,' said Aubrey. 'Only six people knew about

the meeting: myself, Miss Florin, Richards, the gentleman you met yesterday, Anatoli and yourself. We can only assume that the KGB followed him and had orders to kill him if their suspicions were aroused.'

'You don't really believe that do you, Aubrey? As a theory it has more holes in it than my colander.'

'It's the only feasible explanation. MI6 were not notified of the operation and no one other than those you met yesterday in my office knew anything about Anatoli's approach.'

'Well here's a few inconvenient facts for you. According to Anatoli, the men who attacked us were not KGB. They were Bulgarians, part of Service 7. Secondly, they did not just happen upon Anatoli. They knew he would be in the buffet and they were sent to kill him. Anatoli joked when I first saw him that Russian men could visit Kings Cross without raising any suspicions because it was a well-known haunt of prostitutes. They chose the venue because they thought Anatoli would be less cautious in that environment. The man I shot – the man I killed, recognised me. But he didn't see me as a threat. Someone had told him that either I was a retired agent or an old wartime friend of Anatoli's. So again I ask, who talked?'

Unbidden, Richards stood up, turned off the electric kettle and started to make the coffees. Agnes' reasoning was entirely logical.

Collins, freshly washed and shaved, ambled into the lounge. Aubrey viewed him with suspicion but said nothing.

'How much do you know about Mr X?' asked Agnes with more than a trace of sarcasm.

'He has top security clearance,' said Richards.

'So did Burgess and Maclean.'

'Look, even if you are right, you must agree with me that we need to bring Anatoli in without further delay. Only then can we protect him.'

'No,' said Agnes. 'Anatoli is staying where he is until you discover where the leak came from.'

'Very well. I'll leave Richards here as a liaison and head

back to London to review the files.'

'You'll understand why I can't offer you accommodation, Mr Richards.'

'Absolutely. I'll book into a hotel.'

Birmingham, 13.20hrs

The General Hospital was founded in 1779. It had been the brainchild of several eminent citizens of Birmingham including John Ash, Sir Lister Holte, John Baskerville and the businessman and engineer Mathew Boulton, who along with James Watt had led Britain's Industrial Revolution. Much of the funding came from the Birmingham Triennial Music Festival. The first concerts were held over three days in September 1768, and the BTMF continued to fund the hospital into the 20th century. In 1897 the hospital was moved from Summer Lane to Steelhouse Lane, on the opposite side of the road to the city's largest police station, and by 1965 next door to the VD and Urology clinic.

As demands on the hospital had changed over the years, additional buildings and extensions had been added to meet the growing needs of the city. The result was a place where even the staff could get lost, and that was even without venturing into the underground labyrinth of corridors, cubicles and rooms. Agnes had chosen wisely. If anyone was following them, they would have a hard time keeping sight of them here.

Agnes booked in at reception alone. Collins hung back and watched to see if anyone was paying her any undue interest. Nothing. He followed her to the Accident and Emergency department and remained outside for fifteen minutes. Still nothing. He decided it was safe to join Agnes.

The department was strangely quiet. Most of Collins' visits to A&E had been at night, usually after closing time. It was here that he'd seen humanity at its most stupid, like the

17-stone man who had climbed a tree to rescue a kitten. Why he thought a one-inch branch would support him no one knew. Still, he'd have a lifetime to reflect on a possible answer, as he had broken his neck and was now paralyzed from the neck down.

Then there was the 16-year-old lad who had tried to impress his girlfriend by doing wheelies along Great Charles Street on his new motorbike. He hit a pothole, lost control of the bike, and struck the curb with the result that his girlfriend had been catapulted through a plate glass window. She lived but the plastic surgeons were still trying to rebuild her ears and nose which had been sheared off in the crash.

After 20 minutes, Agnes was called and disappeared into a cubicle surrounded by heavy green drapes. In the ten minute examination that followed Collins only heard Agnes cry out once in pain, followed quickly by the apologies of the young houseman.

When she reappeared, Agnes was in a wheelchair. 'X-ray, I'm afraid.'

'I'll keep you company.'

Again Collins hung back and looked for any signs that Agnes was being watched. Still nothing.

An hour later the same houseman who had produced the cry of pain held up the last of five X-rays against the illuminated screen. This one was of her thigh and received considerably more attention than the others. Still holding the X-ray, he said, 'It looks to me like you cracked your hip bone when you fell over. The bad news is that it's very painful, especially when you put weight on it. The good news is that it should heal by itself. I'll write you a prescription for some painkillers. Keep your weight off it for a few days and if you don't see a significant improvement in the level of pain within the week come back. We may have to pin it.'

As they emerged into the sunshine, Agnes said, 'I told you it was nothing.'

'But it is something. It's a cracked bone.'

'Piffle. I'll be fine in a day or two.'

'Well I never thought I'd say this, but it does appear as if you, Clark and I have one thing in common. We all think we know better than the doctors.'

London, 16.00hrs

Sir Aubrey stopped off at Simpson's in the Strand for a late lunch before returning to the office. He was surprised to find a stranger sitting behind Miss Florin's desk. He'd made it quite clear to his secretary on Friday that this would be a working week-end. 'Good afternoon Miss—'

'Ealing, Sir.'

'Where's Miss Florin?'

'She didn't come in today.'

'Clearly. Did she say what the matter was?'

'I'm sorry, Sir, but we've been unable to contact her. We tried again later in the morning. She's probably gone shopping.'

Aubrey absorbed the news like a boxer taking a blow to the kidneys. He felt sick. Miss Margaret Florin had missed two days in the twelve years she had worked for him and the idea that she would fail to call in if she were sick was unthinkable. 'Have my car outside in five minutes and ask for an armed officer to accompany me.'

'Yes, Sir,' said Ealing, a blush of confusion spreading from her neck to face. 'Is everything all right, Sir?'

'Absolutely. You are to say nothing about this to anyone. Is that understood?'

'Yes, Sir.'

Going to the wall safe in his office, Sir Aubrey withdrew his army revolver. Checking that the safety catch was on, he confirmed that the gun was loaded and slipped it into the waist band of his expensive suit trousers. It ruined the line of his suit but his jacket did at least hide the gun from public view.

Thirty-five minutes, later Michael Taylor of MI5 drew to a stop at the top of Russell Avenue, Bounds Park. Miss Florin's home was a small three-bedroom terraced house with a well-tended, but tiny, front garden and an immaculately painted red front door. Aubrey knocked on the door twice without reply. Turning to Taylor, he asked, 'Can you pick a lock?'

'I can, Sir, but we could be here a long time.'

'Very well. Kick it in.'

It took four kicks before the front door snapped open and bounced off the hall wall. The officer led the way into the house, his 9mm automatic drawn, with the safety off. Sir Aubrey followed close behind, his own revolver pointed at the ground.

The front lounge door was open. A quick inspection showed a room that had been ransacked, with books, LPs and china strewn across the floor and furniture. An expensive radio-gram lay smashed and broken. The dining room was the same. Furniture broken and overturned. Pictures missing from the wall. Cupboard doors ripped off and the contents emptied on the floor.

Aubrey approached the stairs. The armed officer moved to go first but Aubrey held up his hand. There was no one in the house and he was fairly certain what he would find upstairs. Miss Florin was in the bathroom. She was wearing bra, panties, stockings, and a white nylon slip, and kneeling next to a nearly full bath. It was clear to Aubrey that someone had held her head under the water. She was dead and Aubrey guessed she had been that way for at least 18 hours.

In her bedroom a new dress, still with the labels on, hung from the back of the door. Her bag and purse lay by the bed, empty.

'Are you all right, Sir?'

'Yes, I'm fine.'

'Do you want me to call the police and report the burglary and murder?'

'No, not yet. I need a few minutes to think. You wait downstairs.' With the officer gone, Aubrey pulled back the sheets. They were clean. Newly changed. But four feet from the top was the unmistakable sign of semen. *Poor, lonely Margaret,* he thought. His mind made up, he went downstairs.

'Taylor, get a team in here asap. I want every inch of the house taken apart, and if any member of your squad so much as mentions this incident to their priest in confessional, you'll be following the Household Cavalry around with a bucket and spade. Do I make myself clear?'

'Crystal, Sir. Is there anything in particular we should be looking for?'

'Proof that she had a boyfriend, and if you're lucky, the identity of said boyfriend. There's semen on the sheets. Now in the twelve years I've known known Miss Florin she has never to my knowledge had a boyfriend. So I doubt whoever it was who left his mark is an innocent civilian.'

Taylor had been too long in MI5 not to appreciate the significance of the Deputy Director's secretary being murdered, especially after what had happened at Kings Cross. Every counter-intelligence service in the country was trying to work out what the hell that had been all about.

Taylor called his three-man search team. They all arrived within thirty-five minutes, and he gave them their instructions. 'We're looking for evidence that the deceased had a boyfriend. That's the silver medal. The gold medal is for finding proof of his identity. Questions?'

'I assume that the local police won't be investigating this murder?'

'Correct. So don't worry about screwing up their scene of crime.'

Whoever had staged the break-in were amateurs compared to MI5, or maybe they just had less time. The officers slashed open every chair, cushion and mattress. Every container in the house was emptied, even the Hoover's dust bag. Carpets and lino were lifted. Photo albums gone through. Book covers sliced open. Every magazine and newspaper was opened, examined and shaken.

Taylor sat on the bed and surveyed the chaos around him. Four hours and they'd found nothing. *We'll have to wait until the morning to check the garden shed,* he thought. Standing, he stretched, as he did so he saw that the small painting of a bird's nest above the chimney breast was very slightly lopsided. Taking it down, he turned it over. The original backing was still in place. It had not been disturbed in 60 years. He threw it on the bed in disgust. Then he saw a tiny sliver of white card peeking out from beneath the brown backing paper. A two-inch slit had been made with a razor blade near the bottom right hand corner. Very difficult to see. Going to the bathroom, Taylor found a pair of tweezers and returned to the bedroom. Grabbing the white card he pulled gently. An unbroken strip of four passport-sized photos was revealed. The photos had been taken in an automatic photo booth and showed Miss Florin sitting on the knee of a dark haired man with thick eyebrows, a thin nose and a full sensuous mouth. Although unclear, it appeared that the man had slipped his hand up Miss Florin's dress in the last photo. She was laughing, her head thrown back.

Still holding the photos with the eyebrow tweezers, Taylor left the room in search of an envelope. With the photo safely tucked away, he rang Sir Aubrey.

Moseley, 16.50hrs

Mary and Clark were in the flat when Agnes and Collins arrived. Kissing her on the cheek, Mary said, 'You're looking a hundred per cent better, Agnes, but I have to tell you that your new Embrocation Bouquet perfume is a real passion killer.'

'How I smell is the least of my worries today.'

Mary smiled and said, 'Well, now that you're all here, I'll leave Anatoli in your hands.'

After Mary had gone Anatoli said 'She's a nice woman, your friend Mary. Is she married?'

'No, she's not, and by inclination she never will be.'

Anatoli smiled. 'I understand. Never mind. She's still a nice lady.'

'I agree, she is. I've known her for years. She runs girls and acts as a mistress, but she doesn't abuse them and she never employs young girls. She is also someone I can trust implicitly because I know she will never let me down.' Not wishing to say any more about her relationship with Mary, Agnes paused, and changing the subject, said, 'Sir Aubrey came knocking on my door this morning.'

'What did he have to say?'

Agnes gave Anatoli a brief outline of what had been said. The Russian listened intently and when she had finished said, 'You did the right thing. The leak must have come from Aubrey or the people you met yesterday. Either that, or someone overheard something. How long do you think it will be before they find out who it was?'

'I have no idea – days, weeks, maybe even months. What I do know is that we need to think about finding you something more permanent and secure than this flat.'

'And where are you thinking of sending me?'

'Scotland.'

'But it's cold and wet in Scotland.'

'Not as cold as the gulag or the grave,'

'This is true.'

Sunday, 11 July 1965

Handsworth, 06.05hrs

The chimes of Big Ben on the Home Service were still resonating in Sir Aubrey's ears when he picked up James Richards at his central Birmingham hotel and drove to Agnes' house.

Aubrey had rung ahead, and after checking who was ringing the bell Agnes opened the door. Sir Aubrey was surprised to find that both Collins and Clark were in the lounge. 'I assume the presence of Constable Clark means that he is aware of what this is about?'

'I think you can assume that,' said Agnes stiffly.

'Very well. But can I remind everyone here that what we are about to discuss is Most Secret.'

'I thought it was Top Secret?' said Collins.

'Listen, you numty, Most Secret is the highest possible classification in Britain,' said Clark.

'But that means Top Secret isn't. So why call it Top Secret?' asked Collins.

Sir Aubrey wasn't sure if Collins was being obtuse, or if he and Clark were playing out a private joke at his expense. 'What it's called doesn't matter. What does matter is that if anyone repeats what I'm about to say, they will be charged under the Official Secrets Act. Is that clear?'

Clark leaned across and whispered in Collins ear, 'Very serious, ain't he?'

Ignoring whatever it was that Clark had said, Sir Aubrey ploughed on. 'Agnes, I can confirm that the leak about Anatoli Petrov came from Miss Florin.'

'Good Lord. She'd be the last person I would expect to...'

'It appears she was the victim of a honey trap.' Aubrey threw a 6 by 8 inch photo of a powerfully built, dark-haired man on the table. 'You were right, Agnes. The man in the picture is Chavda Chilikov, a Bulgarian who works for Section 7.'

'What's Section 7?' asked Clark.

'Essentially, it's an assassination squad, and Mr Chilkov is their top man.'

'How do you know all this?' asked Agnes. 'Did Miss Florin confess?'

'No. She was unable to. Sometime on Friday night Chilkov killed her and tried to make it look like a burglary gone wrong.'

Agnes was shaken by the news but managed to keep how she was feeling from reaching her face. *So much death. What did I start by agreeing to see Anatoli?*

'So how did you identify Chilkov?' asked Collins.

'Miss Florin had kept a strip of photos taken in one of those photographic machine booth things. Chilkov was probably looking for it when he ransacked her place.'

'What does this mean for Anatoli?' asked Agnes.

'It's bad news,' said Richards. 'Chilkov is not going to give up until Anatoli is dead.'

'But we have a plan,' said Aubrey.

'But it's risky,' added Richards.

'Just tell us,' demanded Agnes.

Bearwood, Smethwick 15.00hrs

His near capture at Bright's had shaken Tubbs, and for the last few days he had laid low in his family home. But he had not wasted his time. He had decided to don his Swiss disguise a few days early. His hair was now black and 'A Tan in a Can' had turned his face and hands a light brown. The moustache was an innovation. He'd been growing it for five days and it was almost long enough to dye, but he decided he'd give it another 24 hours. He had also fished out his old black-framed glasses.

More importantly, he'd bought the rail and sea tickets he would require to cross the English Channel and disappear into Europe on his way to Switzerland. All he now had to do was wait until Monday night before setting off. He had plenty of time to finish preparing his two fire bombs. He hoped they would never be used. But he had no intention of the letting the police dig through the house where he'd been born, raised, and planned the death of his parents.

London, 22.00hrs

Sixteen hours after the meeting between Agnes and Aubrey had ended, MI5 Protection Officer Taylor was feeling very cheerful. Three double whiskeys and four pints of beer had that effect on him. He always enjoyed his visits to the Polish Club. Unfortunately, as a non-member he had to rely on an invitation from his friend Danik. As the night wore on he became more and more talkative. When the men started to tell their war stories he decided to tell them about a Russian spy who wanted to defect. When the KGB discovered his intentions, Taylor had hidden him in Birmingham while MI5 sorted things out. The daft thing was that the silly bugger had fallen in the canal basin and they had to fish him out. Unfortunately, in his drunken state he ruined the story by constantly changing between the present and past tenses.

Taylor finished the night by falling down outside the club, twice, before a couple of men lifted him up and bundled him into the back seat of Danik's Mercedes. After two minutes driving, Danik checked his rear view mirror. 'All clear,' he said.

Taylor sat up and said, 'Give me a drink.' Danik passed him a Corona bottle half-filled with water, which he drank down in one go. 'How do you think it went?'

'You make a very convincing drunk, my friend. That communist bastard Karol is probably calling the Soviet Embassy as we speak.'

'God, I'm going to have a thick head in the morning,' said Taylor and sank back in his seat.

Monday, 12 July 1965

Handsworth, 10.30hrs

Clark arrived at work bearing gifts. A coffee and a Belgian bun for Hicks. A tea and a doughnut for Collins, and a tea and a lardy cake for himself. Slumping into his seat, he grinned.

'And what are you grinning at, Constable Clark? asked Hicks.

'The Tax Office said they'd have the stuff for us on Tubbs né Grace by midday tomorrow. The woman at Land Registry obviously fancied me. I don't know if were me looks or charm but she went and looked the information up while I waited.'

'It never ceases to amaze me how quick and efficient blind people can be,' said Collins.

'Yow see the jealousy and disrespect for his betters that I have to put up with, Sir?'

'Cut the crap. What did Land Registry say?

'The property last changed hands in 1957 following the death of Mr and Mrs Grace – in a car fire of all things. Martin Grace is still the registered owner, and it's his name that appears on the Electoral Register.'

'But we don't know if he's living there?' said Hicks.

'No, Sir.'

'OK. Let's take this nice and easy. We don't want to go blundering into another booby-trapped building. First things first. Find some place you can observe the house from. I'll arrange for someone to relieve you at three.'

'That could be a problem, Sir,' said Collins.

'What do you mean, a problem?'

'Do yow trust us, Boss?' asked Clark.

'With my life, yeah. With following orders and procedures, never. Why?'

'We got involved in sommut that is hush-hush and we need to ask for the rest of the day off.'

'What's this sommut all about?'

'We can't say, Sir,' said Collins.

'Holding back information from a senior officer. I'm not sure I like that.'

'I'm sorry, Boss. Wi were told not to say anything.'

Hicks seemed to be enjoying both men's discomfort. 'I'm not sure I can release you without knowing what you're up to. I mean, what if you kill someone? What am I going to say to the Super? No lads, I need a lot more info before I can sign off on this.'

'We're sorry, Sir, but we can't say any more. We have to go,' said Collins.

'And if yow want to discipline us, go right ahead, Boss.'

Hicks glared at both men, 'The bloody cheek of it...' but he couldn't keep up his pretence up any longer, and burst out laughing.

'What's so bleeding funny?' asked Clark.'

'Your faces,' said Hicks, taking a handkerchief from his jacket pocket to wipe his eyes. 'So serious, I wish I'd had a camera. Relax, lads. Sir Aubrey called me last night.'

'I bet he didn't tell you what it were about either,' said Clark.

'No he didn't, and I learnt long ago not to ask, or to piss off any of the MI5 boys – or ladies for that matter. Some of them can be right cows. Just be careful, OK? I think I trust the Russians more than I do MI5 or 6. At least you know the Ruskies are out to kill you. Just check out Tubbs' house first. I'll organise a rota to keep an eye on the house and see if he turns up.'

Bearwood, 11.20hrs

Clark drove past Tubbs' house. The curtains were open, the garden and privet hedge neat and tidy, and there was no mail or milk bottles visible. Collins twisted around in his seat and continued to look at the house until it was out of sight. 'What do you think?' he asked.

'It looks empty to me. But it's worth keeping an eye on it.'

'The question is from where? We can't just park up on the road. Two blokes in a car. Half the people in the road will report us to the police for loitering.'

'Dain't yow see the church hall?'

'What church hall?'

'The one almost opposite the house.'

'How the feck would I see that if I was looking at the house?'

'I've told yow before, yow need eyes in the back of your head for this job, and an extra pair in yowr arse don't go amiss either. Come on, wi need to call Hicks.'

As Clark and Collins drove away, the upstairs curtains in number 86 twitched. Tubbs hadn't been able to see who was in the slow-moving car but he felt certain that it was the police. *Time to go,* he thought.

Birmingham Canal Basin, off Broad Street 12.30hrs

Clark and Collins set up residence in a ramshackle maintenance hut that hadn't seen use since the end of the war. From there they took turns to wander along the tow path between Gas Street and Sheepcote Street. Collins had brought Sheba along as part of his cover. She must have thought it was her birthday, because by 3.30 she'd enjoyed four long walks along nice flat paths with a wonderful array of invigorating smells, including rat. Both men knew that they were seriously under-manned, but supported Agnes in her refusal to bring in anyone from the security services, or even the local police. The risk was too great. Chilkov was the hunter, eventually he would have to show his face.

It was nearly 4pm when Richards spotted Chilkov. He and

two heavies parked at the top of Sheepcote Street and headed towards the wharf. Richards watched them disappear onto the tow path before he left the car. There was plenty of time now. *No need to rush,* he thought.

It had been agreed between the three men that Collins would remain in the hut with Sheba while Richards and Clark went to Moseley with the news of Chilkov's arrival.

After checking who it was, Agnes opened the door and saw the excitement in Richards' eyes. 'They've arrived?' she asked.

'Yes,' said Richards.

'Now the dangerous part,' said Sir Aubrey.

'Only for me, Sir Aubrey, only for me,' said Anatoli, with a grim little smile.

'True,' said Aubrey. 'You'd better get dressed.'

Anatoli took off his shirt and slipped on a heavy nylon vest with numerous pockets. Into each pocket, front, back, and sides Anatoli and Agnes inserted ⅛-inch thick Doron plate, cut into five-inch squares. Each plate was made of a fibreglass laminate that the Americans had produced during the Second World War. With all the pockets filled, the vest weighed eight pounds, and added about two inches to the girth of a man's chest. The vest would stop most small calibre bullets. Larger calibres might be more of a problem. To complete his defences, Agnes slipped a second, one-piece, skin-coloured plastic vest over Anatoli's head, and secured it in place. Preparations complete, Anatoli slipped on his shirt. 'All ready?' asked Agnes.

'Yes.' Pausing, Anatoli asked, 'Gentlemen, could you give me a few moments please?'

Sir Aubrey, Richards and Clark all stepped onto the landing, leaving the door ajar by half an inch. Anatoli smiled and taking Agnes by the arm led her to the small kitchen. 'Agnes, whatever happens, I want you to know I am grateful. You have been a good friend. When I needed hope most in Berlin, you allowed me to hope that you might love me.' Agnes tried to interject, but Anatoli waved her objections away. 'I think I always knew that you didn't love me, but I was only sure when I saw you and Collins together. He is a very lucky man. Don't waste this chance at happiness, my English rose.'

Agnes kissed Anatoli on the cheek and handed him a light-coloured raincoat. As he pulled it on over his shirt, Agnes slipped a small cylinder into his left-hand coat pocket. 'Goodbye, Anatoli, and good luck.'

'Long life my love, and the sense to enjoy it,' said Anatoli and kissed the back of Agnes' hand.

Anatoli started his walk at Gas Street. His mac was open and his right hand buried deep in its pocket. He'd been walking for about five minutes when he saw the man on the opposite side of the canal. There was no mistaking his dark looks, build, posture, and the way he constantly scanned the surrounding area. His reactions were incredibly quick. Unfortunately he'd seen Anatoli a fraction of a second too late. Before he could pull his revolver clear of the shoulder holster, Anatoli had fired without taking the gun from his pocket. The shot hit the man in the groin. He doubled over and dropped to the ground on his knees. Gun now clear of his pocket, Anatoli fired again and the man's chest exploded as a .44 bullet ripped through his heart and lungs.

Turning back, Anatoli started to run. He didn't look back. He knew that Chilkov and his one remaining goon were behind him. Their first shot kicked up the compacted sand and grit a yard ahead of him. He started to zig-zag across the towpath. *Where the hell are Collins and his friend?* The second shot hit him in the shoulder, just above where he'd been shot the previous Friday, and he stumbled, but regained his balance and kept running. A sticky wetness spread down his arm and blood dripped onto the towpath.

Two hundred yards ahead he saw the access slope that led from the canal to the street. Two men were walking down it; Collins and Clark. Anatoli started to wave his arms and shout. 'Help! Help me! They're trying to kill me!'

He was still a hundred yards from the slope when a bullet hit him in the middle of the back and sent him sprawling in the dirt. Staggering to his feet, he lurched forward. Blood quickly soaked through his cheap summer coat, forming a large jagged circle in the middle of his back. Turning, Anatoli raised his gun and fired. The bullet hit the second goon, who doubled over, fell face first to the ground, and lay still. Unsteadily, Anatoli turned his gun on Chilkov, and his shot kicked up the dirt a full two yards in front of the Bulgarian. Chilkov took careful aim. The bullet hit Anatoli just above the sternum. It felt as though he had been kicked by a horse. Spinning backwards, he stumbled and fell head first into the canal.

Chilkov reached the point where Anatoli had disappeared while the ripples were still expanding. There was no sign of the man. Looking to his right, Chilkov waved his gun at Collins and Clark. 'Walk away, English. This is not your war.' Collins and Clark did as they were told.

Chilkov remained by the canal edge looking for signs of life. He could see nothing in the black dirty water except for a smear of oil that covered most of the surface and what might have been black blood. Looking at the blood on the towpath, he thought, *He's dead.* But still he forced himself to stay for a full three minutes. Then, satisfied that Anatoli was indeed dead, he scooped up a handful of blood-stained weeds, turned and ran.

Once Chilkov was out of sight, Collins and Clark sprinted to where they had seen Anatoli fall in. Both men began to slap the surface of the water with their hands. After about twenty seconds, Anatoli surfaced. His head was cut and bleeding, but he was still holding the small cylinder of compressed oxygen that Agnes had placed in his pocket, its small mouthpiece clamped tightly between his teeth.

Grabbing an arm each, Clark and Collins pulled an exhausted Anatoli onto the towpath and propped him up against the wall. 'Are you OK?' asked Collins.

Anatoli nodded, 'The first shot hit my arm. It feels dead. The others all hit the vest. I will be, how you say, be black and blue in the morning, but alive,' and he laughed.

'OK, let's get you out of here.'

Five minutes later, Anatoli and Clark were back in the hut. While Anatoli tried to clean himself up and wipe off the stink of the canal and most of the six pints of Rh-negative type O blood that had been contained in the second plastic vest, Collins was on his way to Mary's flat with the good news.

It was 10.30pm before Richards returned to the hut. Ten minutes later, Anatoli was asleep in the back seat of a Jaguar Mk 2 on his way to the Highlands of Scotland and a lengthy debriefing, followed by a new life.

Bearwood, 23.00hrs

Tubbs had watched the comings and goings at the church hall with a mixture of amusement and regret. Amusement, because the police were so inept. They clearly believed that his house was empty, and therefore had made no effort to conceal their movements. Even the young kids playing on the road knew that the coppers were up to something. Regret, because they had discovered his family home and now he would have to destroy it, just as he had his beloved workshop. How they had found him he had no idea, but he was pleased that he had prepared a welcome for them.

Methodically, he went about his packing. He'd be gone for at least three weeks, but there was no need to take enough clothes to last that time. Once in Holland he'd buy whatever he needed. Levering up the piece of canvas-covered board at the bottom of his rucksack, he placed the envelope containing nine cashier's cheques amounting to £159,000, and the key to his safety deposit box underneath. Pushing the board back in place, he covered it with enough underwear, socks and shirts to last four days. Over those he placed a jumper, in case the weather turned cold, three hankies and his toiletries.

Checking his watch, Tubbs saw it was time to leave. He slipped on his jacket, and examined himself in the mirror. The blond hair and pale skin had been replaced by near-black hair and dark skin. *It's amazing what you can get out of a tin,* he thought and smiled. Picking up a small box, he lifted the lid. Carefully, he selected one of the brown contact lenses and slipped it into place. Blinking, he gently shook his head and then fitted the second lens. Using his thumb and forefinger, he smoothed down his recently grown pencil moustache. Without the hair dye, the blond fluff he had grown would have been barely visible. Now it was quite respectable.

Sitting by the table, he pulled on his new shoes. To get used to them, he'd been wearing them about the house for a week. Tonight would be the first time he'd worn them outside. Standing, he was once more pleased to see that they did indeed make him look two inches taller, just as the advert in the paper had said they would.

Everything done he picked up his bag and went into the hall. The two-gallon tin of petrol was hidden behind the coat stand in the hall. It couldn't be seen by anyone looking through the letter box. Strapped around the container were two sticks of dynamite, a detonator and a cheap alarm clock. A similar package was stashed in the kitchen. He set the timer and walked into the kitchen where he did the same before stepping into the back yard.

Tubbs was confident that there were no police patrolling the back alley, but he couldn't be certain. It was possible that one was stationed out of sight at the end of the alley.

Checking his watch, he took cover in the outside lavatory and leant against the door. Thirty seconds later an explosion ripped through the front of the house. A billowing cloud of flame and debris was hurled across the road, smashing cars, breaking windows and slicing through the bodies of George and Mildred Peace, the oldest residents in the street, who were just returning home after a night out at the social club.

Tubbs waited. He could hear screams and shouts from the front of the house but so far nothing from the alleyway. He used his watch to count off exactly 60 seconds. Satisfied, he shouldered his rucksack and set off down the lane towards Bearwood High Street. Five minutes later, he reached the main road and the second bomb went off. He checked his watch. *Dead on time,* he thought and smiled at his own joke. *I hope some of the police bastards were in the house.*

Tuesday, 13 July 1965

Smethwick, Warley, 00.25hrs

Collins sat in the front of Clark's car rubbing the sleep from his eyes. 'The sod must have been in there all the time,' he said.

'Maybe. Or he could've set it off from outside.'

'You don't believe that.'

'Na. I don't. I just can't stand the thought that wi was within 30 yards of the bastard and missed him again.'

'Do we know if any of our lads were injured?'

'Yow know as much as I do.'

Both men remained silent for the rest of the journey. The local police had cordoned off the road at both ends, and suggested to Clark that it might be better to leave the car and walk to the site of the explosion. They found Hicks talking to one of the ambulance men. When he saw Clark he broke away.

'What's happening, Boss?'

'Henderson and James were in the church hall when the first bomb went off. They saw Mr and Mrs Peace get hit by the blast and tried to help. Both of the old dears died on the spot. Then the second bomb went off. Fortunately, it was in the back of the building. They caught a fair bit of the blast but they'll be OK'

'Any sign of Tubbs?' asked Collins.

'Someone said they saw a man come out of the back alley after the explosion but he doesn't fit Tubbs' description. We're trying to find him just in case he saw anything.'

'This guy ain't going quietly, is he, Boss? I wonder what he's got up his sleeve for us next?'

'So far he's either been lucky or half a step ahead of us. We need to come up with something that puts him on the back

foot. Makes him come to us. Any ideas, lads?' asked Hicks.
'A few,' said Clark.
'Maybe,' said Collins.

Just before Tubbs caught the first ferry of the day out of Dover he posted a letter to Inspector Hicks, Thornhill Road Police Station, Handsworth, Birmingham B21.

Handsworth, 06.00hrs

Collins and Clark had returned to the station in time to join the early shift for breakfast and had then spent an hour discussing possible avenues of investigation with Superintendent Wallace, Inspector Hicks and Sergeant O'Driscoll. They identified a four-stage approach for the investigation, which Collins wrote up.

1) In conjunction with the Fraud Squad, continue to interview all those who had hired Tubbs in the hope that he may have said something to one of his customers that could provide a lead.

2) Work the information that the Inland Revenue and other government agencies can provide, now that we know Tubbs' real name.

3) Sweat the characters at The Strangeways pub who had put Bright in touch with Tubbs.

4) Work with the Press and use what they knew about Grace to annoy, belittle and insult him in the hope that he might retaliate in anger and make a mistake.

'OK who's going to lead on each of the strategies?' asked the Superintendent.

'Sergeant O'Driscoll can work with the Fraud Squad on interviewing those who hired Tubbs. I'll team up with the Inland Revenue and anyone else who might have records on Tubbs under his real name,' said Hicks.

'Mickey and me will have a chat with the guys at The Strangeways,' said Clark.

'Collins did a good job with the press. I think he and I should continue with the briefings and use everything we've got to paint Tubbs as a cowardly, impotent little shit. Hurt his pride. Insult him. Belittle the bastard and hope that he'll snap and makes a mistake,' said Hicks.

'I hope to God he does make a mistake, otherwise we might end up as a couple of human torches,' said Clark.

'That's what I like about you, Clarkee,' said Collins. 'You're always so optimistic.'

When Collins and Clark left the station they barely noticed the bright sunshine and clear blue sky. Both of them were wrecked and ready for a sleep. Hicks' parting words had been 'Get back here for 1.30.' That gave them three hours of blessed sleep in their own beds, unlike Hicks. who was kipping in an empty cell.

Soviet Embassy, London, 10.00hrs

Chavda Chilkov was shown into the Deputy Head of Mission's Office. The assassination had been carried out successfully, but he wasn't expecting unconstrained congratulations. Too much had gone awry for that, which was why he'd rehearsed his answers carefully.

'Comrade Chilkov, please come in and sit down. You know Comrade General Andropov?'

'It's a great pleasure to meet you again, Comrade General,' said Chilkov and standing to attention, saluted the Russian General.

'We only have one question for you, Comrade Chilkov,' said the General. 'Are you absolutely certain that Anatoli Petrov is dead?'

'One hundred per cent certain. Sir. I shot him at thirty yards in the chest. I saw the blood stain his shirt. He fell in the canal and I maintained watch for a full three minutes after his fall. He did not resurface.'

'That is what concerns me, Comrade. You didn't actually see the body. Don't you agree that normally it would have floated for a time before sinking?'

'That's true, General, but we are talking about an industrial canal. All sorts of shit has been thrown in it over the years. Bedsteads, bikes, fencing, and much more. I doubt that half of the bodies surface. They become entangled in the rubbish and weeds. It may be weeks before his remains surface. But dead he is. Of that I am certain.'

'A fifty per cent chance is not the same as a certainty.'

'You are correct, General. But with respect, Sir, you were not there and I was. My second shot took out his heart and lungs. It was because I don't have his body that I scooped up a handful of weeds that had been splattered with his blood. I woke the technician at 4am this morning and asked him to identify the blood group.'

'And?'

'Just before this meeting he confirmed that it was type O, Rh-negative. The same group as Anatoli Petrov. This blood group, as you know, General, is shared by only five per cent of the population. The traitor is dead, of this I give you my word.'

'And what about the death of your comrades?'

'Petrov was a dangerous quarry. He saw them a moment before they saw him, and they paid the full price.'

'Can they be identified as Bulgarian?'

'No, Comrade General. They wore cheap English clothes and carried no identification whatsoever.'

'Well, Comrade Chilkov, it would appear that congratulations are in order. It is a little early for vodka but perhaps you would join us for tea,' said the Deputy.

'Sir, it would be an honour to join you for tea. But perhaps it could contain just a little vodka.'

For the first time, Andropov smiled.

Handsworth, 14.20hrs

The previous press conferences had been well attended. With the news that last night's explosion was also connected to the arsonist, reporters occupied every inch of the room, including behind the counter, with two gentlemen on the counter.

'Thank you for coming, ladies and gentlemen. I have a short statement that I will read,' said Inspector Hicks. '*I can confirm that last night's explosion in Bearwood, which killed Mr and Mrs Peace, was the work of the same man who murdered Anne Johnston and Station Officer Stan Wold. We have now identified the killer. He is Martin Arnold Grace. He also goes by the name of Mr Tubbs. There is evidence to suggest that Grace is mentally disturbed and finds it impossible to form normal human relations. Instead, he seeks satisfaction in starting fires for both commercial gain and personal pleasure.*

'*An Identikit picture of the suspect will be issued to you as you leave the room. We urge anyone who has seen this man or has any information about this person to contact us at Thornhill Road Police Station or their local police station.*

'Thank you,' he concluded. 'We'll now take a small number of questions.'

'*Daily Mail*, Inspector, How close do you think you are to catching this man?'

'You have to understand that we're dealing with someone of very low intelligence who has managed to evade capture only because he remained unknown to the police. Now that he has been identified, it's only a matter of time before he makes a mistake and is apprehended.'

'*News of the World*, Inspector. Have you ruled out the possibility that he might have accomplices?'

Hicks looked at Collins and nodded. *Make it sensationalist*, Collins thought. 'As the Inspector said, we're dealing with a man who has no friends, has never had a girlfriend and who likes to scurry about in the dark where he thinks he's safe. The only way he can get any satisfaction or pleasure out of life is by burning things. I would be amazed if he had accomplices.'

'DC Collins, are you implying that he may be impotent?'

'I'm not a doctor or a psychiatrist, but there are signs that point in that direction. We're dealing with a small, immature, insignificant man who desperately wants the world to take him seriously. He's been a joke all his life and now he thinks he's someone because he's burnt to death some real people who did have families and friends who cared for him.'

Raising his hand, Hicks said, 'I'm sorry, ladies and gentlemen, we're going to have to leave it there. Thank you for coming.'

Pushing their way through the reporters, both policemen ignored the questions that were shouted at them. Back in the office, Hicks smiled. 'You've got a gift for this, Collins. Mind you, you've probably pissed off every small man in the country with what you said.'

'Clarkee is small, but no one would describe him as insignificant.'

Walsall, 20.00hrs

Clark and Collins parked under a broken streetlight outside what looked like a half-respectable semi-detached house and started to walk towards the pub. The Strangeways was off the Bloxwich Road not far from the Wyrley and Essington Canal. It had stood on the same corner for nearly a century and for most of that time it had been known as the place to go if you needed help with an iffy deal of any kind. The main entrance was on the corner. Above the door, a ceramic tile mosaic depicted a deserted beach, cliffs and a shadowy ship at anchor in the bay. A small rowing boat, carrying a large wooden box, was heading for the shore.

Going into enemy territory, Collins and Clark had decided to wear their uniforms. That way, no one could claim that they didn't know they'd been assaulting a police officer when they appeared in court. Like a scene from a Western, the smoke-filled bar went silent when the two men entered. 'Don't mind us. Wem just sightseeing,' said Clark.

Standing by the counter, Clark waited for the barman to walk over, but he was busy acting tough and determined to ignore both men. After a minute Clark took out his truncheon and smashed it down on the counter. Everyone jumped at the sound of wood on wood. But the barman continued talking to his regular.

'Yow know, Mickey, it's a crying shame. Yow try to be nice to people, and they just ignore you. All I wanted were one of them,' said Clark, and pushed a four-pint jar of hard-boiled pickled eggs off the counter. The jar exploded on the floor and sprayed vinegar over the soft drinks, Babycham and bottles of cider stored on the bottom shelves. It would take the barman a week to get rid of the smell.

'Shit. What the fuck did you do that for?' shouted the barman.

'Do what? Did you see me do anything, Constable Collins?'

'Not me. I was too busy looking at that bottle of eggs. They were rocking on the edge of the counter.'

'Fuck you. You knocked them over.'

'Come 'ere,' said Clark and beckoned the barman over with his finger. When he was within range, Clark grabbed him by the tie and pulled. The man's head bounced off the counter but not hard enough to break his nose.

One of the customers put down his cigarette, eased his 15-stone bulk out of his chair, and headed for Clark.

'Go get him, Ted,' said one of his mates.

'Why the fuck did yow hit my mate? He dain't do anything,' said Ted.

The man kept coming, his fists clenched. Clark stood still, his arms by his side. When Ted was within range, Clark's right fist started to move upward. As it passed Ted's chest, Clark twisted his body and wrist. The punch exploded into the man's face with the full weight of Clark's body behind it.

Ted staggered backwards, blood pouring from his nose. He tried to catch the falling blood in his hands, stumbled, fell against his chair and sat down. 'He hit me. The fucker hit me,' he said in total shock. No one moved.

Returning to the bar, Clark grabbed the barman's tie and pulled him to the end of the counter where he raised the flap. Releasing the tie, Clark pushed the man into the room marked Private Office behind the bar.

As Collins followed, he turned to the twenty or so customers in the bar, 'Sorry for the commotion. Tell yow what, why don't yow help yourself to a drink on the house while we have a chat with yowr landlord?'

Clark pushed the barman into the only chair in the office and sat on the desk. Collins leaned against the door, his arm resting on the top of a bookcase that contained nothing but a half dozen empty cardboard boxes.

'Why the fuck did you have to bust me face?' complained the landlord.

'Because yow were acting like a prat and trying to make me and my mate look like a couple of wankers. We can't afford to let scumbags like yow insult us in public. It gives other idiots ideas. And then where does it stop?'

'OK. What the fuck do you want?'

'That's better,' said Clark.

'We want the name and address of one of your regulars. He puts people in touch with hard men and arsonists.'

'For fuck's sake, I can't tell you that. He'd have me, if he thought I'd grassed him up.'

'I don't know the gentleman in question but I'd be more worried about my friend here. He's got a lovely pair of pliers in the car. Hasn't used them in weeks,' said Collins.

'Ah fuck. You wouldn't dare.'

'Yeah, you're probably right. But I'll just pop and get them anyway.' Collins started to open the door and Clark was leering at the barman, clearly looking forward to using his favourite pliers, when the man broke.

'All right. All right. His name's Tony Flynn. Lives on Warwick Lane. I don't know the number. He's got an old Cadillac on bricks in the front garden.'

'Now, that wasn't so hard, was it?' said Collins. 'When's he in next? Tonight?'

'Don't know. He's just hooked up with some tart and she's keeping him occupied.'

'Fair enough,' said Clark. 'In return for your co-operation we'll make this as painless as possible.'

Standing up, the barman said, 'Just get on with it, you bastard.'

Clark hit the barman across the back of the thighs with his truncheon. The blow wasn't hard but it would leave bruises. Then hit him lightly across the chest.

Meanwhile Collins started shouting, 'We're not fucking about any more. What's the bastard's name?' and threw both office chairs against the wall and upended the bookcase.

Grabbing the barman by the arms, both policemen pinned him against the door and then proceeded to kick the door and walls. To end the pantomime, they pulled the door open and Collins punched him in the stomach. The barman doubled over and fell to the floor, crawled a few feet amongst the vinegar and smashed eggs and then lay still. 'Cunts,' he shouted as Collins and Clark walked out of the bar.

Several customers heard Collins say 'Waste of time,' as he closed the door.

Walsall, 22.40hrs

Warwick Lane was less than half a mile away, and just as the barman had said, there was the Cadillac in all its faded glory. A red 1957 model, it had fins and enough chrome work for any three ordinary cars. All it lacked was four wheels. There were no lights on in the house and Collins and Clark settled down to wait. Collins fiddled with the radio and managed to tune into Radio Caroline, which was playing *Looking through the Eyes of Love* by Gene Pitney.

It was five to to eleven before Tony Flynn made an appearance. Arm around a thirty-something bottle blonde who was sharing a bag of fish and chips with him. He said something which he thought was hilarious and she threw a chip at him. 'Now there's a man on a promise,' said Clark. 'Shall wi go and spoil it?

'Why not?'

They waited until Flynn had passed the car then got out. 'Mr Flynn, we'd like a word,' said Collins. Spinning round, Flynn saw the uniforms, pushed the woman into the two men and ran.

Collins went after him, followed a few seconds later by Clark. It didn't take Collins long to realise that Flynn was no runner. Too many fags and way too much beer was weighting him down. Realising that he would catch him in the next thirty yards Collins slowed, allowing Clark to catch up with him. 'What'cha slowing down for?'

'Look at him. He's knackered. Another 50 yards and he won't be able to stand up let alone throw a punch.'

Now at trotting pace, Clark said, 'Yow do realise that with this yow've used up yowr other good idea for the year?'

'Yeah, but I'm going to apply to have me allocation increased.'

'Good luck with that.'

Flynn had stopped running. Hands on knees, he was desperately trying to suck some air into his red-hot lungs and throat. He started to cough and within seconds was spitting up black sputum that had been in his lungs for months. Stumbling backwards, he sat on a low retaining wall belonging to the Baptist Church. Clutching his chest he fumbled for his pack of Players cigarettes. 'What the fuck do yow want?' he gasped. 'I ain't done nothing.'

'So why run, Anthony?' asked Clark.

'Me name's Tony.'

'Tony, Anthony. Them's all the same, ain't they? I bet yowr Mam always calls yow Anthony.'

Flynn looked at the two men with undisguised hatred. 'What do yow want?'

'Yow've been putting people in touch with a certain Mr Tubbs,' said Clark. 'Now, unless yow've been living in a cave, which I admit would be a step up on Warwick Lane, yow'll know that he burnt a poor kid to death. We want to know how yow contact him and anything else yow know about him.'

'Piss off. I ain't no snitch.' Flynn was reverting to his tough guy stance now that he could breathe again.

'Is that right?' said Collins. 'Well I *am* a snitch and a liar. If you don't co-operate, I'm going to let your mates at the pub know that when we caught you, you nearly shit yourself and couldn't wait to tell us about all the guys you act for as go-between.'

Flynn looked doubtful. 'Yow wouldn't dare. I'd get done.'

'Tony mate, yow got to understand that Mickey here don't never make idle threats. He's mean like that. Unless yow start talking in the next ten seconds, yow will be about as welcome as a fart in a two-man lift next time yow visit The Strangeways.'

'OK, OK. I don't know much. I only met him once. The picture yow put out was a good likeness. Small guy. When I shook hands with him it made me skin crawl. His hand were soft like a sponge. But I knew straight off he weren't the type of guy to piss about. He had these weird blue eyes, only there was nothing behind them. It were like he didn't see yow. Scary, it were.'

'How did you make contact with him?'

'He gave me a phone number.'

'Let's have it,' said Clark.

Flynn wrote it down from memory on a scrap of paper and handed it to Clark.

Clark looked at the number. It was for the workshop.

Another dead end. 'The phone that were attached to this number were melted in a fire a few days ago. Unless yow got something else, we're taking yow in.'

''Honest to God, that's all I know about the guy.'

'Cuff him, Mickey.'

'Antony Flynn, I'm arresting you as an accessory before the fact to murder, grievous bodily harm, arson and conspiracy contrary to Section 2 of the Accessories and Abettors Act of 1861. You are not obliged to say anything...'

'OK, OK. I'm trying to co-operate.'

'Yow might be, sunshine, but so far yow've given us diddly squat. Try harder.'

'One of the customers lifted his wallet that night. It had his address in it.'

'Where?' asked Collins, expecting to be given Tubbs' Bearwood address.

'A place in Edgbaston. It's just down from the Botanical Gardens. On the right. You can't miss it. It's like one of those houses you see on chocolate boxes at Christmas with a green roof and a balcony all 'round.'

'And how do you know it has a green roof?' asked Collins keeping the excitement he was feeling out of his voice.

''Me and a mate turned it over about six months later.'

As Clark drove away, Collins said, 'We can't just let Flynn off. He's helped arrange for people's deaths.'

'We ain't going to. We just need to keep him in play for a few days. Then we bring him in and find out just who he recruits customers for. My bet is that he's never arranged a murder. The guys who do that kind of work wouldn't trust a low life like him. He probably only has a few heavies and Tubbs on the books.'

'But why would Tubbs go with him ... because he has no underground contacts?'

'Got it in one, Mickey. Tubbs is a loner. He's never been

in Borstal or prison. He's got no criminal connections. Now that makes him hard to find, but it also means he has no one to turn to for help when things get messy. Fancy having a look at Tubbs' place before we turn in?

'Good idea,' said Collins and turned up Radio Caroline as Judith Durham of the Seekers knocked 15 bells out of *A World of Our Own*. Even Clark had to agree that 'She looks bostin, and can bloody sing.'

Wednesday, 14 July 1965

Harborne, 00.10hrs

Thirty minutes later, they drove past the Teacher Training College on Westbourne Road where Dianna Rigg's aunt was the principal. More than one unsuspecting male student had tripped over, or walked into a wall when he saw the delectable Mrs Emma Peel from *The Avengers* walking about the college or climbing out of her Lotus in the car park.

Passing the Botanical Gardens on the left, they soon found the only house in the road with a green tiled roof. The front gates were closed and locked and there were no cars in the short drive. The house had been built in the style of an Alpine chalet, with white sandstone, a steeply pitched green tiled roof, and a wooden balcony that circled the house.

'It looks deserted,' said Collins.

'Where have I heard that before?'

'Want to take a gander?'

'Ain't that what we're here for?'

The low gates were no problem. Standing in the shadow of a large fir tree, Clark whispered. 'You go right. I'll go left and I'll meet yow round the back.'

Keeping in the shadows, Collins moved silently around the perimeter of the house, checking each window as he went. None of the curtains had been drawn and the interior appeared spotless, with not even a cup on any table or surface. *He's not here,* thought Collins. At the back of the building Collins peered through the French windows. Nothing.

Steeping back, he looked to the left for Clark. The little man wasn't to be seen. Collins walked to the corner of the house. Still no sign. Returning to the French windows, he looked out cross the rear garden. He was just about to call out 'Clarkee,' when he heard the sound of someone landing on their toes behind him. Before he had a chance to move, a hand covered his mouth and in a mock German accent Clark said, 'For you, ze var ist ofer, Tommy.' As he said this, Clark's hold loosened. Instinctively, Collins grabbed hold of Clark's forearm with both hands and pulled downwards. Simultaneously he stuck his bum into Clark's groin and continued pulling. The result was very satisfying, with Clark sailing over Collins' head and landing on his back on the lawn.

'Yow can't do that. I'd already slit yowr throat.'

'Maybe, but it's not me lying on the ground.'

'Cocky bastard. Show him a couple of moves and he thinks he's a bleeding expert.'

'I take it you saw nothing.'

'Nowt upstairs or down.'

'What do you want to do?' asked Collins.

'What do yow think? Wi got two choices. Either we baby-sit the bloody place tonight and spend all tomorrow arranging with the Army to check the house out for bombs, or wi go in.'

Collins could see that Clark was ready to go in. It was a risk. Tubbs had already blown up two properties he was connected to. But for some reason Collins didn't think he'd want to blow this house up. It was the type of place that a working class kid growing up in Bearwood would have lusted after. The house which proclaimed to the world that he'd arrived. 'I think this house is Tubbs' palace. I doubt if it's booby-trapped. So let's save time and go in.'

'OK. But nice and slowly, just in case wem wrong.'

'How do we do this?' asked Collins.

'Wi go in upstairs. People usually load the ground floor with the locks, alarms...'

'And bombs,' said Collins.

'Come on... stay behind me.'

Clark and Collins climbed up the drainpipe and then clambered onto the balcony. Clark pointed at a frosted window and said, 'We go in through the bog.' Slipping his tunic off,

Clark folded it into four and placed it against the glass. 'Give it a tap with yowr truncheon and mind me fingers.'

Collins hit the window and heard the sound of glass falling on the bathroom floor. Clark removed his tunic and held it near the floor, gently shaking it to remove the larger splinters. Leaving his jacket on the balustrade, Clark reached inside the window and eased the catch over. He pushed the window open and climbed in. Standing on the toilet seat, he shone his torch around the room. No wires or any other signs of a bomb or booby trap were visible. Stepping onto the navy blue tiles he said, 'All clear.'

There were four full-sized bedrooms on the first floor, plus the toilet, a separate bathroom and a small box-room that was used as an office. After checking that all the rooms were safe, Clark went to explore the master bedroom while Collins started a search of the office. He started with the wooden tray on the desk top, but found only a couple of bills, before moving onto the desk drawers and the wooden filing cabinet that rested below the window. *There's nothing here,* he thought, *except household bills and copies of the deeds. The solicitor must have the original.* Walking into the main bedroom, he found Clark on his hands and knees, his head and torso buried inside a floor-to-ceiling fitted wardrobe. 'You got something, Clarkee?'

'No. I'm down here praying. What's it bleeding look like?'

Pushing the middle of the three glass panelled doors to one side, Collins saw that Clark was examining a six-inch boarded-in shelf that ran the width of the wardrobe and was about 18 inches deep. It was painted the same colour as the wall and looked as if it had been part of the room's original design. 'You sure it's not just some panel covering up a pipe?' Collins said.

Clark stood up and pointed at what his body had been hiding. There were small flakes of paint between the carpet and the bottom of the ledge. 'There has to be a switch, but I'm dammed if I can find it.'

'Let me have a look.' Clark moved aside and Collins picked up an armful of clothes and threw them on the bed. He continued until the wardrobe was empty, then ran his torch slowly across every inch of the wardrobe's interior, walls and ceiling. Nothing. As an afterthought he directed the torch at the floor. The far left hand corner of the carpet looked as if it had been recently disturbed. Kneeling down, he pulled it back. Set into the skirting board was a small lever. 'Got it,' he grinned.

Clark looked. 'Well done. Of course, pull it and wi could be blown to kingdom come.'

'That's what I like about you the most, Clarkee. Always the optimist,' said Collins and pulled. There was a click and the top of the shelf popped open a quarter of an inch.

'Bloody hell, I dain't expect that. What with the paint flecks I thought there must be a sliding door or summut.'

Clark knelt down and shone his torch into the opening. He could see no wires. Carefully, he felt inside the space. 'I've got something,' said Clark, and withdrew two professionally made wooden boxes each measuring about about 18 inches long, six wide, and 12 high. The boxes were identical except one was decorated with a red dragon breathing fire on the roll top lid and the other featured a blue dragon.

Laying the boxes on the bed, Clark said, 'What's it going to be? Are yow going to take the money or open the box?'

'I'm going to open the box,' said Collins and rolled back the lid on the first box. Inside were eleven small parcels, each wrapped in tissue paper, tied with a ribbon and with a Dymo tape name in red plastic attached to each. Collins picked up the top parcel, marked "Anne", and undid the ribbon. Inside was a pair of white panties, a white bra, a white garter belt with a red rose in the middle of the waist, and a pair of stockings. Neither man said anything. Beneath the last, Collins found three neat piles of 6"×4" photographs showing the burnt remains of various private homes. Finally, there was a diary of sorts listing all the fires Tubbs had set for pleasure.

Clark opened the blue dragon box. This contained a red and black cash book listing the commercial properties Tubbs had destroyed. Each fire had been documented with a series of photos. Some showed the actual blaze as well as pictures of the aftermath, but others only showed the devastated properties.

'Anything else in there?' asked Collins, nodding at the shelf.

'Yow got longer arms than me, Mickey. Have a look yowrself. I'm going to call the station.'

Kneeling down, Collins reached into the opening and felt around. He almost missed it. A yard-long piece of copper wire. There was no tag attached.

Handsworth, 10.30hrs

The night turned into a mixture of interviews, congratulations and bollockings for Collins and Clark. The find was significant, and the Scenes of Crime Officer and his helpers would be kept busy for the next few days going over the house, garage, sheds and garden with the finest of fine toothcombs.

Unfortunately, Collins' and Clark's claims that they had only broken into the house when they heard someone inside, were accepted by neither Inspector Hicks nor Superintendent Wallace. 'You pair of mad bastards. You could have been killed,' said Hicks before relenting and saying, 'The Super says well done.'

Now everyone was ready to go home. O'Driscoll was almost out of the door when Sergeant Ridley came in with a letter addressed to Inspector Hicks and DC Collins. He was wearing a pair of white police dress gloves. 'I thought you should see this. It was posted in Dover yesterday.'

'And why's that important?' asked Hicks.

'The flap of the envelope has TK on it.'

O'Driscoll took off his jacket and Collins and Clark

crowded around the Inspector's desk.

Now wearing the white gloves, Hicks sliced the envelope open with his Swiss Army knife. He withdrew the single sheet of paper it contained and started to read the neatly typed letter.

Dear Detective Inspector Hicks and DC Collins,

Missed me again. What a shame. Even when you stumble across me by chance you can't hold onto me. But then I've always thought you could judge a man by how much he earns. I earn more in a night than you pair do in 15 years.

Well, you'll be happy to know I'm going on holiday for a while. I don't know when I'll be back, but back I will be. You see, I have some unfinished business to take care of. Once I've done that, I'm coming after you and your families. You're going to burn, and so are they. You may think I'm overreacting but you see, I take exception to a couple of retarded cunts insulting me on national TV.

What did you think I'd do when you insulted me? Did you think I'd get angry and come after you all guns blazing like some demented gangster out of a 1930s film? Well bad luck. I've got more brains than the pair of you put together. You've never met anyone like me before. That's why I'm going to kill you pair and there is nothing you can do about it. After that I'm going to disappear and live out my life in comfort. Mind you, I might just burn one or two bitches, now and then, to keep my hand in.

I hope you think about that as you die choking on black smoke.

Bye for now.

Mr Tubbs (TK)

'Well, I don't think he'll be sending yow a Christmas card this year, Mickey.'

'For a man who didn't react to us calling him names, he seems mighty angry,' said Collins.

'Exactly what I was thinking,' said Hicks. 'The only place where he swears is when he describes us as "a couple of retarded cunts." It's when we go after his intelligence more than anything that he gets really angry. He sees himself as some kind of criminal mastermind and you and me as his nemesis.'

'Hang on a sec, Boss. Use of the word nemesis in front of a lowly DC before midday is outlawed in Police Regulations, in case it makes him feel thick.'

'Do you think he's telling the truth about going away for a while?' asked Collins.

'There's a good chance,' said O'Driscoll. 'Sure, he's the number one most wanted man in England. It's only sensible for him to stay low for a while.'

'But the question is, has he gone abroad or is he still in England?' asked Hicks.

'I reckon he's gone abroad,' said Collins. 'He took cashier's cheques when he emptied his accounts. We think he has a numbered account or accounts abroad and he's not going to just post out the cheques. He's more cautious than that.'

'I agree with Mickey,' said Clark. 'This guy is cautious and suspicious. He doesn't trust anyone.'

'Right then,' said O'Driscoll,' I'll send an alert to Interpol and to the French, Belgian, and Swiss police.'

'Send it to the lot of them,' said Hicks. 'He could be anywhere in Europe, or just passing through.'

'Yow do realise that he's changed his appearance by now?' said Clark.

'How can you be so sure?' asked Collins.

'No one's reported seeing the bastard for days now. Plus if he went through Dover he would have been spotted. After all a five foot five, soft, podgy bastard with blond hair and creepy blue eyes would not be difficult to spot. Na. I'm sure he's disguised himself.'

'Include that information in the alert,' said Hicks.

'Do you think he really intends to return, Sir?' asked Collins.

'Yes, I do. Tubbs himself may not have consciously recognised that he's finished with his old life of setting fire to people and places and then slipping back into his old daily routine. Unknown and unrecognised. Yet somewhere in his sick mind, he knows that the life he'd loved is over, and he blames you and me for that. He's going to try and take us out, and when push comes to shove I think he'll be happy to trade his life for ours.'

'Bloody hell, Sir, you really know how to scare the bejeebers out of a man. You don't think that I could explain to Tubbs in the next press conference that the insults were all your idea?'

'No, Constable Collins, you can't. Indeed at our next press conference we will target his arrogance, hubris and stupidity. Now you lot get off and grab a bit of sleep. Be back for a news conference at four. I need to have a think about how we handle the discovery of his house and keepsakes.'

Handsworth, 10.55hrs

Agnes limped into the kitchen and kissed the top of Collins' head. 'You look terrible. Was it worth it?'

'Oh yeah,' said Collins and told her of the new find.

'Why do you think this house wasn't rigged to blow up?'

'When I was outside I had a feeling it was the sort of house a poor kid made good would buy for himself. A house that shouts money and success. But now I think it was his keepsakes. He didn't want to risk damaging them. I think they are the most valuable thing in the world for him.'

'But that will make him even more angry and dangerous when he returns.'

'Maybe. But it'll also make him more careless.'

'You hope. Eat up and go to bed. It's nearly eleven and you have to be back at the station by four.'

'I was going to take Sheba for a short walk first.'

'Bed. You still look like death warmed up. I'll take her. It will do me good to keep moving.'

'OK.'

As Collins wearily climbed the stairs, Agnes took the lead from the back door and waited. Less than ten seconds later, Sheba dived through the dog flap and started to jump up and down and chase her own tail as she waited for the lead to be attached. 'Well, Sheba, it looks like it's just us girls for a walk today.'

'Can I come?' asked Joanne, who had heard the tail end of the conversation.

'Why not? You're a girl just like me and Sheba.'

Zurich, 10.55hrs

Tubbs walked out of the four-star Central Plaza Hotel, crossed the road and gazed at the River Limmat. He was in a good mood. His trip had gone well. All connections had been on time and he'd enjoyed a good night's sleep. Now the sun was high in a startlingly blue azure sky and sparkled on the small waves and eddies that the flow of the river and the pleasure craft using it threw up. Tubbs had discovered the Plaza a few years earlier and immediately liked it. As the hotel's publicity said, it was conveniently situated near the train station, and had an old world elegance that he found attractive. It was also within easy walking distance of the old town, restaurants, bars and most importantly, his bank. Breathing deeply he thought, *Just what I need. Some peace and quiet to think and plan.*

Arriving at the bank, Tubbs was greeted by the staff like an old family friend, which in a way he was. He was invariably polite and willing to chat with any member of staff. The general view was that Mr Hermes was a lonely little man whose dark skin and hair probably meant that he was originally from southern Europe but had obviously spent most of his life in England, which explained his strange accent. None of the staff had ever seen him without his fake tan on.

Mr Fischer welcomed him with a warm handshake and an

offer of coffee which Tubbs accepted. The pastries were always first-class. Once seated, Fischer asked, 'How can I help you today, Mr Hermes?'

'I would like to make a deposit of £169,000.'

'Of course.' Mr Fischer picked up an account card that was on his pristine white blotter and said, 'That will increase your balance to £614,346. Is there anything else we can do for you?'

'Yes, once the cheques have cleared, I'd like you to invest a further £100,000 in Rothschild's Investment Trust through your London representatives, the share certificates to be held here as per our existing arrangements.'

The door opened and Herr Fischer's secretary appeared pushing a silver gilt hostess trolley. The smell of freshly brewed coffee quickly wafted around the room, but Tubbs' attention was on the range of cakes and pastries that resided below the coffee.

Tubbs didn't really notice the secretary until she bent down and lifted the stand with the pastries onto Herr Fischer's desk. Tubbs watched how she moved. How she walked. She was beautiful. Five foot six, with pale skin, a slim face, dark eyes, a thin nose and full lips. Dressed in a white silk blouse and a black pencil skirt, she oozed elegance. She was everything he fantasized about. Except she had black hair, not blonde. *What a pity,* he thought. *Still it would be nice to see her burn* and he felt the familiar tightening in his groin.

Business concluded, the two men drank their coffee, ate their pastries and made the usual stilted small talk about the weather and how good business was before they shook hands and parted.

As Tubbs left the bank he saw Herr Fischer's secretary get into a Porsche 911 with a handsome, suntanned man, twenty years her senior. *Another whore,* he thought and started his walk around the old town.

Handsworth, 15.30hrs

In the CID Room Hicks said, 'I hope you three managed to get some kip,' and inhaled a lungful of blue smoke. Slowly he exhaled. Then sitting there thinking, his cigarette clamped in the corner of his mouth, he continued, 'I did want to keep news of Tubbs' trophies out of the news but it seems either one of the neighbours or, more likely a copper, has leaked the story. So we might as well go for Tubbs' jugular and really lay into him about his keepsakes and stupidity. Anyone disagree?'

O'Driscoll, Collins and Clark all shook their heads.

'Good. Let's go, then.'

The press conference was the biggest yet. A number of foreign journalists had picked up the story and reporters had been forced to congregate in the yard, outside the canteen's open windows, when the corridor could hold no more.

'Detective Inspector Hicks, *Express*. Can you confirm that last night you discovered the home of the arsonist known as Mr Tubbs?'

'I can. The property in Harbourn was discovered following excellent work by DC Clark and DC Collins. The property in question is registered to a Mr Marsden who bought it for cash some five years ago.'

'So what makes you think it's Tubbs' house?' pressed the *Express*.

'We found hidden on the premises keepsakes and photographs from the fires that we believe Tubbs started.'

'What sort of keepsakes and photos?' asked the reporter from *The People*.

'The mementoes were of the most personal nature stolen from the women he killed. The photos showed the aftermath of fires he set and again featured disgusting photos of some of the women he killed.'

'Were these photos pornographic?' asked *The Birmingham Mail*.

'I think it's fair to say that most decent people would find them depraved and sick.'

'Constable Collins, what led you and your colleague to the house?' asked *The Mirror*.

'Just good old-fashioned police work. It was fairly easy, really. Tubbs is not very intelligent. He left a trail of bread crumbs that a blind man could follow. As I've said before, he's only avoided capture because he's been lucky and a loner. It's always harder to find someone who has no friends or acquaintances. It's now only a matter of time before he makes another major mistake and we pick him up. '

'Inspector Hicks, if you were to sum this man up in a sentence how would you describe him?' asked *The Telegraph*.

'A small, insignificant man of limited intelligence who desperately wants to be important, but whose ego will ultimately be his downfall. Thank you.'

As the reporters filed out, O'Driscoll stood to one side of the door. When the man wearing earphones around his neck and carrying a Phillips tape recorder came through he grabbed him by the arm and pulled him to one side. 'The Inspector wants to see you.'

The man from the BBC entered the CID Room with a mixture of arrogance and trepidation. Arrogance, because he was part of the world's premier broadcasting organisation, and trepidation, because he was young and was worried that he or the BBC might have done something to anger the police.

Inspector Hicks, DC Collins and a small man who the reporter hadn't seen before were standing in the middle of the office. Behind them on a desk, the reporter caught sight of a number of parcels that had been wrapped in tissue paper. Each had been opened, and he could see that they contained ladies' lingerie. *They weren't kidding when they said he kept intimate items as keepsakes.*

'Mr Douglas, isn't it?' said Inspector Hicks, holding out his hand.

'Yes.'

'Can I get you a drink, tea, coffee or maybe a little tipple of something stronger?'

Douglas relaxed. The police don't offer you a drink if you've annoyed them. 'No thank you. I'm fine.'

'Good. Well, I have a favour to ask of you. What I'm about to tell you is in confidence and must not be broadcast or reported at this time. You understand?' Douglas nodded yes. 'Good. We have reason to believe that Tubbs has left the United Kingdom. We also believe that he will return to the UK in the near future. We would like him to return sooner rather than later.'

'I see. And how can I or the BBC help you?'

'I'm aware that the World Service is the responsibility of the Foreign Office. However, I am asking the BBC to prevail on the World Service and to report on and broadcast as much of today's press conference as possible. If you do so, I believe that lives will be saved. In return, once Tubbs has been arrested, we will acknowledge the part that you and the BBC played in his capture.'

'I'm not sure that the BBC would like the World Service to be seen as an arm of the British Police. How about you and DC Collins give me an exclusive interview?'

'Done,' said Hicks.

This time it was Douglas who held out his hand and said, 'I'll have that drink now.'

Clark left the station at 6.15 and followed Collins' bright red MG Midget out of the car park and along Thornhill Road. As they approached the junction with Holly Road. Collins pulled the car over, blocking the road, jumped out and ran across the street. As Clark came to a halt he saw the problem. A group of four men were laying into a black man outside the Park Gate Stores. Although there were four of them, they weren't having it all their own way.

Clark immediately piled into the fight. He punched the man who was grappling with Collins in the kidneys. The man let out a cry and sank to his knees, unable to move. Clark slapped his face and said, 'Stay there.' Next he grabbed one of the two men who were trying to punch the black man senseless. Spinning him round, he hit him with a right jab. The punch landed plumb on the point of the man's jaw, his knees buckled, and he fell to the ground unconscious.

Meanwhile Collins was wrestling with a tall lanky bloke who was surprisingly strong. Clark was about to help when Collins grabbed the man by the lapels, stuck his right foot in the man's stomach and simultaneously pulled on the jacket and fell backwards. The man sailed over Collins' head, and landed on his back in the middle of the road and lay there unmoving.

Clark turned back just in time to see the black man lift the fourth rocker off his feet with one of the best uppercuts he'd ever seen outside a professional bout. The man landed on his feet, then crumpled onto the ground, senseless.

'Winston, are you OK?' asked Collins.

For the first time Clark looked at the blood-covered face of the black man and realised that he was just a kid. 'Is this the lad you were talking about?'

'Yep. Clarkee, I'd like you to meet Winston.'

Clark held out his hand and felt his fingers being crushed. 'Steady, big boy. That's the hand I write with.'

Winston let go and said, 'Sorry, sir.'

'I ain't a sir, lad. Just a Mr. This lot jump yow?'

'Yeah.'

'Want to press charges?'

'No. Them's just trash with no sense.'

By this time all four men were on their feet and Clark had been through their pockets. The reason for their attack was clear. They were all members of the Greater Britain Movement and had been distributing leaflets on the street corner, advocating the repatriation of all coloureds, when Winston had walked past.

Collins and Clark corralled the men against the window of the Park Gate Stores. 'Listen to me, yow trouble-making bastards,' said Clark, 'If I see yow trying to rough up anyone again, white, black, blue or purple, I'm going to put a few of yow in hospital. Is that clear?'

There was a muffled mumblings from all four that sounded vaguely like 'Yes.'

'Right then, piss off home and don't let me see yow on the street again tonight.'

As the four men stumbled away Clark turned to Collins and Winston. 'Anyone fancy a coffee? There's a new place on Soho Road.'

By the time three frothy coffees were on the table and Winston had washed his face, he looked fine, except for a cut lip and some bruising around his left eye. His shirt was ripped, revealing a set of pectoral muscles that would give Steve Reeves a run for his money.

'How long were they on yow before we turned up?' asked Clark.

'Not long. Thanks for the help.'

'You're welcome,' said Collins.

'I suppose this has happened to yow before?' said Clark.

'Yeah, but this was the first time in the daylight.'

'I'm sorry, but there's not much we can do to help you at the moment,' said Collins.

'I know,' said Winston looking down at the table.

'Listen, Mickey tells me yow want to join the Army.'

'Yeah.'

'Well, I'll ask around for yow. See if anyone I know can get yow in. But it'll be hard to get in. And if you do get in, yow'll face more prejudice than yow've ever seen in civvie street. Yow'll have to prove yow're better than every other recruit, every single day just to survive.'

'I know. I just want a chance.'

'OK. I'll see what I can do. But don't hold yowr breath. Coloureds aren't welcomed in the Army, except when a war is on. Do yourself a favour and read about the French Foreign Legion. They'd have you in a shot.'

As they returned to their cars, Collins asked, 'What do you think of him?'

'An absolute bloody natural for the Army. Calm, fearless, knows how to handle himself and as a strong as an ox.'

'So you think he has a chance of getting in?'

'I'd say it's slim to non-existent. The Legion is the way to go, although at the moment them in the dog house for trying to bump de Gaulle off. But they'll come back and when they do it would be good to be on the ground floor.'

Zurich, 23.00hrs

Tubbs was truly content. He'd enjoyed a good dinner in the old town and now he was heading back to his hotel. Ahead were a young man and his blonde girlfriend. The man's hand continually moved down from her waist to her backside and she kept pushing it back up. As they neared an alleyway, he whispered something to her and she pushed him away in mock horror. When he took her by the hand she seemed happy to follow him down the passage without protest.

Tubbs stopped and looked at the menu outside a restaurant that advertised Genuine Swiss Cuisine. Tubbs wasn't at all sure that Switzerland had its own unique cuisine. He'd always thought of it as a mixture of French, Italian and German. Perhaps he was wrong.

At the mouth of the alley, he stopped again. Looking around the corner he saw that after 30 yards the passage turned sharp right. The young couple were nowhere in sight, but he could hear the sound of muffled voices from around the corner. He edged into the alleyway. As he neared the corner, the voices grew louder and more urgent and excited. He recognised the language as Italian, but didn't understand what was being said, although the low moans and the slap of flesh on flesh could mean only one thing. He had to look.

She was standing against the brick wall her dress pushed up, her top open and one breast peeking out from the top of her pink bra. Her matching pink knickers around one foot. The young man's trousers and pants lay at his ankles. His left hand cupped behind the girl's right knee held her leg up as he drove into her. Despite the light that escaped from a second floor window, Tubbs couldn't see much. But the mere thought that they were unaware of his presence excited him. He decided to store the memories away for later when he was in the more comfortable surroundings of his hotel room.

As he turned to go, a large man blocked his path. 'Did you enjoy the show, little man?' he asked in English with a heavy Italian accent.

'I don't know what you mean.'

'Yes you do. Alonzo, Gabriela, I have another pervert here. What do you want me to do with him? Call the police or beat him up?'

Alonzo appeared around the corner. A smirk covered his face. The girl joined him, twirling her knickers around her index finger. She didn't look annoyed or upset that her love-making had been interrupted. Walking over to Tubbs she tickled him under his chin. Then holding her knickers in front of his face asked in broken English, 'You get the eyeful little man? You get the hard-on? You wank, I think, later. Or maybe time next you fuck your wife you think about me? But maybe little man has little cock and no wife.'

'Who'd marry that cunt?' said Alonzo in Italian and laughed.

'You haven't said what you want me to do with him,' said the big man.

'Beat him,' said the girl. 'The little cunt is pervert.' This time her English was very clear.

'No, wait,' said Tubbs. 'I have money.'

'How much?' demanded the big man.

'About $800 in Swiss francs.'

'Show me.'

Tubbs took out his wallet. As always it contained no identification – just the spending money he had allocated for the next few days. The big man grabbed the wallet and counted the money. 'He's loaded.'

Alonzi flicked through the wallet and said in English, 'Not bad. Let the cunt go.'

'Wait. I've had no fun yet. I want my fun?' said Gabriella in Italian, bit the second knuckle of her index finger and pouted like a spoilt teenager.

'Oh for God's sake, let her have some fun or she'll sulk all night,' said Alonzo.

'OK,' said the big man.

Tubbs had very little idea of what had been decided when the young woman approached. He smiled his funny little smile in an attempt to appear friendly. Standing in front of him, the girl rubbed her body against his. He stood there terrified of what the two men might do if he moved. He wasn't expecting the girl to knee him in the groin. He fell to his knees, unable to breathe or cry out.

Gabriella grabbed his hair, pulled his head back and punched him in the face. He fell to the ground and she kicked him in the face once, then moved on to his stomach and chest.

'That's enough,' said Alonzo. 'We've got his money and had some fun. Leave the shit for the garbage collectors.'

'Alonzo, just one more kick in the balls please. Pretty please,' she pleaded in Italian.

'All right.'

Tubbs lay defenceless on the floor. Gabriella kicked his legs apart and then taking careful aim booted him in the groin. Tubbs' body jack-knifed before he fell back on to the cobbles. Giggling, she stepped back and kicked him again.

'Enough, let's go,' said the big man.

'One for good luck,' said Gabriella and kicked Tubbs again before grinding the heel of her shoe into his groin.

As soon as they had gone Tubbs started to crawl towards the wall. Once there, he slowly pulled himself up. He couldn't go to hospital or the police. He had to get back to the hotel. The house doctor would look after him – discreetly. After five minutes, he felt strong enough to let go of the wall and walk unsteadily to the end of the alleyway. Stepping onto the main road, Tubbs looked at his reflection in one of the overpriced antique shop windows. The damage was not as bad as it might have been. His nose had swollen to twice its normal size but it didn't look as if it had been broken. Wiping the worst of the blood off his face, he willed himself to walk in a straight, steady line. He'd hail a taxi as soon as one appeared. Unfortunately, none did.

As he walked slowly along the riverside road a Volkswagen camper van passed him on the opposite side of the road. The big man was driving. Tubbs clocked the van's colour and a pair of flowered curtains on the back window before it sped away.

Fifteen excruciating minutes later he reached the Plaza. The doorman recognised him and immediately and went to help the battered guest. 'Mr Hermes, are you all right?'

'I'll be fine. I'd be much obliged if you would help me to my room and call the house doctor. I'm afraid I fell down some steps.'

'Surely we should take you to hospital, sir?'

'No hospitals,' said Tubbs, almost shouting. Then in a lower voice, 'I hate hospitals. You see, I spent too much time in them as a child,' he lied.

On arriving in his room, Tubbs took a shower. His whole body was starting to stiffen up. He stood under the cold shower for nearly three minutes as it washed off the grime and blood that had covered his body. When he could stand the cold no longer, he stepped from the shower and examined himself in the full-length mirror.

His face had two large bruises – one on his left cheek, the other around his left eye and the bridge of his nose. His chest and ribs were a rainbow of colours, and when he breathed in deeply he could hear the crepitus of the broken bones grate together. However, it was his testicles that were worst affected. They had ballooned to twice their normal size and were very badly bruised. *I'll be pissing blood for a month,* he thought.

Gingerly, he took the dressing gown from the hanger, slipped on the terry towel slippers that the hotel supplied to all guests and hobbled out of the bathroom. Holding on to various items of furniture, he crossed to the bed, lay down on the covers and waited for the doctor.

Within minutes, the house doctor, a tall, austere German with a thick mane of silver grey hair, arrived. He was too well-mannered to comment on the difference between the colour of Tubbs' face and hands and the rest of his body or on the fact that it was obvious his injuries had been caused by a beating and not a fall. Instead he tutted ostentatiously as he examined each bruise. When he finished, he said, 'I understand, Herr Hermes, that you do not wish to go to hospital. That, of course, is your prerogative. I am, however, concerned that there may be some internal bleeding. Therefore, I strongly recommend that you have nursing care for the next 72 hours.'

'Very well. However, I would prefer a male nurse.'

'That can be arranged. A nurse will be with you within two hours. In the meantime I am going to dress the worst of your abrasions and strap up your ribs. The strapping should be left on for the next 10 days at least. I will also arrange for a bag of ice to be delivered to your room every three hours. You should wrap this in a small hand towel and apply it to your groin area. It will reduce the swelling.'

'How long before I can travel?'

'I would not think of it for at least two weeks. Three would be better. I will also give you an injection for the pain which will help you sleep. I'll call again in the morning.'

Thursday, 15 July 1965

Zurich, 06.55hrs

When Tubbs awoke he was immediately conscious of the pain emanating from every inch of his body. Without opening his eyes, he reached for the painkillers on the bedside cabinet. 'Allow me, Herr Hermes,' said a male voice. Tubbs opened his eyes, and saw that his male nurse had arrived. 'My name is Johann and I will be with you from 8pm until 8am, after which my colleague will take over for the day.'

'Can you help me sit up, please?'

As he was helped up, and an extra pillow slipped behind his back, Tubbs saw a large bowl of fruit and an overflowing vase of flowers on the table by the window. In addition, there was a radio. 'Where did they come from?' he asked.

'The hotel management sent them up along with a card wishing you a speedy recovery. The radio is shortwave. They thought you would enjoy listening to the BBC World Service. Will I plug it in?'

'Please.'

The radio was switched on just in time for Tubbs to hear the chimes of Big Ben announce the news. He was not expecting to hear mention of himself. "British Police have made a major breakthrough in the hunt for the sadistic arsonist known as Mr Tubbs. His house in Harborn, Birmingham was raided by police in the early hours of yesterday and a cache of pornographic pictures and intimate keepsakes he had taken from his victims was discovered. As he said in a press conference, Inspector Hicks from Birmingham City Police believes that the search for the arsonist is entering the end game."

Tubbs listened to the press conference with a mounting sense of shock, loss, anger, and despair. The bastards had taken his mementoes. How the hell did they find the house? No one knew about Westbourne Road. No one. As the devastating news sank in, he began to shiver with shock, quickly followed by tears. Huge gasping sobs of anguish shook the little man's body. He was hysterical with grief and hate. Hate directed at Hicks and especially Collins. That arrogant, good-looking prick.

Johann put his arms around Tubbs and let him cry. Clearly the shock of last night's attack was only now registering fully. It was right that he should let it out. It would do him good.

Handsworth, 11.30hrs

Following the latest press conference, the station received numerous sightings of Tubbs. He'd been spotted as far north as Dundee and south in Cornwall, at Bude. Given that everyone in CID was sure that he'd gone abroad, very little action beyond recording the call was taken. Tubbs' house and garden had been taken apart. Other than his keepsakes, there was not so much as a pack of firelighters to link Tubbs to the house or the fires.

At 12 noon Hicks summed up what everyone working on the case knew, 'He's gone. He'll be back. I'm sure of it but for now he's gone. While we're waiting for the bastard to return we need to pick up all the stuff we've been ignoring for the past few days. O'Driscoll will continue working with the Fraud Squad on interviewing those who hired Tubbs and liaising with the Inland Revenue, Land Registry and anyone else who might have records on Tubbs under any of his names.'

'What do yow want to do with me, boss? Go back to uniform?' asked Clark.

'No. The Tubbs case isn't finished. The team stays together until it is or York returns. I'll talk to the Super and clear it with him.'

'That's fine with me. Anything in the tray you want Mickey and me to look at?'

'I haven't looked today,' said Hicks and picked up the contents of his in-tray. Five or six pages into the pack he smiled. 'I've got just the job for you pair. Ridley had a call from the vicar at St. Basil's. Seems he's worried that there is either a gang of vandals smashing up his church or we've got a group of Satanists on the loose. Go and have a chat with him.'

On the way to the car Clark said, 'I'll interview the vicar while yow have a look about the graveyard. See if yow can find any disturbed graves or dead animals.'

'How come you get to interview the vicar about Satanists and I'm inspecting the graveyard?'

'Because yowm only just finished your probation, and that makes me the senior officer, which means yow get all the shit jobs. Besides yow have a much higher boredom threshold than me. It comes from yow having a lack of imagination.'

'I don't know about that. At the moment I'm imagining a bloody horde of Satanists sacrificing a small copper to their great god Lucifer while I hand them the daggers.'

'That's not imagination. That's yowr pagan Celtic past rearing up.'

'I'll have you know that Ireland was civilised when you lot were still running around with your arses hanging out of fur skins. Ireland's not known as "The Isle of Saints and Scholars" for nothing.'

'And I bet it was the Irish Tourist Board dreamed that one up.'

The day was hot, very hot, with barely a breeze to disturb the shimmering heat. Clark whistled the tune to *Dam Busters* as he drove to St Basil's. In retaliation Clark hummed *Danny Boy* – loudly. The church had been built when there was plenty of cheap land available and people still wanted to build great monuments to both God and their own

Christian generosity. Clark followed the drive to the church door where it broadened out into a large turning circle. *Perfect for hearses,* he thought as he parked. Climbing out he looked around the churchyard. It backed onto Handsworth Park and was immaculately kept, with neat, well-tended graves, trimmed privet hedges and the grass cut to within half an inch of its life.

'Have a quick shuftie, Mickey. Then join me in the church.'

'OK.'

Pushing the heavy wood door open, Clark stepped into the church. The pews, old and scarred, had been polished to a gleaming dark brown. Light streamed through two stained glass windows. One showed the crucifixion of Christ, and the other the risen Christ walking from his tomb on Easter Sunday to be met by Mary Magdalene and her companions. From what little Clark knew about such things, he thought they were well done.

To the right of the altar, the sacristy door was open and Clark could hear movement. Walking down the centre aisle, his steel-tipped heels sounded like rifle shots on the ancient stone flags. Clark immediately recognised the vicar who emerged from the sacristy to see who was in the church. He'd seen him on TV in one of those late night discussion programmes where very earnest young men dressed in black polo-neck jumpers, and the occasional woman, pontificated on topics of the day in very earnest tones that no ordinary person ever used. Clark couldn't remember his name but he was known as The Bikers' Vicar.

'Morning, Vicar. I'm Constable Clark. I'm here to talk to yow about the recent damage to yowr church.'

'Welcome. Welcome,' said the vicar in that overly effusive tone that so many people find annoying and false. 'I'm so glad that you're here. I'm at my wit's end. Wit's end, I tell you. There have been two desecrations of the church in the last month.'

Holy man or not, Clark found the vicar irritating. 'Perhaps

yow could tell me what happened.'

'Indeed, indeed. Please sit down.'

Clark sat on the front pew and was joined by the vicar. 'It was three weeks ago that the first attack took place. Someone gained entrance to the church and removed the cross from the wall behind the altar and left it propped against the front of the altar turned upside down. There were also the bloody remains of a chicken on the altar steps.'

'Did yow report it to the police?'

'No. We get this sort of thing fairly regularly. I thought it was just some children playing around. But the second attack, which took place last Monday was much worse. I am now certain that there is a band of Satanists behind this sacrilegious behaviour.'

'What did they do this time for yow to reach that conclusion?'

'Again, the cross had been taken from the wall and placed upside down. A statue of Christ was knocked from its plinth and smashed. Also blood and what may have been semen was smeared on the bare altar alongside two used condoms.'

'I see and yow say that this happened last Monday night?'

'Yes.'

'Did the other attack occur on a Monday?'

'Why yes, it did, as a matter of fact.'

'Did yow find out how they broke into the building?'

'No there was no damage to any of the doors or windows.'

'How many entrances are there to the church?' asked Clark uncrossing his legs and readjusting himself on the hard pew before he got pins and needles in his backside.

'Three. The front door, through the sacristy, and through the church hall.'

'Who has duplicate keys?'

'Well, the verger and I are the only ones with keys to the church and sacristy but several groups who meet in the church hall have keys to the hall.'

'Is the connecting door to the church kept locked?'

'No, no. Many people attending a function like to pop in and say a prayer. Only last Monday two members of the 101 Motor Cycle Club came in to pray.'

'That's the club where yow have to ride yowr bike at 101 miles an hour to join?'

'That's right. But they always take care. They wait until the morning hours before their "chicken run".'

Clark said nothing, but he could remember attending a road fatality in 1960 where a biker had crashed doing over 90 at 1am. The top of his skull had been sheared off when he lost control and slid under a lorry. He'd never been able to prove it but he'd been convinced that the 101 club were involved in the death.

'Do yow have a list of groups meeting in the hall, please?'

'Yes, there's one on the noticeboard.'

Rising, both men went into the hall, which was typical of its kind. A stage at one end for amateur shows and recitals. A door and serving hatch in one wall which led through to the kitchen. A dance floor took up most of the remaining space with about a hundred chairs stacked around it. The vicar crossed to the noticeboard, unpinned a schedule of bookings and gave it to Clark.

Clark quickly scanned the list. 'I see that the 101 Club is in every two weeks on a Monday.'

Yes, but I'm certain that they wouldn't be involved in anything like this.'

'Yow're probably right. It could be the Scouts or knitting circle.' Looking at the list again, Clark asked, 'The bikers meet fortnightly. How come they're in again next Monday?

'They break up for the summer next week. It's their year-end party.'

'What time will that end?'

'About 11.'

'I'll be here.'

'I told you that the Club wouldn't do this.'

'I know, and I'm not saying that they caused the damage,

but it's a bit of a coincidence that both attacks happened on their Club night.'

Clark had been sitting in the car with the door open for five minutes before Collins appeared from behind the church. 'Where yow been? I said have a quick look see and come in the church.'

'I was having a talk with my new friend Patrick Murphy, ex-boxer, ex-sailor and now a gentleman of the road.'

'Yow mean a tramp?'

'I do, but a very interesting tramp. He's set up his summer residence under a couple of sheets of corrugated zinc in a briar patch between the churchyard and the park. It's very private.'

'And what did he have to say?'

'We're not dealing with Satanists.'

'Hell, I already know that.'

'Well, in that case what are we going to do about it?'

'Come back next Monday and pinch the sods.'

'Seems fair enough. But can we do it quietly? I don't want to disturb Patrick, he's a light sleeper or so he tells me.'

'Get in the car, you numty.'

Saturday, 17 July 1965

Oxford Street, London, 11.00hrs

It was a typically busy Saturday morning on Oxford Street. The sunshine had brought out the crowds, and they had abandoned their jackets and cardigans, for the weekend at least. A gentle breeze ran down the street and it was difficult not to feel alive and joyous on such a beautiful day.

Chavda Chilkov had left his flat in Holland Park at 9.20 that morning and phoned his girlfriend from a phone box near the local Underground station. They had decided to spend the morning shopping before taking his Ferrari 250 GTO for a spin in the Kent countryside, followed by dinner at one of the many discreet hotels which boasted an excellent menu and soft beds.

Miss Emily Lincoln, aged 39, a plain but very likable secretary at the United States Embassy, had been only too happy to accept the invitation. It was with excitement that she had showered, dried her hair and put on her make-up. There was never any doubt in her mind as to what she was going to wear. Just the previous week André had bought her a beautiful set of cream lingerie, a red dress with matching jacket and black patent leather kitten heel shoes. She was so lucky to have met him. André's wife sounded like a truly awful woman, completely incapable of understanding the complex and sensitive man she'd married and was now stifling him. Soon, very soon he would leave her and then they'd be together.

Stephen Rhodes followed the happy couple at a discreet distance of twenty yards. His military bearing was obvious in the way he walked. Left leg and right arm swung gracefully in unison. On every second step, the steel tip of his umbrella struck the ground simultaneously with his left foot. Rhodes knew that it was extremely unlikely that Chilkov would spot him. The man's entire attention was directed towards the dowdy secretary who was one of three who provided secretarial support to the CIA Station Chief at the Embassy. For her part, she clung to the Bulgarian like one of the doomed passengers on the *Titanic* who had held on to floating debris in the freezing water.

Breaking into a trot, the happy couple ran to catch the traffic lights before they changed. Too late – they were left standing on the curb. Almost instantaneously other pedestrians started to gather around them. Rhodes eased his way into the waiting mass. He was now barely a yard behind Chilkov. When the lights changed, Rhodes pressed a small black button at the base of the umbrella handle and stepped forward. Left leg, right arm swinging. But this time, in the crush, his umbrella did not strike the ground but caught the left heel of the Bulgarian. Chilkov spun around, and Rhodes immediately offered his profuse apologies.

Chilkov ran through all known British and American security agents that were currently operating in London and the Home Counties. This man wasn't on his list. With a smile he said, 'No harm done.' On reaching the other side of the road Chilkov and Miss Lincoln turned left and the newest recruit to MI5 and retired Coldstream Guards Captain Stephen St. Claire Rhodes went right.

Sitting in the restaurant, under black oak beams that were 400 years old, Emily felt wonderful. André had been gentle at first but as her passion had built, so too had the ferocity of their lovemaking. She had never felt anything like it in her life. Her desires had been fully sated in a way that she had thought only existed in books. Sitting opposite the man she loved, she felt complete for the first time in her life.

After this afternoon there would never be the need for small talk again. She and André were now one. He smiled at her and lifted a forkful of chicken chasseur to his lips. Suddenly his eyes bulged and he grasped at his throat. Standing, he knocked his chair over. Emily watched her lover's face turn from red to blue. Blood appeared in his mouth and then he said, 'Help m—,' and spattered food and blood across Emily's face. She started screaming. Guests and staff rushed to help.

Andre fell to the floor. His body shook with convulsions and he lost control over his bladder and bowels. A final fit lifted his back, buttocks and thighs off the ground before he collapsed and lay still. Emily continued to scream.

Later that evening, the London CIA Station Chief and a Marine Staff Sergeant from the Embassy arrived to take Emily back to London and a debriefing session that would destroy her even more than the death of her lovely André.

Sunday, 18 July 1965

Birmingham, 10.50hrs

The Meeting for Worship at Bull Street Meeting House had reached that state of deep silence which occurs when late into a service no one has offered ministry and a genuine silent union has been achieved between all those present.

Agnes was glad of the silence. She had much to contemplate and pray about. For the last week, she'd found herself constantly replaying the shooting at Kings Cross. The look on the Bulgarian agent's face as he realised he was dying. The spreading bloodstain on his shirt. The smell of gunfire. The ease with which her old training had allowed her to renounce her non-violence principles and to use deadly force without conscious thought. Which was the real Agnes? The trained killer of long ago, or the committed Quaker? Agnes was no longer sure. She thought she'd left that killer back in the 1950s.

With just ten minutes of the Meeting left, Agnes was still struggling to justify her actions. She'd saved Anatoli's life but only by killing another person. She found no peace in the thought that the man she'd killed had lived a life marked by violence and death, because she knew that Anatoli had also done unspeakable things for the security of his country. Nor was she herself without sin. At least 14 men and women had died at her hands during the war and immediately after. But that was before she had committed herself to non-violence and joined the Quakers. She thought she had changed for ever. Had she been deceiving herself?

Suddenly Agnes was aware that her left leg had started to shake. *No,* she thought. *I'm not going to speak.* But now her right leg was moving and her stomach turning somersaults.

Quaking head to foot, she was compelled to stand, as if someone had taken her hand and pulled her out of the chair. Now that she was standing, she realised that her mind was blank and she had no words to express what she was feeling.

The Friends present recognised the turmoil that was churning within Agnes. To see someone quake at a Meeting for Worship was not rare but it was uncommon and all who saw it realised that the person affected required their prayerful support. The Friends remained silent, content to let Agnes have as much time as she required to compose herself and organise what she so obviously needed to say.

When she finally spoke, her voice was unsteady at first but quickly grew in strength as the words stared to flow. 'As Quakers, our fundamental belief is that there is "That of God" in every person. It is this belief that informs our commitment to non-violence. But what happens when we find ourselves in a violent situation and we have to choose who lives and who dies? I'm not talking about choosing who to save in an accident. In such situations our decisions are often made instantaneously and socially conditioned. We choose the child over the adult, the friend over the stranger. No, I'm talking about the case where we are active participants in the events taking place. When it is our actions that directly determine who will live and who will die.

'It is easy to live by a set of principles as long as they are never tested. It is only when our espoused beliefs crash into reality that we really know what we stand for. If we cannot live up to our principles, yet continue to call ourselves a Quaker, are we just hypocrites like the Pharisees of old?

'How often can we fail and still claim adherence to a principle? It is this clash between what I say I stand for and what I actually do that has occupied much of my thinking this past week. To date I have failed to reach a conclusion.' Agnes sat down and the sixteen pairs of eyes that had been watching her either closed or turned to look for a suitable focal point to rest their gaze on.

With less than five minutes left of the allotted hour, an old man, whom Agnes had never seen before at Meeting, rose unsteadily to his feet. 'Friends, I am in my ninetieth year on this earth, but I am far from wise. I know this to be true, because I still continue to make the same mistakes now as I did in my twenties. Although I seem to make fewer mistakes these days when it comes to women. One of the worst mistakes I have made is to believe that because I am a Quaker I must be perfect. That my beliefs and actions must be perfectly aligned at all times. This ignores one essential truth; there has never been a perfect man or woman on this earth.

'Every one of us fails to live up to the ideals that we set ourselves. That does not mean we are hypocrites or evil. It just means that we are human and we should forgive ourselves for our failings, as God does, and resolve to do better in the future. God does not expect perfection from us. Only that we constantly seek perfection while knowing that in this world we will never achieve it.'

As the old man sat down, Agnes felt a gentle warmth flow through her body. Silently she turned to God and said a prayer for the unknown Bulgarian she had killed and the other 14 men and women she knew for certain had died at her hand. When the Meeting ended she remained seated, contemplating her own humanity in all its glorious failure.

After ten minutes she went to join the small congregation for a cup of coffee. She particularly wanted to thank the old man for his ministry and was disappointed to find that he had left.

Monday, 19 July 1965

Handsworth, 23.20hrs

Clark made himself comfortable in the Italian Gothic presider chair he'd taken from the altar earlier, while Collins contented himself sitting on the cabinet that contained the chalices, wine and wafers used for services. They'd been ensconced in the sacristy since nine that evening, and both were glad that the vestibule had been extended to include a small room where the vicar could talk to parishioners in private, and a toilet.

'Strewth, I'm bored,' said Clark. 'It's bad enough attending a church service but sitting in a church for two hours doing nothing is worse.'

'Well you could always try praying,' said Collins. 'Or having a chat to God about your sins.'

'No chance. I ain't got the time, and he don't have the patience.'

'God exists outside of time. Time is meaningless to him.'

'In that case he has something in common with Ruth. She also operates in her own sweet Fanny Adams time.'

'What can I say, you're a .... .' Collins stopped and held up his hand for silence. 'Did you hear that?' he whispered.

Clark nodded.

Both men moved silently to the sacristy door which they had left open half an inch. Peering through the gap, Collins saw two teenage boys enter the church from the meeting hall. The dark-haired one, a head taller than his friend and his face covered in spots, led the way. 'Come on, Johnny. We haven't got all night.'

Johnny was smaller, with fair hair that covered his ears. Even at 15 yards Collins could see that he was scared. Moving aside, Collins gestured Clark to take a look. 'Wi wait until they do summut then have 'em,' whispered Clark.

'I don't think we should do this, Will,' said Johnny.

Will turned and grabbed Johnny by the shoulder and shook him. 'Come on, we agreed. Those fucking greasers slapped us about. This is how we get them back. The coppers are bound to think it were them.'

'Well how come the police haven't been around to talk to them?'

'Because the vicar's shit scared of 'em and dain't call the cops. After tonight, he'll have to. Now come on. We'll do it together.' Walking behind the altar he took the four-foot cross down from the wall and returned to the altar steps. Johnny was standing beside a three-foot statue of St Basil. 'OK,' said Will. 'Three, two, one,' and smashed the cross on the altar steps, breaking it in two. At the same time Johnny grabbed the side of the statue and pushed it. The hollow statue sounded like a bomb going off as it shattered into a myriad pieces on the stone floor.

Throwing the sacristy door open, Clark shouted, 'Right, yow little shits, yow're under arrest.'

For an instant both boys froze. Terrified. Then Will shouted, 'Run.'

Johnny was nearest the hall and was the faster runner. He was in the hall and heading for the front door before Will even made it out of the church. Clark grabbed the big lad by the collar and pulled him back. Off balance, the boy fell and banged his head on the side of a pew.

Collins ignored Clark and went after Johnny. The lad had made it into the graveyard and was heading down the path when Collins came out the door. Collins increased his speed and started to gain when a dark, dishevelled shape that was barely human in appearance reared up from behind a gravestone. Arms spread wide, a wailing cry on its lips, it lunged towards the boy. Johnny screamed in fright, changed direction and ran straight into Collins' arms.

'Don't let it get me. Don't let it get me,' he pleaded.

Collins was barely aware of what the boy was saying. His entire attention was focused on the overpowering stench that was emanating from the lad and which could only mean one thing.

'Have you got the little bastard, Mickey?'

'I have, Patrick. Many thanks for your help. Will you be around tomorrow?'

'Sure, other than meeting the Queen at 11 I've nothing else planned.'

'I'll see you then with a little something. Thanks for your help.'

'I'm always happy to help a fellow Dub, Michael.'

'Look, yow caught him. Yow take him back to the station. He ain't going in my car, and that's final.'

'But it's over a mile back.'

'So? It's not my fault yowr little plan scared the shit out of the lad. Is it?'

Clark drove off leaving a very smelly Johnny, the vicar, and Collins standing at the church gates. 'I'm sorry, Vicar, but can the lad get cleaned up before we head back to the station?'

'Very well, and I'll see if I can find him a pair of trousers to wear.'

'That would be grand, Vicar.'

Collins took the still snivelling Johnny by the arm and led him back into the church. Opening the toilet door Collins said, 'Clean yourself up and leave the door open a couple of inches just in case you're daft enough to try going out that window.'

A dispirited and despondent, 'Yes, officer,' was enough to convince Collins that the lad was going nowhere.

Twenty minutes later Collins and Johnny set off to the station. The lad was now wearing a University of

Oxford rugby jumper and a pair of grey shapeless track suit bottoms. Both items were several sizes too big for him. At 1.30 in the morning, though, no one was around to comment on how he looked and Collins was just pleased that he no longer smelt.

As they walked, Collins chatted to the lad. After five minutes' talk about his school and Will, he asked, 'Why did you do it?'

'It was Will's fault. We were sitting on the church wall a few weeks back and this girl went past. We knew she hung out with the greasers, so Will said, "How much do you charge for a fuck," and she said, "A lot more than your pocket money." Well, that annoyed Will and he started calling her names. You know, slag, scrubber, cunt. Anyways, one of the bikers coming up the street heard him and grabbed him by the collar. I thought he was going to thump him, but he told the girl to get the gang. About fifteen of them came out to see what was going on. That's when he put Will across his knee and gave him a right spanking. They were all pissing themselves laughing but Will was really angry. He wasn't that hurt, but he was really embarrassed.

'The next day he said he had a plan to get his own back. He'd read about how the bike gangs in America were into voodoo and black magic so he said we'll frame 'em.'

'And you just went along with it?'

'Yeah. He's me mate.'

By the time the lad's parents had been woken up, travelled to the station, listened to their sons confess to sacrilege under the Section 24 of the Larceny Act 1916 and been told that the maximum sentence was penal servitude for life and bailed to appear at Juvenile Court it was after 6am.

'Yoe reckon they'll ever do it again?' asked Clark.

'Na, the threat of a life sentence scared the bejesus out of them.'

'Always does the trick,' said Clark. 'They'll probably get probation.'

Collins and Clark wandered to their cars in the clear, bright early morning sunshine. It was a fresh start to a new day, but both men would spend most of it trying to sleep as the temperature soared and even the lightest of sheets made them sweat like visitors to a Turkish bath in their airless bedrooms where the windows were kept firmly shut to keep out the noise.

Wednesday, 21 July 1965

Zurich, 12.00hrs

Doctor Bachman was astonished at the progress that his patient had made in just a week. 'Herr Hermes, another week like the last one and you will be back to your old self. How do you feel?'

'Better every day, doctor. I can walk normally again and I think my ribs are healing well, although I still find it difficult to take a really deep breath.'

'Have you been out at all?'

'Yes, I've taken a stroll to the old town the last two nights.'

'Excellent. Excellent. But please do not overdo it.'

'Rest assured, I won't,' and for the first time since he had heard of his mementoes being stolen by the police, he smiled his private little smile with his tongue showing between his teeth.

With the doctor gone, Tubbs picked up the large sports bag he'd purchased that morning and walked over to the bathroom. Closing the door, he opened the bag and took out three cheap bottles of wine, a can containing four litres of petrol, a black funnel, and a role of medical lint. He opened each bottle in turn and poured its entire contents down the sink. He then placed the bottles in the bath, and used the funnel to fill them with petrol before replacing the corks. Wiping down everything he'd touched, he returned the items to the sports bag.

The smell of petrol was strong in the bathroom. Tubbs opened the window and turned the on fan, then sat on the toilet seat. Checking his watch he smiled, *just 11 hours until they all start to be sorry,* he thought.

Zurich, 23.40hrs

Tubbs had spent the previous two nights searching for his attackers. He was sure that their attack on him hadn't been the first time they had enticed a man into an alley and taken his money. They had been too confident for first timers. No, they knew what they were doing.

Amazingly, he'd found their van on the very first night. They had parked just yards away from where he'd seen them drive past. It was a side street off the road that ran alongside the River Limmat, quiet, dark and secluded. Ideal for his needs. The second night he'd confirmed that they arrived about 8pm and returned to the van just after midnight. He was now ready for them.

Standing less than six yards away from the empty van, Tubbs hid behind an electricity substation. His three Molotov cocktails, each now with a petrol-soaked lint fuse, rested at his feet along with the quarter-full petrol can. When they turned the corner he saw that they had linked arms and were laughing. The woman, Gabriella, was in the middle. She pulled open the rear door of the Volkswagen camper and clambered in.

Tubbs waited until the big man turned the ignition key and nothing happened. Then he lit the fuses. Without a distributor cap the van was going nowhere. Picking up the three bottles, Tubbs approached the van from the rear. Walking quickly, he pulled the back door open, stepped back, and threw the first bomb at the woman. The lethal cocktail landed on the van's metal floor inches from Gabriella's feet and exploded, covering her and the men in burning petrol. Stepping further back, Tubbs threw the remaining two bombs into the van. One exploded behind the front seat and the last hit the windscreen and exploded in the men's faces.

Kicking the back door shut, he ran to the side of the van and watched the three occupants screaming and writhing in agony as they were consumed by burning petrol and choked by filthy black smoke. Tubbs especially enjoyed watching

Gabriella burn. For an instant, she looked straight at him and he had the feeling that she recognised him. That look. The feeling of absolute power it provoked in him, caused him to grow hard.

Spotting a trickle of petrol from the tank dribble under the van, he moved further back. Soon the trickle became a thin fast-moving flame that raced down the road to the petrol tank. This explosion that followed lifted the camper off the road.

Tubbs dropped the petrol can into the sports bag and set off down the road. As he passed the burning van, he threw the sports bag into the centre of the flames. Just as he turned onto the main road, he heard the final explosion as the petrol can ignited. *I bet the little bitch isn't laughing now.*

Back in his hotel room, he stripped off his clothes and placed them in a paper shopping bag. He would dispose of them tomorrow. As he lay luxuriating in the bath, the woman's face kept coming back to him. He was sure she'd recognised him in the moments before the fire had engulfed her. The thought pleased him. He lay back and stroked his lamb's tail. Just as he had that night long ago when he'd seen Mrs Sims screaming for help outside her house. He thought about how hot the flames must have been in the van, of the pain Gabriella had felt and the choking smoke, and he came for the first time since he'd been attacked. The blood-streaked semen stored up for over a week kept coming and he smiled as it covered his hand and watched as it dripped off his fist into the water. Satisfied. Relaxed. He stood up and stepped out of the bath, and started to dry himself. Tonight had been wonderful, but now he had to plan for Hicks and Collins.

Part 4

Monday, 26 July 1965

Handsworth, 09.40 hrs

The day had started without a cloud in the sky or sign of a breeze. A dirty haze hung over Birmingham and would remain there until a stiff wind dispersed it. Every officer in the station was in shirtsleeves and every window was open, and it wasn't even 10am.

Hicks was reading the overnight reports but there was nothing of any consequence. Clark was half-heartedly working through the interviews with Tubbs' customers for the umpteenth time. But still he couldn't find even the thinnest of clues as to where Tubbs was or what he'd been doing.

Tubbs' Identikit picture and description had been issued to every major European and Scandinavian country. Special attention had been given to Switzerland. Hicks himself had called the Commissioners of Police in Bern, Basal, Geneva, Lucerne and Zurich. Nothing. The only fire-related incident involved three known criminals who had been killed by a rival gang using Molotov cocktails in Zurich.

Collins, carrying a tray of three teas and two rounds of toast for each man, pushed the door open with his backside. He was in danger of spilling the tea until WPC Carol Milne held the door open and followed him into the room.

'Morning, Sir,' said Milne. Amazingly, she still had her jacket on, buttoned up as per regulations and she didn't appear to be at least bothered by the heat. 'Sergeant Ridley asked me to bring this round to you. It's just arrived with the rest of the post.'

'What is it?'

'Looks like a book, Sir,' said Milne turning over the slim

package in her hand. 'It says "Return address Police Review." Want me to open it, Sir?'

'No, give it to me.'

Milne handed Hicks the package and stood by his desk as he ripped it open to reveal a taped-up cardboard box. He ripped a corner. Milne saw the wire first and immediately understood its significance. Grabbing the box from Hicks, she threw it out of the window behind him and dived on top of the Inspector, knocking him out of his chair and onto the floor.

Clark reacted before the package hit the concrete in the yard and pulled Collins down, sending three teas and six rounds of toast flying.

When it came, the explosion wasn't large, but the fireball that erupted in the yard was 25 feet across and sent flames licking through several ground floor windows. A strangled cry of pain came from Collins.

'Anyone hurt?' shouted Clark, as the fire alarm sounded and running feet and shouted instructions echoed down the hallways.

'We're fine,' said Hicks.

'I'm OK. But I'm bloody covered in toast and tea,' said Collins.

'Stop yowr complaining. If it weren't for Milne we'd all be dead.'

'Yeah, but you didn't spill three full cups of hot tea on your crotch.'

Ridley evacuated the building and took a full head count, including prisoners, at the front of the station. No one was missing. There were no casualties, except for Collins, who left as soon as he could to find the nearest chemist and get something to relieve the pain of scalding.

The first fire engine arrived within two minutes. The watch had been playing volleyball when they saw and heard the explosion just one street away. However, on arrival there was little for them to do. WPC Milne had thrown the package into the middle of the yard where there was nothing to feed the initial explosion. Without fuel, the fire had quickly consumed itself. All that was left was a dark patch and a small pothole in the concrete.

'Don't hose it down, lads,' said Inspector Hicks. 'We might be able to find something in the debris that may help us.'

One of the leading firemen asked, 'Is this the same bastard that killed Stan?'

'I'm afraid it is.'

'About bloody time you caught the fucker, ain't it?'

'I can't argue with that.'

'Yeah well, when you do, give him to us for half an hour, would you?'

Hicks smiled and said nothing. He understood only too well how the men felt.

Birmingham, 18.30hrs

Tubbs finished listening to the six o' clock news on the Home Service and its report on his failed attempt to kill Hicks and Collins. Standing, he walked to the table, picked up the cheap Bush transistor radio he'd bought and threw it against the wall. 'Fuck, Fuck and double fuck.' he shouted and upended the table, sending his ham sandwich and half-full cup of tea skidding across the dust-covered floor. 'Fucking bastards,' he screamed.

The radio bulletins throughout the day had been full of the attack on of Thornhill Road Police Station but only the Home Service evening news had carried an exclusive interview with Inspector Hicks. 'The gloating cunt. I'll kill the bastard. How dare he call me an incompetent, little man of low intelligence and less worth?' The words "of low intelligence and less worth," continued to resonate in his head.

Looking in the mirror he'd propped up on the battered sideboard, he fought to control himself. Slowly his breathing returned to normal, and the tension in his arms, back and neck started to dissipate. Looking directly into his own eyes he promised himself, in a voice little more than a whisper that, 'They'll pay. I'll make them all pay.'

Picking up the table he started to rummage in his case for pen and paper. He had a plan to prepare.

Handsworth, 18.35hrs

When Sheba's ears pricked up, and she trotted out to the front door Agnes followed. There was no sign of Michael's car yet, but Sheba was never wrong. He'd be here soon. Thirty seconds later, at the sound of the MG, Agnes opened the front door.

Michael had called her after the explosion to reassure her that he was safe, but there had been something in his voice that concerned her. When he stepped from the car she immediately saw that he was walking with some care. Concern flooded over her. Sheba ran to meet him, but instead of playing with her as usual, Collins seemed to be trying to fend her off. As he approached the front door Agnes asked, 'What's happened? Are you hurt?'

Stepping past Agnes, Collins walked stiff-legged to the lounge. 'What's happened?' she demanded.

'It's nothing, honest.'

'What's nothing?'

'I was holding a tray of tea when Clarkee pulled me down. I was scalded. It's not too bad. It'll heal in a few days.'

'Where were you scalded?' Collins said nothing. 'Where were you scalded?'

Collins looked shamefaced. Unwilling to reply.

'Where?' demanded Agnes, her voice rising.

'Three cups of tea landed in me lap.'

As relief chased away the fear she'd been feeling Agnes felt her lips twitch. She fought to control it. 'I better take a look at that,' she said straight-faced.

'You've got no bloody chance,' said Collins.

Unable to control herself any more, she started to giggle.

'You're as bad as the rest of the station. Bloody Clark told everyone what happened. Every woman from the cleaner to Milne has offered to rub it better.' Standing, he waddled towards the door and mustering what dignity he could he said, 'I'm going to put some cream on it.' Agnes bit her lip but as Collins walked wide legged up the stairs he heard her stifle a laugh by sticking a cushion in her mouth. 'Typical. No bloody sympathy for a wounded man,' he shouted. That was the final straw and his ascent to the top of the stairs was accompanied by hysterical laughter from the lounge. By the time he'd reached the bathroom door he was smiling too.

Joanne joined Agnes and Collins for dinner. Joanne had relaxed since she had arrived and the bruising had started to fade, but still she had not said who had beaten her up.

The conversation was light and cheerful but turned more serious when Joanne asked, 'How long can I stay here, Agnes? I mean, I'm nearly better and I can't just stay here. Can I?' There was a note of pleading in her voice as she finished speaking.

'You can stay until you have a place to stay and a job to support yourself,' said Agnes and reaching across the dinner table, held Joanne's hand. Tears appeared in the young woman's eyes and she quickly wiped them away with her fingertips.

It was the first time that Collins had seen tears of gratitude in Joanne's face, and he felt that she was ready to open up and tell Agnes what had happened. Instinctively he realised that it would be easier for Joanne to say what she had to say if he wasn't there, so standing up he collected the plates and asked, 'Who wants ice cream?' Both women said they did and Collins left for the kitchen where he took a long time finding and cutting the ice cream. When he returned Joanne looked as if she had been crying, with red eyes and a hankie held tight in her right hand.

Whatever had been said was not going to be repeated now, and the conversation turned to what they could watch on TV that night.

It was nearly 11pm, and he was lying in bed with Agnes when she told him who had beaten Joanne up and why. The story made him angry and chased the sleep he needed from his mind. For two hours he thought about the problem and how best he could help Joanne. He still hadn't settled on a course of action when he fell asleep at a little after 1am.

Tuesday, 27 July 1965

Handsworth, 09.20hrs

Every morning paper had at least one, usually more, photos of the station and officers milling about after yesterday's explosion. The result was that every copper in the station had bought at least one morning paper – just to see if their picture was in it. Headlines screamed that the police in the United Kingdom were under the worst sustained attack since the IRA Border Campaign of 1956 to 1962.

Questions were to be raised in the House, and the Home Secretary had issued a statement condemning the attack and offering all the resources of the state to Birmingham City Police in their endeavours to capture this madman. Several papers mentioned the quick thinking of WPC Milne and there was a good picture of her in *The Birmingham Post* being congratulated by the Chief Constable.

Strangely, the atmosphere in the station was one of quiet celebration. They'd survived an attack and escaped unscathed. Tubbs had failed for the first time. People saw it as an omen. Clark saw it for what it was. 'A bloody near thing. Next time wi might not be so lucky.'

'We need to catch him before he tries again,' said Collins holding the office door open. Before he'd walked ten yards, Sergeant Ridley asked, 'How's your knackers, Mickey?

At the doors to the canteen the WPC Milne said,' I hope your goolies are better, Mickey.'

Turning to Clark, Collins said, 'This is all your bloody doing. The next one who asks how me testicles are, I'm going to punch.'

Turning the corner Collins bumped into Superintendent Wallace, 'Morning DC Collins, how's your bollocks?'

'Fine, Sir,' replied Collins and kept walking.

'Coward,' said Hicks.

'Bollocks,' said Collins.

'That's yowr problem, Mickey. Yowm obsessed with your ...'

'Don't say it,' said Collins drawing his fist back.

After a morning spent checking yet more possible sightings of Tubbs, it was nearly 2pm when Collins and Clark went to the canteen for lunch. Settled in a corner table both men looked at their dinners, and grinned. Sausage, mash, peas and thick brown gravy. Everyone's favourite. After eating in silence for a few minutes Collins said, 'You know Joanne, Agnes' latest lodger?'

'Yeah.'

'She told Agnes last night who had beaten her.'

'Who was it?'

'Her father.'

'Why did he beat her?'

'That's the thing. It seems her Mother died when she was eight. Before she was nine Daddy was using her as his wife.'

'So what happened? Did she decide that that she wasn't going to play mommy anymore?'

'No the father did. Seems she has a younger sister aged ten, and Daddy fancies her more than Joanne. She doesn't want her kid sister to go through the same things she's had to. So she threatened him with going to the police and he beat her black and blue and threw her out of the house. He told her to sod off and not to come back. Said she was old enough to fend for herself.'

'So open a case file and arrest the bastard for GBH and see what he has to say about playing mummies and daddies with his daughter.'

'Easier said than done. He's a copper. Works in Aston and is a part-time minister at the Church of the Holy Risen Christ.'

'Bloody hell. What are yow going to do?'

'According to Agnes, Joanne doesn't want any court case. She just wants to get her sister away from him. So a legal case isn't going to work. I was thinking we could go and see the sod and have a few hard words with him. Get him to give up the sister. What do you think? Are you up for it?'

'OK. But first wi listen to what Dad has to say. She could be lying about the whole thing.'

'Yeah, I know. But I doubt it.'

'OK, then. When do wi go and see the man?'

'How about after work tonight?'

'Why then?'

''Cos that's the time I made an appointment with the Inspector.'

'A bloody Inspector. Yow're treading on very thin ice. Wi could both get in serious trouble if things get rough tonight.'

'I'll say a prayer to St Jude for us. He's the patron saint of lost causes,' said Collins with a smile.

'I'd feel happier if he was an Assistant Chief Constable and he'd told us to speak to Inspector what's-his-name.'

'Monroe's, the name. Inspector George Monroe.'

Erdington 18.25hrs

Monroe's house was a large semi-detatched house near Wylde Green train station. It was a substantial house with a long front garden in the middle of which stood a monkey puzzle tree towering above the house. Collins knocked on the door and he heard movement and the sound of feet running up the stairs before the door was opened by Inspector Monroe. The inspector was in his early 40s and looked fit. His handshake was firm, and his clear blue eyes that stared back at Collins gave nothing away.

'So can I get you lads a cuppa before we start?' the Inspector asked.

'That would be good, Sir,' said Collins and sat down in the

armchair nearest the door.

Collins and Clark sat and waited while they heard the kettle come to the boil and tea was made and biscuits found. Placing the tray on the coffee table Monroe asked, 'How is Joanne? Is she all right?'

'She's fine. She's staying with a woman who looks after women and girls who have been beaten.'

'What do you mean, "beaten"?' Monroe asked. The concern and confusion in his eyes looked real to Collins. 'How can she be all right if she's been beaten?'

'She's fine, Sir. Honestly. Someone gave her a bad beating after you threw her out.'

'Is that what she told you? That I threw her out?'

'Yes, Sir, and she said it were yow who hit her.'

Monroe slumped back into the settee and, putting his hand over his eyes, started to cry. The sobs started small but grew into great heaving sobs that Jenny, his younger daughter,r heard and she came running down the stairs. Seeing her father crying, she ran to him and threw her arms around his head. He held her tightly and slowly his tears ended.

Collins caught Clark's eye and the message that passed between them was simple and clear. *This is not what we'd expected.*

'Jenny love, I'm all right now. You go and play while I talk to these men about Joanne,'

'All right, Daddy,' the young girl replied and left the room to take up residence, out of sight, on the bottom step of the stairs.

'All right, I suppose she's also told you that since her Mother's died I've been using her as my wife and that now I've turned my attention on Jenny.'

'Something like that. Would you like to tell me what's going on?'

'Jenny's mother died soon after Jenny was born. Joanne has always believed that she died because of the birth. But the truth is it wasn't connected. A brain tumour killed my wife four months after Jenny was born. But Joanne believed that differently. She started to act strangely towards Jenny. Small accidents suddenly happen. Insignificant at first, but gradually they grew more serious.'

'Such as?' asked Clark.

'Well first she had her hand scalded when a cup of tea split on her hand. Then she fell down the stairs – twice. Then she was poisoned. It was then that I called the police in, and they spoke to Joanne and searched her room and found the poison she'd used.

'She was diagnosed as having depression and paranoia and committed to a secure hospital seven years ago. She was only released from it six weeks ago. At first she seemed fine, but she quickly deteriorated. When I searched her bedroom I found that she'd been stockpiling her drugs. When I asked her why, she said they were to kill Jenny.' A great shudder ran through his body as he said this and his eyes filled up again.

'So how come she were black and blue when picked up by the Salvation Army in Birmingham?'

'I've an idea, but you won't believe it.'

'Try me,' replied Clark.

'She hurts herself. That's what the scars are on her arms. When I found the drugs I locked her in her room and called the hospital. She started to run into the wall and doors and to punch herself in the face. When I finished the call I went to her room and she hit me with a brass candlestick. I kept it. It's in the kitchen. It's got my blood on it and I've still got the scar, here,' he said and pulled the hair on the side of his head apart to show a two-inch red scar. 'When I came around she'd gone.'

What about the hospital? What did you tell them had happened when they called around?' asked Collins.

'Oh, they never came. They'd told me that she was cured and unless I had proof that she was a danger to herself or others there was nothing they could do. Fucking idiots.'

'So you just let her go?' asked Clark.

'If you exclude looking for her every day since she left, then yes, I just let her go,' Monroe shot back, and for the first time there was an edge to his voice. 'I found I couldn't even lodge a bloody missing person, as she was over 21 and had every right to leave home. But the Super at my nick was good. He had it as a standing item on each roll call. If it had been official we could have gone citywide and you'd have spotted her sooner.'

'So what are you going to do now, Sir?' asked Collins.

'Go with you and pick her up. Take her to see the psychiatrist that committed her first time around. Can I ask, will you be willing to speak to him?'

'Yes,' said Collins. 'But for now we'd best go and pick her up from Agnes.'

Thirty minutes later Collins drew up outside the front door with Inspector Monroe beside him. Stepping from the car, he heard Sheba's whining in the kitchen interspersed with scratching and the occasional bark. The front door was ajar. As he entered the hall Collins felt the blood drain from his face. Agnes was lying unmoving on the parquet floor at the bottom of the stairs.

Crossing to Agnes, Collins knelt down and searched for a pulse in her neck. He found a strong one. As he moved her, Agnes started to regain consciousness. Slipping his arm under her shoulders he said, 'Easy, darling. You're all right now.'

'Who's that?' Agnes asked looking at Monroe.

'That's Inspector Monroe. Joanne's father.'

'Your daughter knows how to punch, Inspector,' said Agnes before adding, 'Help me up please, Michael.'

The rest of the evening was taken up with calling Clark at Monroe's place and arranging for him to ferry Jenny over to Hamstead Road. Agnes, having being seen by the station's on-call doctor who pronounced her fine, followed by Inspector Monroe, Jenny, and Collins, all provided statements to O' Driscoll and Clark about the events leading to Joanne's second disappearance within two weeks. During the course of the evening Jenny met Sheba, and the two became firm friends as the ten-year-old girl chased the dog around the garden.

When everyone had left, Collins asked for the first time. 'What set Joanne off?'

'She heard one end of our conversation and when I hung up, wanted to know who I'd been talking to.'

'I tried to calm her down, but when I said her father was on the way over she went to her room without saying a word. When she reappeared she had that small suitcase that the Salvation Army had given her and said she was leaving. I tried to dissuade her, but she was adamant and became more and more agitated. Then suddenly she punched me in the stomach. I was so surprised that I never even saw the right hook which knocked me down and I banged my head on the floor. It's very unusual for a girl to be such a good boxer.'

'She's an unusual girl all round, I'd say.'

'You do believe Joanne's father, don't you? He's not lying about her?'

'No he's not lying,' said Collins. 'And do you know something? Despite everything she's done, he still loves Joanne.'

Wednesday, 28 July 1965

Winson Green, 22.30hrs

Tubbs moved silently across Bright's rear car park. There was a three-quarter moon and visibility was excellent. In its light, he and the sports bag he carried would be visible to anyone looking out of a window, but he wasn't worried. He was safe from prying eyes. There was nothing but the backs of factories overlooking the deserted parking area and at 11.35pm no one was working – not even the night watchmen.

He found the window he'd used before, slipped the paint stripper's blade between the sash windows and pushed the latch to one side. Sliding the window up, he stepped into the warehouse then, reaching back, picked up the sports bag. The warehouse hadn't changed since his last visit. But he had.

There was no longer any need to conceal his identity. He wanted them to know it was him. He wanted to rub their noses in their inability to capture him. Yes they had damaged his business and destroyed his mementoes, but they had not caught him. Instead of disguising the cause of the fire, he now wanted to advertise to the entire world his skill and show how he'd outwitted the police. There were now only two things on his mind, utterly destroying the warehouse and getting out safely.

The loss of his workshop and most of his supplies had forced him to improvise. His four incendiary bombs were simple and unsophisticated, but he felt confident that they would get the job done. Each bomb had just two elements. A plastic bottle containing two pints of petrol and a quarter-stick of dynamite attached to the side by insulation tape.

He placed the bombs in a square, 20 paces apart, in the centre of the warehouse. Each rested on material that would burn easily and quickly, fabrics, plastics and bedding. Satisfied with their placement, he returned to each bomb in turn and lit the five-minute fuse. Only one of them needed to work to ensure total devastation of the building, but he wanted to put on a show.

As he walked quickly to the rear of the warehouse he took out a bottle of acetone and sprinkled the stock as he went. By the time he climbed out of the building the fumes from the chemical, so reminiscent of nail varnish, hung in the air, just waiting to be ignited by the first touch of flame.

He was standing by the back wall, forty yards from the warehouse, when the first explosion occurred, quickly followed by a blinding flash of flame that smashed windows and burst into the night sky as the acetone vapour ignited. Seconds later, the three remaining bombs went off almost simultaneously. He felt the ground shake and smiled as sheets of flame spiralled into the night sky and the wonderful smell of an untamed fire filled his head.

Turning, he saw in the glare of the flames the four-foot-high heart encircling the letters TK that he'd painted on the back wall. *The stupid bastards will never know what it means.* He waited for two minutes more, enjoying his work, then clambered over the wall and headed for his van.

The fire lit up the night sky for miles around. A huge plume of black foul-smelling smoke hung over the warehouse and was drifting over the canal and heading for Winson Green Road and the prison. Not surprisingly, only a small number of people had gathered to watch the free show. The nearest residential road was Heath Street, a depressingly long road of two-up, two-down back-to-back houses that provided a lot of the manual labour required for the local factories and warehouse. If the people living there were interested in the fire, they could watch it from their rear bedroom or standing on the roof of the outside toilet.

'You know, Mickey, this bastard is starting to seriously piss me off. He's ruining me sleep,' said Clark as he parked 100 yards away from the still burning warehouse.

'He is irritating, I'll give you that. But you've got to admire his persistence. He likes to finish what he starts.'

'So do I, and there's only one way this thing is going to end.'

Collins looked at Clark but said nothing. Everything he needed to know was written on the small man's face.

Inspector Hicks was watching from a safe distance as the men from two fire stations tackled the blaze. Two pumps were cooling down the buildings that adjoined the warehouse and four more were engaged in fighting the fire itself.

'Evening, Sir,' said Collins. 'Have they got it under control yet?'

'God knows. There are another two engines at the side and around the back. They can't get inside. The building is unstable and there's a danger it will collapse. They could be at it for hours yet.'

'I don't suppose there is any chance that Tubbs didn't do it?' asked Collins.

'There's always a doubt. But I think the 4 foot heart painted on the back wall with TK in the middle gives him away.'

'Cocky bastard,' said Clark. 'He's taunting us.'

'Listen, there's nothing we can do until the morning. You pair might as well get off home. No need for all three of us to lose a night's sleep.'

'Decent of Hicks to send us home,' said Collins. 'But I've no idea what we can do in the morning. We've got no leads on Tubbs. He's running rings around us.'

'Yam not wrong. But we ain't out of the game yet. He wants yow and Hicks. He missed you the first time. I reckon he'll try again. Yam unfinished business. Just like the warehouse were.'

'But if he keeps sending bombs instead of facing us I can't

see how we catch him.'

'Tubbs wants you bad. That will make him impatient. The bomb failed and he ain't going to want another failure.'

'Do you think he'll try for me at home?'

'Possible. That's why the Superintendent asked the Chief Constable to have your place and Hicks' watched.'

'Bloody hell. They must be good. I haven't seen them.'

'That's the general idea. If you can't see 'em, neither will Tubbs, until it's too late.'

Thursday, 29 July 1965

Winson Green, 10.00hrs

After an interrupted night's sleep Collins and Clark returned to Bright's. Two fire engines were still there, damping down the smouldering mass of bricks, wood, metal and fabrics. Even from fifty feet away, both men could feel the heat radiating from the debris.

A quick visit to the back wall confirmed that the heart and initials were indeed Tubbs' trademark. 'OK, Sherlock, tell me what yow think.'

Climbing up the six-foot wall, Collins looked over and then dropped back into the yard. 'Well, I reckon he came in from the canal side and went out that way. There are no houses around here. It's all factories. No one would have seen him come or go. He probably slipped the catch on a sash window, did the dirty deed, and then disappeared back the way he came.'

'I think yow're right. But he ain't as big as yow...'

'So how did he climb over?' asked Collins.

'Exactly. Give me a hand and I'll see what's what on top.'

Placing his left foot in Collins' cupped hands, Clark stepped onto his friend's shoulders and then pulled himself up. The drop to the canal towpath was a good nine feet, compared to the mere six-foot factory side. *No way he got up here without help,* thought Clark. Walking along the wall, he spotted what he was looking for. A climbing wedge had been driven into the wall about four feet from the ground. There was no sign of any rope. Sitting on the wall, Clark pushed himself off and dropped back in to the yard. 'There's a climbing wedge the other side. I'll send a bobby to pick it up. We might be able to find out where he bought it.'

'So he came in off the canal towpath. Maybe someone saw

him.'

'Possibly, but it's a long shot. Yow don't get many people walking along the canal at night. This ain't Venice. And I'm pretty sure that if yow were in your back bedroom and looked out you'd see nowt. He'd be in the shadows. No, house to house is a waste of time. We'll put up some notices asking for anyone who was walking on the canal between 10pm and midnight. We might get lucky with a courting couple.'

Collins and Clark returned to the station in time to join those officers waiting to go on duty at 2pm for lunch. They were joined by Sergeant Ridley. 'You two look knackered.'

'That's what I admire most about yow, Ridley. Yow're a man of sage-like perception. Of course wem bloody knackered. Wi been up half the night.'

'He gets terrible grumpy, Sarge, when he hasn't had his eight hours.'

'More likely, when he ain't had his cocoa,' said Ridley and laughed.

Clark smiled at the old joke.

'What the feck has cocoa to do with anything?' asked Collins and both men collapsed into laughter.

Before they were finished eating Hicks joined them. 'Find anything at Bright's?'

'He used a climbing wedge to get over the wall from the canal side. I sent a bobby to collect it. Wi think it's a waste of time doing a house to house. Only Heath Street has a view of the warehouse and them's nearly 100 yards away. It might be worth putting up a few posters asking for anyone who were walking the canal between 10 and midnight to contact us.'

'OK, do that. The Chief Constable wants a briefing on the case and last night's events. The Super and I are off there at two. You could check in with Superintendent Patterson or his sidekick. See if they have anything.'

'Will do Sir,' said Collins. 'Yow going to be back today?'

'Doubt it. I can hardly keep me eyes open.'

All the windows in the CID office were closed and the place was stifling. Collins opened all three windows than sat down. A gentle breeze ruffled the top papers on his desk.

'Mickey, can you contact Patterson for me? Find out what the Fraudies have found out?' I need to pop out.'

'Sure. Where you going?'

'It's your mate, Winston. Yow were right. There's something about the kid. He deserves a chance. It ain't worth calling anyone. I need to speak to someone.'

'Who?'

'Me old Captain. He's a Colonel now at Whittington Barracks.'

Collins smiled. 'OK. No problem.'

Whittington Army Barracks, 14.30hrs

Clark rolled down the car's front windows and headed for Perry Barr and the A38. It was a beautiful summer's day with a cloudless sky and the sun cracking the stones by the side of the road. Jacket off, he enjoyed the rush of cool wind through the passenger window. Turning to the Light Programme on 1500m long wave, Clark settled down to listen to Mantovani and other band leaders as he headed for Whittington Barracks. The barracks were situated between Lichfield, one of the oldest cities in Britain, and Tamworth, ancient capital of the Mercian kings. The A5 road which linked both towns had been built by the Romans and was still known as Watling Street.

The current Whittington Barracks had been built in 1877 and been intended to house the 38th (1st Staffordshire) Regiment of Foot and 80th Regiment of Foot (Staffordshire

Volunteers). However, under the Childers Reforms these regiments were amalgamated and became the North Staffordshire Regiment.

During the Second World War the barracks had been occupied by the United States 10th Army and was used as a Replacement Depot where soldiers were housed until they were shipped out as front line replacements. By 1965 the barracks had become the regional centre for infantry training and was known as The Mercian Brigade Depot.

As he drove past Lichfield on the Tamworth Road, Clark saw a young policeman sitting on a grass hillock by the side of the road, his jacket off, a 50cc police bike near-by. He was sketching a herd of cows in a nearby field. As Clark drove by, he waved at the young constable who saluted back. *Now there's a man who's got his priorities right,* thought Clark.

Nearing Whittington Barracks, Clark rehearsed what he was going to say. He was going to see the man responsible for selection and recruitment of the entire North Staffordshire Regiment. If anyone could ease Winston's way into the Army, it was him.

Colonel Freddie Winthrop didn't keep Clark waiting long. As soon as he heard who was in the recruitment office he flung the door open and bellowed the length of the office, 'Sergeant Clark, get your fucking arse in here.'

Every head in the twenty-strong office shot up. The gaffer was angry. Someone was going to get it in the neck. Looking up, they saw the small civilian who was waiting to see the Colonel stand up. He was grinning from ear to ear. Coming to attention, he shouted in return, 'Yes, Sir. Right away, Sir. Should I bring me box, Sir?'

'Bloody right you should, and your tin hat,' said Winthrop, before dissolving into a huge smile.

Clark marched smartly up to his old CO and saluted again before shaking hands. 'Come in, Clarkee. Come in.' Turning to his admin assistant Winthrop said, 'Bring in some tea please, Sergeant, and find some whiskey.'

Seated in the Colonel's Victorian office, Clark admired the high ceilings, which kept the temperature down, the oak picture rail, skirting boards, fireplace and windows, all of which looked as new as the day they had been installed. Dropping into a Pompeian style wooden armchair without cushions, Colonel Winthrop asked, 'What brings you here today, Clarkee?'

'A favour.'

'Well, ask, and if it's within my power, you shall receive.'

Clark was about to launch into his story when the Sergeant appeared carrying a tray of tea and biscuits. As he laid the tray down he looked at Clark. Stepping back he saluted the Colonel, which he didn't need to do, as he wasn't wearing his cap, and then turning to Clark, he came to attention again and saluted the small man saying, 'Sir, honour to meet you.' Turning in a smart about-turn, he marched out of the office.

'Word didn't take long to get out,' said the Colonel.

'I find it embarrassing.'

'Don't. You deserve it. Not many of these guys have met a VC. Anyway, tell me what you want.'

Without mentioning the fight outside the Park Gate Stores, Clark spoke about Winston's ambition to join the army and his own view that he was an ideal candidate. When he'd finished, the Colonel said, 'So what's the problem? Has he got a record? If so, that's no bother.'

'The lad's as black as a chimney sweep.'

'Oh, I see. When you called him Winston I'd assumed it was his surname. But you still think he has what it takes to make an "outstanding soldier"?'

'Yes, I do.'

'You know the squaddies will have him for breakfast?'

'They'll try, but the lad has something about him. Something that makes yow like him. He's also tough, he'll give as good as he gets. And he can definitely hold his own in a scrap. I've seen him in action against four toughs from The British Movement.'

'OK. I'll tell you what,' said Winthrop, pulling out a writing pad from his desk. Have him come and see me informally. Tell him to catch the train to Lichfield and we'll talk. If I like what I see I'll encourage him to apply. You'll need to supply a reference, and one from Collins would help also. And for once in your life will you please sign it Mr Clive Clark VC and the rest of the fruit salad you picked up.'

'That's great, Sir.'

'I've not finished yet. He'll have to pass the entrance exams. Do all that and I'll make sure he's not blackballed. Sorry for the pun.'

Clark smiled. 'Thanks, Sir.'

'Don't thank me yet. The poor kid will have to put up with hell if he gets in. Now,' said the Colonel. looking at his watch 'Do you fancy a drink in the Officers' Mess as my guest before you go home?'

'It's a bit early. But I'll have just the one. I need to get off.'

Four hours later Clark drove out of the main gates. He'd lost count of the number of whiskies, gins and vodkas he'd poured into the pot containing the giant rubber plant.

Friday, 30 July 1965

Handsworth, 09.30 hrs

Clark had been in the office since six. He wanted to write Winston's reference and type it up before the official day started. Pulling the finished document from the typewriter, he signed it and placed it in a police envelope. Seeing Collins drive into the back yard he stood up, slipped the letter into his desk drawer and set off to intercept Collins. He needed a strong cup of tea and a piece of dry toast to settle his stomach. Never a spirits drinker, he was suffering from the two pints and two single whiskies which he had downed the previous night, and were wreaking havoc on his stomach and head.

With a cuppa and a piece of toast in front of him, he told Collins the good news.

'That's bloody marvellous.'

'Is it? That poor lad's going to get it in the neck every day – starting as soon as he applies.'

'Maybe. But at least you've given him the chance to find out if it's really for him.'

Changing the subject, Clark asked, 'Do yow know what's happening with Patterson?'

'They're building cases against nearly forty people spread over the last eleven years. But they've found nothing new that would enable us to find Tubbs.'

'So all wi can do is sit and wait. I hate bloody waiting.'

'Me too.'

Winson Green, 14.00hrs

Tubbs had been out for nearly three hours when he returned from shopping. Except for the occasional twinge from his ribs, he was fully recovered from the beating in Zurich, and despite his failure to kill Hicks and Collins, he was more like his old self. The answer for this lift in his spirits was simple; the Bright's fire had been very satisfying, plus he had something to do. Something to keep his mind engaged.

Just that morning he'd visited several hardware, gardening and paint shops buying odd items from each. He now had everything he needed. A few hours' work and the bomb would be finished and ready to deliver to Thornhill Road Station, and no one would be able to throw *this* bomb out the window. He smiled his little smile at the thought of the utter devastation that it would cause, and went to make a sandwich. *Soon,* he thought. *Very soon.*

Handsworth, 17.30hrs

'Well, I'm off,' said Clark.

'Me too. I'll walk out with you.'

As Collins and Clark walked past the Charge Room, Sergeant Ridley stuck his head round the glass petitioned door. 'Clarkee, you know you were asking about Zatopek? Seems he's moved to pastures new. I've got Dudley Road Police on the phone. They've just picked him up. He had thirty quid in his pockets and the saddle bag on his bike, all in shillings.'

'What do they want, a medal?'

'It's Zatopek. Seems he's demanding to speak to you. Says he has some very important information and will only give it to you. Won't speak to anyone else.'

'Bloody hell. I were just going home. If he's wasting me time I'm going to nail his scrotum to the notice board.'

'Does that mean I can tell them you're on your way?'

'Yeah. I'm on me way.'

As they left the station Collins looked at his watch. 'It's a bit early to clock off. Why don't I come with you? It's not every day you get to meet a guy who's committed 10,000 offences.'

'Oh, he's nowt special. A right little creep really. His one redeeming feature is that he's popular with the householders. In about three-quarters of the thefts he does, he shares the takings 50-50 with the gas meter's owners.'

'I can see why he's popular then.'

'No, that ain't it. Others offer the same service but he's the neatest and cleanest.'

Sergeant Cowell of Dudley Road and Clark were old friends. They'd served together in the 50s at Thornhill Road. They shook hands warmly and Clark introduced Collins as "the guy with the scalded dick." Nearly a week after the bombing every police officer in Birmingham knew the full medical details behind the only casualty of the bomb. So far 27 tubes of TCP ointment had been delivered to the station from well-wishers. Other solutions had been sent by Collins' enemies.

Sergeant Cowell showed Collins and Clark into Interview Room 2. A few minutes later he brought Zatopek up from the cells. 'I'll leave the little shit with you pair. Can I just remind you that this interview room is soundproof? We can't hear anything outside the room. You could be beating the shit out of him and we wouldn't hear a thing,' he lied.

As the door closed behind the Sergeant, Clark asked, 'So, Zatopek, what's so bloody important that yow dragged me all the way over here?'

'Please, Mr Clark,' snivelled Zatopek. 'don't call me that name. I hate it.'

'What would you like me to call yow?'

'Archie would be fine.'

'OK, Archie, what do yow want?'

'You've always treated me fair, Mr Clark. Never thumped me, so I reckon you'll treat me fair on this. I've got some real important information.'

'And what do you want for your information?' asked Collins.

Archie looked at Collins for the first time. 'I want a deal.'

'What kind of deal?' asked Clark.

'The kind that keeps me out of jail.'

'Yow've been out of the nick for less than a month and were caught with thirty quid in yowr pockets all in shillings. It will have to be bloody great info to keep yow out of Winson Green.'

'It is. And if it works out I want the ten grand reward as well.'

Collins pushed himself away from the wall. There was only one reward of £10,000 on offer at the moment and that was from the insurance companies who wanted to see Tubbs locked up.

Neither Clark's demeanour nor voice changed, 'Tell me what yow've got and I'll see what I can do for yow. I can't promise to keep you out of clink but if yowm entitled to any reward I'll make sure yow get it. Fair enough?'

'Fair enough.' Archie Mellon took a deep breath and said,' I know where that arsonist you're chasing is hiding out.'

'Like fuck yow do,' said Clark.

'It's the truth, Mr Clark.'

'I ain't sure yow've ever been introduced to the truth, Archie.'

'Why would I lie, Mr Clark? If I'm wrong I get nothing out of this. Pissing you about would only make it worse for me.'

'Go on,' said Clark.

'I've been doing meters all round the streets off Rotton Park and City Road for the last few days. Yesterday I went down Gillot Road. I was doing all right. I did this house that were let as flats. It had six separate meters. Anyhow, when I comes out I saw him. The small geezer you've been looking for. He'd changed his appearance a bit. But it were him.'

'How do you mean, changed his appearance?' asked Collins.

'He'd dyed his hair and grown a moustache and he were

wearing a pair of specs. You know, like Buddy Holly used to wear.'

'That's a lot of changes. How can you be so sure it was him?' asked Collins.

'I'm good with faces. You can't change their shape, can you? I mean the hair and skin were dark but the face was the same. I'd bet a ton it were him. Small little guy with round face.'

'Yowm betting more than a hundred quid. Yow're betting 12 months in prison.'

'So where did you see him?' asked Collins.

'That's what made me look at him. He was going through the wire fence into an empty hotel on Gillott Road.'

'What's it called?' asked Clark.

'The Finlandia. It looks like one of those places you see in the 1930s gangster films. Now, it's a right dump. The tatters have had all the lead off the roof and the place is falling apart. You can't miss it.'

'OK,' said Clark. 'I'll ask the Sergeant to hold off changing yow for now. But if yow'm lying I'll make sure yowr sentence is doubled. Is that clear?'

'I ain't lying. He's there and it's him.'

In the corridor, Clark asked, 'What do yow think, Mickey? A lead or a wild goose chase?'

'I don't think he's lying. He saw someone but it might not be Tubbs.'

'We better go take a look, then?'

'Yeah, but we need to tell Hicks what we're doing, just in case.'

'OK. Yow call Hicks. I need a chat with me old mate.'

Clark found Cowell alone in the Charge Room. 'Steve, can I have a word?'

The Sergeant looked up and read Clark's face, 'For God's

sake, don't tell me the little rat-faced shit has something.'

Clark sat down and told him what Archie had said.

'Bloody hell. What you going to do?'

'Mickey's calling our boss for instructions. If there is a chance to catch the bastard we can't pass it up. Wi have to take a look and go in if needs be.'

'OK. I can get you a couple of guys to act as backup until the cavalry arrive.'

'Ta, that would be a help. What I really need though is a couple of guys outside the building with shooters. Just in case.'

'You know we don't have any guns here except those belonging to the Divisional Shooting Team.'

'They'll do. How many you got?'

'There are two rifles and two pistols. They're all single-shot .22s. Do you want the pistols?'

'No, I've got a couple in the car for Mickey and me.'

'How come you always travel with two guns?'

'Ain't yow heard? I'm very insecure I am.'

Cowell and four other officers remained out of sight on the corner of Wheatsheaf Road while Collins and Clark started to walk along Gillott Road. The Finlandia Hotel, or what was left of it, was on their right and backed onto the Edgbaston Reservoir.

'What did Hicks say?' asked Clark.

'Observe and take no action until he arrives with support.'

'Fair enough, but if I see Tubbs I'm going in. He ain't getting away this time.'

'I know.'

Clark and Collins crossed the road and disappeared into the mouth of a back alleyway running between two houses. Hidden from anyone in the Finlandia, they had their first good look at the hotel. Standing just 30 yards away, it was as Mellon had described, totally dilapidated. Built in the art deco style of the 1920s, it was a squat, four-storey building with rounded corners and a flat roof. Originally, the external brickwork had been plastered and painted white, but now much of the rendering had peeled off to reveal the red bricks beneath.

The original metal window frames had been ripped out during the war and used for munitions. Their cheap wooden replacements were rotten and broken. The only window panes still intact were on the fourth floor, where the kids' stones had failed to reach. Through the broken windows they could see parts of the main staircase that ran up the middle of the hotel. On each floor the stairs gave way to a landing which branched off to the right and left. The ornate exterior cast iron fire escape that had run down the side of the building had proved particularly attractive to the tatters. There was virtually nothing left of it except a few anchorage points embedded in the wall.

Clark dug in his pocket and handed Collins a handful of .44 shells. 'These are yowr spares. Remember, the Bull Dog only has five rounds. It ain't a six-shooter and while it's bloody effective over 15 yards, it's almost useless at 30. Got it?

'Yeah,' said Collins. "What do you think? Is he in there or not?'

'Yowr guess is as good as mine. Although, I could have sworn I just saw someone on the second floor.'

'Well in that case, we have no choice, we have to go in.'

'I thought yow might say that. Yow go round the back and I'll go in the front. Meet me on the ground floor.'

Re-crossing the road, both men covered the remaining distance at a fast trot. They stopped at a gap in the wire fence that ran the entire length of the hotel's frontage and slipped through. The front drive was overgrown and litter-strewn with bottles, old newspapers and the remnants of many a night's quick passion. Only the silver birch trees that had been planted in a semi-circle around the sides and back of the hotel had retained a hint of grandeur. They soared 80 feet into the clear blue evening sky and spread their untended branches in every direction.

Collins sprinted for the back garden, keeping low as he went. Clark ran up the drive and pushed the unlocked door open. As the evening sunlight fell on the floor, he saw recent footprints in the white dust that covered everything. He moved lightly across the boards, silent and quick. In many places the plaster had peeled from the walls revealing the wooden slat laths beneath. Odd pieces of broken furniture lay scattered across the room. The entire reception area felt hot, dry and oppressive.

Turning left, Clark walked into the front bar. The damage here had been made worse by the broken wall mirrors and smashed bottles littering the floor. He slipped behind what remained of the bar and looked for the trapdoor to the cellar. After descending just three steps into the darkness he realised that the entire basement had been flooded by the reservoir. Tubbs was not down there.

Returning to the bar, he walked to the end of the room where there was a connecting walkway into the restaurant. Like the bar, the restaurant had seen its fair share of vandalism but there were still some tables and chairs which were serviceable. He'd just reached the foyer when Collins appeared from the back. 'Anything?' he asked.

'Just a blue Morris Minor van with a grocer's sign on it,' said Collins smiling. 'He's here. We've got him.' Half way across the reception area a creaking floor board made Collins turn and look up. Tubbs was standing on the first floor landing, taking aim with a sawn-off double-barrelled shotgun. Collins dived at Clark. The shotgun went off and threw up dirt and splinters as the two men scrambled for cover in the restaurant doorway.

'Come out, come out wherever you are, Mr Policemen. It's time for you to die,' Tubbs sang out as he walked down the stairs.

'The fucker doesn't know we're armed,' whispered Clark.

'Yow stay here and if he comes within range, shoot him. I'm going to try summut.'

Clark moved quickly through the restaurant to the walkway and into the bar. Knowing it would it impossible not to crunch the glass underfoot, Clark sprinted for the foyer entrance.

Tubbs heard him coming and stopped halfway down the stairs. He'd not expected them to charge him. They had no guns. He was the one with the guns. But what if he was wrong? What if they were armed? Indecision and fear gripped him. Turning, he ran up the stairs.

He'd almost reached the first floor when Clark emerged from the bar. Clark now had a clear and uninterrupted view of the stairs and landing. He raised the Bull Dog and fired. The shot was uphill and beyond the limit of the gun's accuracy. The bullet hit Tubbs in the shoulder. He cried out in pain, stumbled, regained balance and ran along the landing and into the left-hand side corridor. A second shot hit the wall behind him.

Collins emerged from the restaurant door. 'Did you get him?'

'I winged him. We'll have to go in and winkle him out. Be careful, he might have more ammo or even another gun. I'll go up first and cover yow.' Clark took the stairs two at a time and flattened himself against the landing wall. A quick peek down the corridor revealed a trail of blood in the dust, but no sign of Tubbs. Clark waved Collins up.

'What now?' asked Collins.

'I'll follow Tubbs. Yow take the corridor on the right.'

Collins trotted across the landing, took a quick look, and then stepped into the corridor. Nothing. There were four doors on his right and three windows on the left that overlooked the side of the hotel and the silver birch. Reaching the first door, he eased it open quietly. The bedroom was 12 foot by 16, with peeling wallpaper, no furniture and an old torn carpet square that covered most of the floor. The room was empty.

A hole in the ceiling allowed him to peer into the room above, but the angle made it impossible to see if anyone was up there. Moving on, he pushed open the second door. Again nothing. The third room was also empty but he distinctly heard the sound of footsteps in the room above. *How the feck did he get up there?* he thought and walked quietly to the end of the corridor where it joined the rear service passage. In the corner was the answer to his question – a back stairway. Clark appeared from the left and asked,' 'What's up?'

'He's on the next floor,' said Collins, pointing upward with his thumb.

In single file and with a space of six yards between them, both men edged up the stairs, conscious that in the narrow stairwell they were sitting ducks. Reaching the second floor, they stopped. 'OK,' said Clark, 'Let's do this quick and together. Kick in each door and follow up with one of us going high and the other low. OK?'

Collins nodded in agreement. Moving quickly, Collins kicked in each door in turn as Clark crouched in the middle of the corridor waiting to fire at anything that was short and flabby. They'd reached the last room in the corridor when again they heard Tubbs moving about above. 'Bollocks,' said Clark. 'This guy is starting to seriously piss me off. Come on let's finish this.'

Taking the stairs two at a time, they stopped at the old fire door. A crash from above them sent them once more scurrying up the remaining stairs. At the top they paused, then cautiously opened the door onto the fourth floor corridor. This was the top of the building. Tubbs was trapped. He had nowhere to go. That made him dangerous.

As Collins and Clark stepped onto the fourth floor, Tubbs was moving silently towards the main stairs carrying a sports bag. On the fourth floor landing he left a plastic bottle filled with petrol. Taped to it was a half-stick of dynamite. Shortening the fuses to three minutes, he lit them. On the third floor he left and identical device. He now had only 90 seconds before the first bomb went off. As he raced down to the first floor he felt pure joy. A feeling he usually only had when he went hunting. *Now I've got you. You cocky bastards. Now we'll see who the morons are.* And despite the pain in his shoulder he smiled broadly, the tip of his tongue clearly visible.

On the first floor he stopped and opened the small door beneath the stairs that neither Collins nor Clark had spotted. Used by maids and cleaners to store their supplies, it now contained the partially constructed car bomb that Tubbs had been working on for two days.

The bomb on the fourth floor blew up and he felt the landing shake but his hands were steady as he pulled the device out. Without the ammonia nitrate-rich fertilizer that was in the van parked out at the back, his bomb had lost 90% of its explosive power. But it didn't matter. He was no longer aiming to blow up Thornhill Road Station. In this tinder-dry hotel he only needed a fraction of that power to ignite the acetone and petrol he'd packed around four sticks of dynamite.

He quickly placed a detonator in the centre of the four sticks of dynamite and led the 30-second fuse across the landing. The bomb on the third floor exploded. He smiled broadly as he lit the fuse with his Ronson lighter and ran down the stairs and took up his position where Collins and Clark had stood in the restaurant doorway. As he waited for the big one he imagined Collins standing on the landing as the vapors from the acetone ignited, immolating him in a flash fire, sheets of flame racing across the floor and walls. *Such a pity I won't be able to see it.*

On the fourth floor, Collins and Clark burst into the last room at the back of the building and stopped. This room was unlike any of the others. One wall was covered with newspaper articles and photos about Hicks and Collins.

The camp bed in the corner was unmade, and a Primus stove and a cache of basic foodstuffs including a bucket of water, bread, eggs, bacon, tinned corned beef, milk, and biscuits sat on a couple of orange boxes against the rear wall. In the centre of the room was a worn and scratched table on which lay Tubbs' tools: a small pair of pliers, hacksaw, wire clippers, a full set of screwdrivers, copper wire, a broken alarm clock and a couple of cheap Timex watches.

'So where's the sod gone?' asked Collins, walking over to the corner and pulling a small tarpaulin off a mound of rubbish.

Clark took one look at the discarded acetone bottles and petrol cans, and said, 'Oh shit.'

At the corner of Gillott Road and Wheatchief Road, Inspector Hicks arrived with the reinforcements. 'Who's in charge?'

Sergeant Cowley raised his hand. 'I am.'

'Where are Clark and Collins?'

Cowley hesitated. He knew they'd be in for a rollicking. 'They went inside.'

'When?'

'About ten minutes ago.'

'Anything happen?'

'There were a couple of shots just after they went in. Sounded like a shotgun followed by a handgun. Nothing since then.'

'Bloody hell. They went in unarmed?'

Again Cowley hesitated. 'They ain't unarmed.'

'Why aren't I surprised? Clark and his personal bloody arsenal.' Turning, Hicks looked at the four PCs with Cowley. 'What are they carrying?'

'Two single-shot target rifles and two target pistols, also single-shot.'

'Better than nothing, I suppose. You and your mates are coming with me.' Calling Sergeant Ridley over, Hicks said,

'Take our lads and clear the nearby houses. And for God's sake keep your head down.'

As Ridley and his six men moved off, Hicks turned to the officers from Dudley Road. 'We're going to set up position behind the two cars opposite the hotel. Keep your eyes open and remember there are two friendlies in the hotel. Now let's double time it.'

'What's the matter?' asked Collins.

'He's conned us. We're up here and he's setting off fucking bombs downstairs.' As if to emphasise Clark's point, the fourth-floor bomb exploded quickly, followed by the one on the third floor. Then there was a loud thud, like a heavy wall collapsing onto soft turf. The building shook and the windows rained down shards of glass like a heavy April shower onto the ground below. A whooshing sound like the roar of a tornado was quickly followed by long forked tongues of fire that erupted from the hotel's front windows.

'Bloody hell,' said Clark.

Hicks heard the Molotovs go off and instinctively ducked and pulled Cowley down with him. Shielded by the cars, both men stood up just as a the hotel was shaken by a dull explosion and a spectacular twenty foot sheet of red, yellow and blue flame shot out the front door. 'Fuck me,' said Hicks. 'The bastard's blown the place up.'

'What now, Sir?'

'We call the fire brigade and wait.'

Tubbs stood in reception looking up the stairs, and smiled. The fire was already blazing across the landing and down the corridors. He could hear the crackle of dry walls, floors and doors as they started to burn. The smell of old varnish filled the air. He'd won. Now he had to get out before the police and fire brigade arrived. By tomorrow he would be back in Switzerland, and by next week, who knows where? Not even the constant throbbing in his shoulder could dampen his spirits.

As he stepped from the front door he froze, dumbfounded by what he saw. Two rifles and two pistols were pointing at him and Hicks was standing there, a look of determination and hatred on his face. *Where did they come from? They shouldn't be here. I heard no bells.* He had been so sure that only two coppers had entered the hotel and that there was no one else outside that he'd become overconfident and careless. *Fuck, fuck and double fuck. How could I have been so fucking stupid?* He looked back. The door was ten feet away. He'd never make it before they shot him.

He raised his arms and shouted, 'I surrender.'

'What now, Sir?' asked the Sergeant, before he added, 'I'm sure I saw a gun on him.'

Hicks understood fully the implications of the statement. For a moment he remained undecided. Then he looked at the hotel. Fire was now streaming out of windows on every floor and grey clouds of stinking smoke were rising high into the evening sky. The fire brigade was five minutes away. Even if they arrived within the next ten seconds, it would be too late for Collins and Clark. They were already dead, as was Anne Johnson and God knows how many other women.

'I also saw a gun,' said Hicks. 'But when you fired, he ran back into the building. Understand?'

'Yes, Sir.' Turning to the best shot in the Division, Cowley said, 'Smithy, crease him a bit.'

The first bullet clipped the lobe off Tubbs' right ear. Tubbs screamed in pain, grabbed his ear and shouted, 'I surrender.' Switching rifles, Smithy's next shot hit the heel of Tubbs' shoe, making him dance with pain. When he tried to step forward, Cowley handed Smithy the reloaded first rifle. The third bullet creased the side of Tubbs' head and sent him spinning into the dirt.

Finally, Tubbs understood what was happening. Standing up he shouted, 'This isn't fair. I surrender. You can't do—' His words were cut short by the fourth shot that went through the side of his flapping white shirt without hitting him. Crying with frustration, self-recrimination and rage he backed off into the reception area. *I'll show those bastards. I'm not finished yet. I can get out of this. Out the back way and onto the reservoir.*

It didn't take long for wisps of smoke to make their way along the corridor and into Tubbs' workshop. 'Well, Ollie,' said Collins, 'this is another fine mess you got us into.'

'There yow go again, Stanley, always the pessimist.'

'So what are we going to do?'

'Find a way out, of course.'

'Now why didn't I think of that?' said Collins, and coughed as the smoke found its way into his lungs.

'Come on, let's check the back staircase.'

Stepping into the corridor, both men could see the advancing column of dark filthy smoke that was rolling down the corridor. Now and again they could just discern a flash of fire in the darkness. Already the temperature was rising, and the floorboards felt warm though their shoes.

Reaching the stairwell, Clark placed his hand on the stairwell door. It was warm to the touch but not hot. He grinned and gave a thumbs up. Easing the door open, they stepped into the velvet darkness. Dirty black smoke, two foot high, was swirling and eddying around the landing. On the third floor, they could see the fire running along the walls as ancient varnish bubbled, burst and gave off thick, black, noxious fumes.

'What do yow think?' asked Clark.

'Not a chance. We'd be running straight into the fire. How about the main staircase?'

They retraced their steps and were halfway down the corridor when they heard a great crash of wood. Sparks and flames leapt upwards and clouds of dirt and smoke were pushed down the corridor like water in a pressure hose. Covering their mouths, stumbling, their eyes stinging and noses running, they felt their way to Tubbs' workshop at the back of the building and slammed the door shut. The floor was a damn sight hotter than it had been just 50 seconds earlier.

Bent double, both men were overcome with a fit of coughing. 'Sweet Jesus, Mary and Joseph, that bastard knows how to start a fire,' shouted Collins over the increasing noise. The building was screaming in fury and pain as it raced towards its death. Meanwhile, the fire continued to hunt for its twin needs of oxygen and fuel. Bone-dry doors and old furniture burst into flame at the beast's merest touch. Walls caved in and sections of the floor collapsed in a series of muti-coloured pyrotechnic displays while all the time the beast exhaled tendrils of deadly gases.

'What about the remains of the fire escape? Can we get down that way?' asked Collins.

'It's worth a try.' Taking a dirty towel from the table, Clark ripped it in two and handed half to Collins. 'Soak it in the water. It'll keep some of the muck out.'

Collins tipped half of Tubbs' drinking water over the rag and tied it round his face. Clark did the same. 'Ready?'

Collins nodded and opened the door. A rolling ball of flame ran across the corridor ceiling faster than Collins could sprint. He slammed the door shut. His face felt as if someone had used a blowtorch to give him an instantaneous tan. He could smell the singed hair on his head and eyebrows. 'Fucking hell,' he said.

Clark pulled him back from the door, waited 30 seconds, and then very carefully eased the door open. The fire was licking at the adjacent room's door and the ceiling was crackling away like jumping jacks on the Fifth of November. The smoke seemed to have abated. Not a good sign. It meant the fire was burning bright and was hot enough to burn without smoke.

'Let's go,' said Clark. Turning left, they followed the corridor to the service passage at the rear of the building. The fire was moving both upwards and backwards from the front of the hotel. It was now only a matter of minutes before it punched its way through the end bedroom walls and consumed everything in its path.

Reaching the left-hand wall, Clark stuck his head out the smashed window. Ripping off his towelling mask, he took a deep breath of hot air. It was far from sweet, but infinitely better than anything inside the building. Stepping back, he grabbed Collins and shoved his head out.

Coughing, eyes still smarting, Collins looked down at the ground some 70 feet below. *No chance of jumping,* he thought.

Pulling Collins back in, Clark leaned out, looking for the remains of the fire escape. It was to his left. He counted nine bits of wrought iron extending up to six inches out of the wall. Stepping back he said, 'First the good news. We can probably make it down to about mid-way on the third floor. After that we'll have to jump.'

'How far to the ground?'

'Well these old places have high ceilings and good gaps between the floor boards. I'd say we'd have at least a 40 or 50 foot drop.'

'So a couple of broken legs apiece. Better than burning to death,' said Collins.

'OK. Let's do it.'

Both men straightened up. They knew the risk. Broken legs for sure. A broken back or neck and a lifetime in a wheelchair, a strong possibility.

'I'll go first,' said Clark, and pushed the sash window up and sat on the window sill. Collins stood behind him. Grabbing the side of the window with his left hand, Clark started to swing his right hand across his body, reaching for the first handhold. As he did so, a disconnected gas pipe exploded near the front of the building. The entire hotel shook. Clark's grip loosened and he started to slip off the sill. Collins grabbed him by the shoulders and pulled him back through the window.

As Clark landed on the floor, both men heard the building creak loudly. Instinctively, Collins grabbed Clark's collar and pulled him away from the wall. As he did so, a gap appeared in the ceiling between the wall and the roof. Both men watched in fascination and horror, as in slow motion a twenty-foot length of the side wall crumpled, folded, and dived gracefully into the ground, sending a huge plume of dirt and brick dust into the air.

Looking at Clark, Collins said, 'Typical. You caused that. You're getting fat in your old age.'

'Bollocks. It were probably yow swinging me around that did it.'

'Yeah, it could have been,' said Collins, conceding a point to Clark for the first time in his life. 'So what now?'

'It's too far to jump and I don't fancy burning,' said Clark and sat down with his back to the rear wall. After a short pause he took out his revolver and held it in his lap. 'I think wi just sit here and enjoy the fresh air coming though that bloody great hole in the wall and look at the sky. We have a minute or two before the flames arrive.'

Collins took out his gun and sat down beside Clark. The wall felt hot. Soon it would be too hot to touch. 'It's a shame I never got to marry Agnes.'

'Yeah. And it's a shame Ruth never had a nipper. She would have liked that.'

Putrid black smoke with its stinking acrid taste was rapidly filling the corridor. Fire had reached the back wall. It was now only a matter of seconds before it reached them. The heat was excruciating. It hurt their lungs to breathe. Sweat dripped off their noses and chins, and turned their clothes into a sodden uncomfortable mess.

Collins started coughing, and Clark joined in with great heaving coughs as the air turned grey and flames lapped along the walls and ceilings like waves. Soon it would be high tide. Clark and Collins exchanged looks and nodded. There was nothing more to say.

Collins turned his head to look out at the sky one last time and a sudden gust of wind stirred the branches on the silver birch tree. For a moment it seemed that they would brush against the hotel. 'Stop,' he shouted and started coughing again. His voice dry and hoarse he said, 'I know how we can get out.'

'Well, why the fuck didn't yow say so before?'

''Cos I only thought of it now.'

'Typical of yow bloody Irish,' coughed Clark spitting a glob of tar-like saliva at the advancing fire. On contact it sizzled and burned. 'Yow Irish always have to make a drama out of everything. So what do we do?'

'We jump.'

'What?'

'Trust me.'

Stumbling to his feet, Collins edged to the gaping hole in the wall and looked across at the silver birch. The tree trunk was about eight yards away. But the top branches were only six yards away at this height. Lower down the branches were longer. There might only be a five yard gap between the branches and the hotel. It might just work. The fire was now three-quarters of the way along the passage. 'We'll jump for the trees and hope that the branches lower down catch us.'

'Are yow fucking mad? Even if wi make it, we'll break every bone in our body.'

'No we won't,' shouted Collins over the crackle of the fire. 'Silver birch is a soft wood. They throw out a lot of thin branches high up. With a bit of luck they'll slow us down.'

The floor lurched to the left beneath their feet. Looking down, Clark said, 'OK. Let's do it.' Backing up to the edge of the flames, he accelerated as fast as he could in the 15 yards available. At the end of the floor he pushed off hard, jumped high into the air and sailed out into the evening sky.

Smithy saw him and shouted, 'Look!' Hicks watched in terrified astonishment. Astounded that Clark had survived, and terrified that the little man would miss the trees and plummet to the ground.

For the longest single second in his life Clark fell through the air, and then brushed against a branch. Desperately he tried to grasp it. Then he collided with a bigger branch, which broke beneath his weight. Now branches were tearing at his face and clothes. He was tumbling. Out of control. He had no idea which way was up or down. He hit a thick branch and felt the air driven out of his lungs and an excruciating pain in his side. This branch didn't break. He tried to grab it but slipped off and fell further. Suddenly there were no more branches and he hit the ground hard, landing head first. A blackness swelled up all around him and he was helpless to resist it. His last thought was, *Where's Mickey?*

Collins had watched Clark career out of control through the upper branches of the tree but had lost sight of him before he reached the ground. It was time for him to go. Crossing himself he prayed, 'Into your hands I commend my spirit. Your will be done.'

Then he stepped back. The fire was now running the full length of the ceiling and smoke was making it difficult to see more than a couple of yards. *Not much fecking room,* he thought. Crouching down like a long jumper at the start of his run, he charged along the passage. A yard from the hole, the floor bucked again and Collins stumbled. Too late to stop, he kept going and launched himself into space as the top floor collapsed. Flames, dust, smoke, bricks and wood showered down around him as he fell towards the tree.

He could see nothing. Prepare himself for nothing. When it came, the first branch drove into his back and broke four ribs. The second broke his collar bone and dislocated his shoulder. One branch caught the side of his arm and opened up a cut from his elbow to wrist. Falling out of the tree, he landed on his dislocated shoulder and broke his arm.

He was barely conscious when a fireman rushed up to him and pulled him away from the crumbling building. The pain of being pulled along the rubble-strewn road was intense, and tears came to his eyes. 'How's Clarkee?' he crocked.

'What was that, mate?' shouted the fireman.

'How's Officer Clark?'

'He's on his way to hospital, pal. He'll be OK.'

Collins smiled and let the world fade to black.

Running across the foyer, Tubbs felt the intense heat that was radiating from the stairs. The stairs were fully alight and flames had engulfed the first floor landing. *The fire's spreading upwards. If I'm quick I can get out through the kitchen. I'll beat the fuckers yet.* The kitchen was down a short passage that ran alongside the staircase and under the landing on one side and into the restaurant on the other. *If it's clear. I'm home free.*

He smiled as he entered the kitchen. It was untouched and relatively cool. The cupboards and shelves had been ripped from the walls and the old chef's chair lay in splinters on the floor. Only the main preparation table, a massive oak monstrosity, was still standing proudly in the centre of the room.

He could hear the fire above his head, consuming everything in its path and smiled. Moving quickly, he tried to open the kitchen door. It was locked, with mortice locks top and bottom. 'Fuck.'

There were only two windows, one over the sink, the other beside the door. Both were boarded up. He tried to move a plank with his hands. Nothing. Whoever had nailed them up had used six-inch nails. 'Shit,' he cried and returned to the passage door. As he opened the door he was hit by a searing blast of heat that made him close both his eyes and the door. The side of the staircase had collapsed and was blocking the entire length of the hallway. He was trapped.

Starting to panic, he turned and flung open every cupboard door and drawer that might contain a knife or length of metal he could use to lever off a window plank. The drawers were empty. The cupboards bare. Fear was starting to take control. Thinking was becoming harder.

Bending down, he examined the legs of the table. They were stout and strong. Hope returned. *If I can get one off, I can use it as a battering ram.* Upending the table, he examined the leg joint. The carpenter had used mortise and tenon joints to attach the legs. Tubbs started to pull at the leg. It felt immovable. Lying on the floor, he started to kick the leg inwards with the heel of his foot.

Smoke was now seeping under the door, filling the kitchen with a deadly mix of poisons and the ceiling had begun to sag. He tried to ignore his fear and just concentrate on kicking the table leg. Slowly, he felt movement in the leg. Changing feet, he renewed his attack with greater force, fuelled by a desperate belief that he could still escape. Suddenly the leg broke. He fell back on the floor and started to laugh with relief.

Despite the pain in his shoulder, he grabbed the leg and worked it from left to right to break the remaining wood fibres connecting it to the table. He started to cough. His eyes streaming, he could taste the bitter acrid smoke in the back of his throat. Seconds later the leg broke free.

Tucking the table leg under his arm like a lance, he charged at the window by the door. The oak leg hit the boards and bounced off. Tubbs went sprawling on the floor. Regaining his feet, he selected a single plank, then holding the middle of the leg in his left hand, he used his right to power the leg into the plank. He aimed to strike the plank's centre where the greatest flexibility was. After a dozen blows he felt the first movement in the wood. Five more and he could see daylight though the splintering wood.

Stepping back, he placed both hands on his knees. It was getting harder to breathe. The room was now completely filled with soft grey smoke. Worse, the hall door was on fire and Tubbs could hear the bubbles of varnish pop as they expanded. Straightening up, he lent backwards to relieve the stiffness in his back. The ceiling seemed to be moving. Smoke was billowing through the hole where the light fitting had been. Then, like a dam bursting, a stream of plaster, burning floorboards and dust poured down on him.

Knocked to the floor but still conscious, he lay there, unable to move his legs. Struggling to sit up, he raised his chest and head from the floor and saw that he was covered in timber, plasterboard and rubble from ankles to waist. He started to remove the debris and then he felt the gas pipe explode outside. The building shook from side to side and seemed to flex in the middle.

Looking up, he saw the second floor collapse, and burning joists, floorboards, plasterboard, carpets and furniture rained down. Tubbs covered his face with his arms and screamed as he was engulfed in half a ton of hot rubble. Dust and dirt mixed with the smoke in the kitchen, and total darkness descended on him.

As the dust settled, Tubbs stirred. Miraculously, he'd survived, but there was a terrible pain in his left leg and he was having difficulty inhaling. He couldn't expand his chest or stomach. Tilting his head and shoulders up, he saw the cause of the problem. He was now completely buried up to his sternum by hot debris. *I've got to move. I have to get out* and he tried to slither free of his burial mound. But it was useless. He was pinned. He could feel his legs and thighs being slowly roasted by the debris and he started to scream and cry with long, wailing howls of anguish and pain. As he scrabbled at the dirt, his fingernails broke.

A second crash in the hallway blew in the door, and flames leapt into the kitchen. Tubbs' panic escalated into hysteria. He screamed, but barely a sound escaped. Both his mouth and throat were clogged with smoke and dust.

Tubbs watched in terrified fascination as the fire curled over the top of the door frame and spread along the walls and ceiling at an amazing pace. Worst of all, the hot debris covering his lower body was reignited by the heat. 'No! No!' he whimpered. He scrabbled wildly at the burning rubbish, oblivious to the pain in his burnt hands.

Another collapsing floor or wall sent a ball of fire barrelling down the passage. It exploded into the kitchen and expanded to fill the entire room momentarily. When it drew back, Tubbs' face, hands and chest were blistering and his hair was alight. His sightless eyes were filled with pain. Boiling rage fought with madness as he thrashed about. The heat continued to rise and the fire was now dancing across all four walls.

The skin on Tubbs' face began to bubble and burst. His lungs were burnt and nearly shut down. His heart rate was over 190 beats per minute. What was left of his mind was squirming and slithering into total madness and hatred. Then the last of the staircase collapsed into the hallway sending yet more flames into the kitchen. They enveloped Tubbs in their searing embrace and he felt the agony of the damned as his eyes closed for the last time and he was fully consumed by his one true love.

Saturday, 31 July 1965

Dudley Road Hospital, 04.00hrs

Some time around 4am Collins started to wake up. He was propped up in bed and was surprised how well he felt. There was no pain at all. In fact, he felt wonderful. *Must be the relief at being alive,* he thought.

Turning his head he saw that his arm and shoulder were encased in plaster of Paris and suspended in the air by a system of wires and pulleys. His arm was bent at right angles at the elbow and was level with his chin. Moving slightly, he realised that the reason his breathing was so shallow was the heavy strapping around his chest and waist. With the latest revelation he decided to revise his previous conclusion. How he felt was clearly down to the drugs.

Trying to sit up further, he looked down the bed and saw Agnes. She was sitting in a chair, arms folded on the bed, her head resting on them, asleep. She felt him move and sat up. A smile tried to cross Collins' lips, but his face was too bruised to comply. Seeing the look on Agnes' face, he said, 'Honest, darling, it wasn't my fault.'

'Maybe not,' said Agnes, 'But what are you going to tell Jamie when he gets home tomorrow?'

Agnes and Ruth stayed by their men's bedsides until 6am, and then left arm in arm only when they were certain that both Collins and Clark would be all right. The men slept fitfully and awoke more than once coughing and spluttering.

By 8am strings had been pulled, and Collins and Clark were given a two-bed side ward to themselves. Reporters were in the corridors trying to see the heroes who'd tracked down Tubbs and only escaped his last fire by jumping from a fourth floor window into trees. They were held at bay by one formidable Sister of indeterminable age, a young Staff Nurse, and an orderly with a mop whom Sister had ordered to continually wash the same twenty feet of corridor.

The two orthopaedic surgeons who had operated on the men arrived at 8.30 to see their patients before they went home to a well-earned sleep. As each man's injuries were read off, Collins and Clark kept score.

Collins had a dislocated collar bone and a broken elbow and arm, plus four broken ribs, along with multiple cuts, bruises and abrasions. Total breakage score, 7.

Clark had a dislocated shoulder, three broken ribs, plus a broken ankle and wrist. He too had suffered numerous cuts and bruises in the fall and there was barely a square inch of unbruised skin on his stomach and chest. Total breakage score, 6.

Neither man wanted to talk about the fire and how close they'd come to death. That would come later. For the moment, they were happy to compare injuries and argue over which was more serious, a broken arm or ankle and whether a dislocation was worth as much as a break. After lying in silence for ten minutes, Clark asked, 'How did yow know the jump would work?'

'Sure, I worked it all out in me head. It's amazing how quick you can think when you have to. I saw the branches through the hole in the wall and I did a rough calculation of our speed at lift-off, distance to the branches, acceleration of descent and trajectory of fall. All that stuff.'

'Now, I really don't know how yow keep all that crap in yowr tiny head.'

'I don't. I told you before. I just make it up as I go along and sure some ejit nearly always believes me. Personally, I was certain we'd both be killed.'

'Then why the hell did yow suggest it?'

'It was a chance, a long shot. But I thought it was worth a try.'

There was something in Collins' voice that made Clark think he was hearing only half the story. 'And what else?'

Collins said nothing and closed his eyes as if embarrassed by what he was about to say. 'It's a mortal sin to kill yourself. I didn't want either of us to die with a mortal sin on our soul.'

'But yow thought we were going to die anyway?'

'Yes. But by jumping we weren't committing suicide. We were trying to save ourselves. It's all about not giving up hope and the reasons behind your actions…or that's what Father McGoogan told me when I was nine.'

'Well if yow tell me where I can find Father McGoogan, I'll buy him a drink.'

'Ah sure, he's dead. He committed suicide years ago.'

'Yow sod. Tell me the real reason or I'll break yowr other arm.'

Epilogue

The only remains found of Mr Tubbs, (aka Martin Grace), in the ashes of The Finlandia Hotel consisted of a badly burned skeleton that was missing several small bones which had been incinerated by the fire. He was buried in a pauper's grave with just a minister and two gravediggers in attendance. No one has ever been able to identify, with certainty, what TK stands for.

His savings and investments remain unclaimed in a Zurich bank, accumulating interest and dividends.

Miss Florin was buried in her home village of Ashworth, in Sussex. Agnes, Collins, Sir Aubrey and several other members of MI5 attended the funeral, along with numerous members of Miss Florin's family and villagers who knew her.

Miss Emily Lincoln returned to the United States and resigned from government work. She currently teaches first graders in Hope, Michigan. She remains unmarried.

Archie Mellon was unable to escape a custodial sentence for his latest one-man crime wave. However, on the basis of information provided by Detective Constable Clark the judge sentenced him to 12 months' imprisonment, nine months of which were suspended for three years. On release he received £5,000 reward for his part in tracking down Mr

Tubbs. On his wife's insistence he invested his windfall and opened a small lock and key shop. The business is thriving.

The remaining £5,000 reward money was split equally between Mrs Williams and Mr Wilson who had provided the police with an excellent likeness of Mr Tubbs.

After they recovered from their injuries, Collins and Clark contacted the Commonwealth War Graves Commission and tracked down the burial site of Mr Williams. Through the Royal British Legion they then arranged for Mrs Williams to visit her husband's grave, almost exactly 50 years to the day he had died.

Tony Flynn was not as lucky as Archie Mellon. He was sentenced to 12 years for accessory before the fact to grievous bodily harm, arson and conspiracy contrary to Section 2 of the Accessories and Abettors Act of 1861. There was no evidence that he had ever provided anyone with the contact details of a hired killer.

Superintendent Patterson spent a year investigating all those named in Mr Tubbs' records and anyone who had transferred funds into any of his bank accounts. On completion of his meticulous investigation, 27 business owners were charged with conspiracy to defraud and conspiring to cause arson and endanger life.

Mr Bright was given a suspended sentence on the grounds that the fire had not been set under his direction and he had co-operated with the police. He was declared bankrupt 11 months later.

As a result of role played by several officers at Thornhill Road Police Station there were a number of changes. WPC Milne received a commendation for her quick thinking in saving the lives of Inspector Hicks, DC Clark and DC Collins. She was promoted to Sergeant five years and eight months after joining the police, and went to work in the Chief Constable's Office. DC Collins' secondment to the CID was confirmed as permanent following the closure of the Tubbs case. DC Clark returned to the uniformed branch duties at his own request. Inspector Hicks was promoted to Chief Inspector following the closure of the Tubbs case.

Station Officer Stan Wold's funeral took place at St Paul's Cathedral, Birmingham. Mourners from the fire brigade, police force and the public filled the church, and much of the surrounding graveyard. He was posthumously awarded The Queen's Fire Service Medal for Gallantry for saving the lives of DC Clark and Detective Inspector Hicks.

Anatoli Petrov spent three months in a Scottish country house being debriefed by MI5 officers. Information he provided led to the identification of four double agents, two within MI6 and one each in MI5 and the Security Service. He also identified 11 prominent Labour MPs who were supporters of the Soviet Union and several international businessmen who had been compromised by the KGB, including two from New York.

After his debriefing he bought a property near Edinburgh

and is writing a book entitled *My Life as a KGB Agent,* to be published only after his death. -

Joanne Monroe was picked up by a police officer in the centre of Birmingham on 7 September 1965. After a court hearing she was returned to the secure hospital she had left barely four months earlier.

Winston Chambers joined the North Staffordshire Regiment in September 1965. Six weeks later, he passed out top of his platoon. His story has only just begun.

The End

Until...

A Death in Spring: 1968
Jim McGrath

See preview below.

From Death in Spring:1968

Smethwick, Monday, 13 February 1967, 22.40hrs.

Phillip Mabbit was a loser. He lost at everything he did. Jobs, friendships and especially betting. Sitting in the car, he remembered his first bet. It had been in 1956 and he'd put his entire week's wages of £9 10s. on Devon Loch to win the Grand National.

With just three jumps remaining, the Queen Mother's horse had taken the lead and cleared the last fence half a length ahead of E.S.B., and took a commanding lead on the final stretch. Then, in front of the Royal Box, with only 40 yards to the winning post and five lengths ahead, he inexplicably jumped into the air and landed on his stomach, allowing E.S.B. to overtake and win. Afterwards, the Queen Mother said: 'Oh, that's racing.'

However, for Phillip it was walking to work for a week, going without any lunch in the canteen and having to stay in and listen to his father moan at the news twice a night for a week. On the last day of the week he'd met Liz, and they'd been married two years later in 1958, by which time he was betting daily on the horses and the dogs. Always chasing the big win which would set him and his kids up for life.

Instead of living the good life, he was he was now sitting in a car, near Warley Park, waiting for a man he didn't know to leave the Bear's Head. A man he was going to run over and kill, in order to settle a gambling debt of nearly three grand he owed.

He checked his watch. It was 10.45pm and the pub was starting to empty. He'd sat in the same place for three nights over the last ten days and the man he was to kill was always last out. This wasn't because he was a drunk, but because he was the leader of the local gang in Smethwick which ran gambling, protection and prostitution on the dark streets of this small town just three miles from Birmingham, and people were too afraid to ask him to leave.

At 11.05 the man left the pub and walked to the traffic lights on the corner. He waited patiently until the lights turned green and then stepped into the road. As he neared the far side of the road Phillip Mabbit crashed into him at forty miles per hour and sent him tumbling down the road. Mabbit saw him lying in the road ten feet away and pushed his foot to the floor and ran over him a second time. Clear of the body, he put his foot down and sped away towards Birmingham and the scrapyard where he was to deliver the car.

As he drove he felt a mixture of emotions – relief that he'd been able to do it, fear that someone may have seen him, and a desperate desire never to get involved in anything like this again. 'I'm never going to have another bet again,' he said, and meant it, for he knew that he'd just played the biggest hand in his life.

As he drove to the scrapyard, the same question he'd asked Johnny kept returning, 'Who wants him dead?'

Lightning Source UK Ltd.
Milton Keynes UK
UKHW02f2050150218
317900UK00011B/313/P